A
BRILLIANT
VOID

A
BRILLIANT
VOID

A SELECTION OF CLASSIC
IRISH SCIENCE FICTION

EDITED AND INTRODUCED BY **JACK FENNELL**

TRAMP PRESS

First published 2018 by Tramp Press
www.tramppress.com

A CIP record for this title is available from The British Library.

1 3 5 7 9 10 8 6 4 2

ISBN 978-1-9997008-5-0

Tramp Press gratefully acknowledges
the support of the Arts Council.

Thank you for supporting independent publishing.

Set in 11 pt on 15 pt Caslon by Marsha Swan
Printed and bound in Great Britain by Clays Ltd, Elcograf S.p.A.

Contents

INTRODUCTION
The Green Lacuna

JACK FENNELL

So, yes: it turns out that there is such a thing as Irish science fiction. In fact, if you look at the history of Irish storytelling, it becomes clear that Ireland has always been inclined that way.

In the 11th-century *Book of Invasions* (*Lebor Gabála Érenn*) we can spot a number of images and characters that have become recurring tropes of present-day sci-fi. Lugh, the hero of the Tuatha Dé Danann, was the grandson of Balor of the Evil Eye, the chief villain of the Invasion Cycle – at least nine hundred years before Luke Skywalker learned who his real father was. Balor, meanwhile, was basically a mutant with laser-vision, and in what would later become a comic-book tradition, he acquired his power through a laboratory accident. Also featured in the Invasion Cycle is the warrior Nuada, who was provided with a substitute arm made out of silver after losing his own, thus becoming 'Nuada Silver-Arm', a Celtic proto-cyborg.

Later, the *immrama* – early Christian fantastic-voyage epics – routinely included encounters with strange creatures that can be read as forerunners of modern sci-fi aliens and mutants. In 'The Voyage of Maeldún', collected in the twelfth-century *Book of the Dun Cow* (*Lebor na hUidre*) and the fourteenth-century *Yellow Book of Lecan* (*Leabhar Buidhe Leacán*), the titular hero and his crew come up against gigantic ants (resonating with Gordon Douglas's 1954 shocker *Them!*), a carnivorous dog/pony hybrid, a beast with revolving skin and muscles, cannibalistic horse-monsters, blazing pigs and sapient birds. As the whole point of the *immrama* was to show the protagonists' eventual submission to the will of God, none of these encounters is ever explained: the strangeness of them is the whole point.

Another important precursor of modern science fiction was the nineteenth-century Gothic, and Ireland was home to one of the most celebrated varieties of Gothic literature. While the Ascendancy Gothic presented with all the mystery, secrecy, horror and tension seen in other Gothic traditions, it was Irish philosopher and statesman Edmund Burke who first linked these sensibilities with the 'sublime' – a profound feeling of awe that comes when one is confronted by something so powerful that it shatters pre-existing conceptions of reality. This made paradigm-shifting encounters with the Other, and the implication of cosmic scales of time and distance, central to one of the most popular literary genres being produced and read in Ireland. Elsewhere, Gothic tropes soon started to appear in 'scientific romances' in the style of Jules Verne and H.G. Wells, and out of this cross-fertilisation came the pulp sci-fi and weird fiction of the early twentieth century.

Given our literary heritage, then, it's no wonder we're mad for science fiction, even though the very idea of it might seem a bit bizarre, and to some people, pointless. As I will argue below, plenty of established Irish literary genres (such as *aisling* poetry) intersect quite well with sci-fi, and could conceivably be read as proto-science fiction when it comes to the idea of seeing into the future. In spite of its compatibility, however, science fiction is often subject to oddly utilitarian gatekeeping.

When I was putting my doctoral thesis on Irish science fiction together, one member of a progress review panel asked (to paraphrase), 'So what? What's the point of "recovering" this stuff? I mean, you might find an abandoned car in the middle of a field and spend ages restoring it, but why should anyone care?' I hasten to add that this person is really sound; I don't want to paint them as a villain here, but the fact remains that this is a question that would never be asked of a more 'respectable' genre. This idea that science fiction must justify its existence is derived from, and reinforces, an assumption of disposability that has led to the loss of an important part of Ireland's literary history. At the time of writing, most Irish people would probably be hard-pressed to name an Irish sci-fi writer, or at a push, might tentatively point to the stranger works of Samuel Beckett or Flann O'Brien; the likelihood that they might know of any sci-fi works by women, or in Irish, is lower. Outside of science fiction fandom, genre-savvy readers might know one or two examples – though, tellingly, they will each mention two different titles. The history is fragmented, because the material was not thought to be worth preserving.

There are two reasons why this material matters. First, the science fiction of the past gives us an insight into how our ancestors imagined their future: it tells us what they hoped for, what they were afraid of, and what they considered inevitable. Secondly, it allows us to look at the commonplace from a hypothetical remove: what, for example, would an alien make of a hurling match, a referendum, the St Patrick's Day parade or a banking inquiry?

This kind of extrapolation, I argue, has always been a part of the Irish imagination. This book contains fifteen samples, from 1837 to 1960, including short stories and excerpts from longer works; there are authors in here who were important literary figures in their day, along with writers who were unknown or wrote under pseudonyms. The one thing they all have in common is that the science-fictional material they created has been somewhat neglected.

Until quite recently, science fiction was regarded as marginalia by Irish literary critics, if it was acknowledged at all. Dismissive rather than openly hostile, this lack of attention reflected a commonplace assumption that the genre was frivolous and not worthy of serious consideration. From this point of view, science fiction is an inherently ridiculous genre by virtue of the imagery it uses, and irrelevant by dint of its abstraction from the here and now.

In this collection, you will find time-travelling nationalists, a sad dinosaur, educated apes, subatomic universes and a reanimator collecting the 'brain gas' of Europe's intelligentsia, among other things. Taken at face value, such things are indeed absurd, but science fiction uses such images to ask deeper hypothetical questions that go to the core of who we are as human beings – questions that might not be as easy to articulate in other kinds of writing. What would happen if we learned that our world (read: existence; way of life) wasn't unique? What if we could see ourselves as outsiders do? Given a choice, would we use our knowledge for noble or selfish ends? How far would we be willing to go in pursuit of what we assume to be the common good? Like Emily Dickinson, sci-fi tells the truth, but 'tells it slant'. The only *literal* thing you will learn from these stories is that if you ever hear someone described as 'the cleverest man/woman in all of Ireland', that's your cue to run away as fast as you can.

The most frequently asked hypothetical question in this collection is: what if you could see the future? Several of the authors collected herein extrapolate different answers, some from a perspective of hope, or a need for reassurance, others with meditations upon free will and determinism. In Amelia Garland Mears's story, visions of the future confirm that the moral arc of the universe bends towards justice, so that predestination vindicates those who have been victimised; Jane Barlow and Art Ó Riain, by contrast, see it as a Nietzschean 'eternal return' – horrifying to those unable or unwilling to submit to it.

It is not difficult to perceive the baleful influence of Irish history in this fascination with prophecy: that history has been punctuated by war, starvation, economic hardship, dramatic reversals of fortune (for better and for worse), political corruption and miscarriages of justice. With all that in our past, it would be handy to know if more of the same is on the way. Ireland's traumatic history subtly influences all of the stories collected here, but it looms particularly large over the pieces by Dorothy Macardle, Tarlach Ó hUid and Cathal Ó Sándair.

The desire to see the future is so ingrained in Irish culture that prophecy has long been part of our literary tradition, most obviously in the form of *aisling* or 'dream vision' poetry. One pronounced feature of Irish folk-culture was a strong belief in literal dream interpretation, prophetic dreams and revelatory dreams, and this soothsaying tendency persisted for longer than one might guess. The twentieth-century Irish philosopher John W. Dunne, a known influence on the work of Flann O'Brien and J.R.R. Tolkien, formulated his theory of 'serialism' to explain a number of his own prophetic dreams: in his view, these were normal dreams occurring on the wrong nights, proving that time is not uni-directional, and that the human mind can travel through time more or less at will. In Irish science fiction, dream-endings are not the cop-out they are in other contexts: just because 'it was all a dream', that does not mean it isn't *going* to happen, that it *didn't really* happen, or that it isn't *happening right now* in the world next door. Besides, dream-endings are no more of a narrative dodge than *Star Trek's* use of the holodeck to tell stories that contradict the rules of the franchise's setting. The issue of what is permitted in sci-fi, of course, speaks to how one defines it, and these questions are highlighted by the issue of gender.

It was important to try to achieve a gender balance for this collection (insofar as a simple binary can still be considered 'balanced'). As it happens, we ended up with six men and eight women (two of Clotilde Graves's stories are collected here, because they are both strikingly odd, and I wasn't willing to lose either one).

One frustrating thing about looking for this kind of material is that historically, writing by women has been treated dismissively, if not with outright contempt. Reviewers and bibliographers of the nineteenth century tended to be rather inexact in their descriptions of genre fiction by women, meaning that a bona fide sci-fi story was as likely to be classed as a fairy tale or melodrama as it was to be called a 'scientific romance', with very few critics bothering to write synopses of the content. By the time Luxembourgish-American pulp publisher Hugo Gernsback invented the term 'science fiction' in the late 1920s, such material tended to be written by multi-tasking hacks who made their living from churning out men's adventure stories; it was assumed that women and girls just weren't interested. As was the case with literature generally in previous centuries, many women authors disguised their gender with masculine or neutral pseudonyms to be taken seriously – one of the most notable of these was Alice Sheldon, who won renown as a sci-fi writer under the name 'James Tiptree Jr'.

One explanation for the apparent gender imbalance in early science fiction writing emphasises the societal mores of the time. For much of the nineteenth and twentieth centuries, the genre was mostly concerned with exploration, warfare and invention – meaning tales of conquest and colonisation, future battles fought with devastating super-weapons, and clever feats of engineering rather than scientific abstraction. Obviously, women were excluded from the military and bureaucratic apparatuses of empire-building, discouraged from pursuing scientific education, and simply barred from many institutions where such education or training might be acquired. This, combined with the attitudes of the Irish literary establishment toward genre fiction, might lead one to the conclusion that Irish sci-fi by women 'fell between two stools'. I laboured under that faulty conclusion for ages myself, until I turned over the 'Gothic' box, and dozens of mislabelled sci-fi stories came tumbling out.

However, the operative word in science fiction is *fiction*, at the end of the day, and it's reductive to conclude that women didn't write this kind of thing because they were excluded from the real-world practices that informed it. For one thing, officers and bureaucrats frequently brought their families with them to the imperial frontier, and Europe was so permeated with imperialist ideology anyway that women who remained 'at home' were no less exposed to it; for another, this is a genre where manned vessels regularly break the speed of light, so fidelity to accepted science isn't exactly a deal-breaker. Rather, science fiction is a genre where the fantastic-seeming accoutrements are stated or implied to have been accomplished in accordance with the scientific method, rather than the supernatural; how much 'actual science' goes into it after that is up to the author. Fans today acknowledge a division between 'Hard SF' and 'Soft SF', with the former being more crunchy and technical, and the latter more philosophical; there is nothing inherently 'masculine' or 'feminine' about either variety. In this collection, for example, L.T. Meade's scientific detective story gestures toward Hard SF, while Æ (George William Russell) sketches out an entirely mystical account of the creation and renewal of the universe. If any 'gendered' difference can be discerned in the stories collected here, it seems that the women writers are more inclined to irony, occasionally verging into world-weary cynicism.

Though the scientific method is centred as a key defining element, these stories are as ambiguous in their genre as an initialled pseudonym is in its gender. Wary of compromising their cultural identity, most of these authors seek some kind of compromise with pre-modern tradition: see Fitz-James O'Brien's mad scientist consulting a ghost for advice on building a microscope, Frances Power Cobbe's rather cynical attitude to the approaching 'Age of Science', and Charlotte McManus's interesting blend of science and folk magic. Indeed, many of the stories gathered here could just as easily be classed as 'weird' fiction, the quasi-scientific, quasi-occult genre that emerged through the writings of H.P. Lovecraft, Algernon Blackwood and countless others. As with the dream-endings mentioned previously, this kind of indeterminacy is something that many science fiction fans and readers might baulk at, but I would argue that it is integral to understanding what Irish sci-fi is and how it works.

The title of this collection comes from a sentence in Fitz-James O'Brien's story: 'It was, however, no brilliant void into which I looked.' The paradoxical phrase 'brilliant void' calls to mind the night sky and outer space – a desolate hard vacuum that is nonetheless full of matter and starlight – which seems a nice metaphor for the whole subject of Irish science fiction. Ireland is not perceived as a place where sci-fi 'happens', but when you look deeper into the apparent void, you'll find an entire cosmos waiting to be explored.

The New Frankenstein

WILLIAM MAGINN (1837)

The first of our many Mad Scientists reckons that he can improve upon Doctor Frankenstein's achievements by fashioning a mind for the monster – thus revealing that author William Maginn had probably not read the original 1818 novel by Mary Shelley, in which the reanimated creature proves to be both intelligent and eloquent. In the absence of any major connection to the book he's referring to, however, Maginn sutures together a patchwork of allusions and references to Dante Alighieri, William Beckford, E.T.A. Hoffman, Alain-René Lesage and several others in the following abridged version of this story.

AT THE LAZARETTO OF GENOA, by good fortune, I met with a German who was travelling to the Vatican, in search of Palimpsests. He was scarcely thirty, though he might have passed for ten years older, as is often observed to be the case with those who have devoted much of their time to intense study. His shoulders inclined forward, and his light, flaxen hair hung much below his travelling cap. In his eye there were a wildness, and a glassiness, that bespoke, if not alienation of mind, at least eccentricity.

During our captivity in quarantine, we endeavoured to kill time by relating our several adventures; and, one evening, the German, having been called upon to continue our soirées, looked round for a while, as though he were waiting for the dictation of some familiar spirit – some monitor, like a second Socrates; and, with a voice not unlike a cracked instrument, without preface, in his own idiomatic language, which I will endeavour to translate, thus commenced:

I came into the world on the same day as Hoffman's celebrated cat Mürr – ay, not only on the same day, but the same hour of the day, if the obstetrix kept a good reckoning. Who does not remember Mürr – that back which outvied the enamel of the tortoise in the brilliancy and variety of its colours; that coat, finer than ermine; that voice, whose purr was more melodious than the whispered voice of lovers; and then, his eye, there was something in it not feline, nor human, nor divine? I will now let you into a secret … Mürr was strongly suspected of being more than a familiar – an emanation, an incarnation, of one to whom Hoffman, like Calcott, was so much indebted; it being to a certain dictation that he owed so many of his nocturnal and diabolical tales, and, among the rest, that marvel of his genius, the *Pot of Gold*. I wish to show you, gentlemen, what gave the bent and impulse to my genius, and how seemingly insignificant causes are the parents of the great events of our lives.

At twelve years of age I was sent to the university of Leipsic, and at fifteen was thoroughly master of the dead languages; but my favourite author was Apuleius, the most romantic of all the ancient writers; and I had got almost by heart the first book of the *Golden Ass*, fully believing in all the wild traditions, the fantastic fables, and visions that it embodied. I thus early divided the life of man into two sets of sensation, but not of equal value in my eyes – a waking sleep, and a sleeping sleep; for it seemed to me that no one could dispute the superior advantages of the latter in perceiving the only world that is worth perceiving – the imaginary one. Natural philosophy was the great object of my pursuit; and it must be confessed that my tutor – for I had a private one, and seldom attended the public lectures – was admirably qualified to direct this branch of my studies. How he had acquired all his learning was a mystery; for he never read, and yet had hardly, to all appearance, passed his twenty-fifth year. Where he had been educated, or from what country he came, was equally unknown, for he spoke all languages with equal fluency. As Goethe says of the meerkats, 'Even with those little people one would not wish to be alone.'

Thus, he was a man in whose company I never felt quite at ease, and yet was attracted to him by a kind of resistless impetus. Though his features were good, his face was a continual mask; his eyes, dark and lustrous, had in them an extraordinary and supernatural power of inquisition. There was an expression in his countenance the most gloomy, a desolateness the most revolting; the depravity of human nature seemed to him a delight. He was never known to laugh but at what would have moved others to tears. Though he watched over me as if his own life depended on mine, there was hardly a drunken orgy, or a duel, its natural consequence (for you know such take place daily at our universities), that Starnstein – for that was his name – was not the exciting cause. You saw me look round just now. I often fancy him at my elbow; and thought, since I began talking of him, that he whispered in my ear.

Being destined for a physician, I repaired, after taking my degree, to Paris, for the purpose of attending the anatomical school. There, however, the only dissections in which I took an interest were those of the brain, which opened to me a new world of speculations – one of which was that all our sentiments are nothing more than a subtle kind of mind, and that mind itself is only a modification of matter. I now set no bounds to the power of *Mater Ia,* and soon attributed to her all creation, being much assisted in coming to this conclusion by Buffon and Cuvier. Their researches, particularly those of the latter great naturalist, proved to my satisfaction that there was a period when this planet was inhabited by a nameless progeny of monstrous forms, engendered by a peculiar state of the atmosphere – a dense congregation of putrid vapours that brooded over chaos; that all this Megatherian and Saurian brood, those flying liquids, long as the 'mast of some high admiral', disappeared at the first ray of light, and gave place to a new and better order of existences; but as inferior to man, or the present race of the inhabitants of our globe, as man is to the ape – himself the original of our species.

But I was the first to discern that chrystals are to be produced by the galvanic battery, and animal life from acids; to detect in paste, by means of the solar microscope, thousands of vermicular creatures, which could not have arisen from the accidental depositions of ova – this genus being, like that of eels, viviporous. I got some volcanic dust from Etna, which I pasted with muriatic acid, and after a time distinguished, though inaudible save with an ear trumpet – or thought I could distinguish – a hum, like that of fermentation. What was my delight to find that there was vitality in the mass – that these atoms daily grew in size! They were of the *bug* species; not unlike what the French call a *punaise*. Their kinds were two; the larger soon began to devour the smaller, till they were completely destroyed; and in their voracity the survivors preyed on each other; so that at last only one, the great conqueror, was left, and he, I speak it to my infinite regret, was crushed in handling – so crushed, that scarcely anything but slime, not of the most agreeable odour, was left upon my fingers. I had promised myself to present him to the Luxembourg, for its splendid entomological collection. He would have been a prize, indeed.

I pass over several years of my life, and find myself, in the summer of 18--, at Manheim. It is a curious old town, but I shall not stop to describe it. There it was that I first met with a German translation of that very ingenious history of *Frankenstein*. Such was my predisposition to a belief in what might have seemed to others prodigious, that I read it without a question or suspicion of its being a fiction. The part, however, that most interested me was the creation; the scene that riveted me most, the creation scene. One night I had the passage open in my hand, when who should walk into the room, arm-in-arm, but my old tutor and that anatomical man – that identical phantasmagoric hero.

Starnstein, after having posted him against the oak panelling, turned towards me with one of his old Sardonic grins, pointed to his protégé, and slipped off before I could have detained him, had I been so inclined, which, to tell you the truth, I was not. I had never seen him since I left college; but wished to renew his acquaintance, and sometimes doubt whether it was not his apparition. But not so the other. He was too palpable to view, and without any mistake. Thus he was standing in *propriá persona* – the human monster; the restored ruin; the living phantom; the creature without a name. I put my hand before my eyes more than once, to convince myself that it was only a vision such as a feverish imagination conjured up. No rattlesnake could have more fascinated its victim. Yes, there he stood in all his horrible disproportion. His back, as I said, was against the oak wainscot, and his face turned towards me.

Everyone knows the effect produced at Guy's Hospital on the medical students, when the corpse of a criminal, under the effect of a powerful galvanic battery, opened its eyes, made one step from the table against which he was placed, erect, and stiff, and fell among them. Such was the feeling I experienced, lest he should advance. Horrible sensations for a time came over me; there was a lurid glare on all the objects in the room; everything took, or seemed to take, the most fantastic forms, and to bear some mysterious relation to the strange being before me. But by degrees I became familiarised with his person, and at length thought I should not dislike his company; I therefore took up the lamp, and with measured and stealthy steps began to approach my visitor. But this rashness had nearly proved fatal, for that which had given him life had well-nigh caused my death: so powerful was the galvanism with which he had been charged, that the shock struck me to the ground like a forked flash of lightning.

How long I lay I know not; but, on recovering, had learned sufficient prudence to keep a respectful distance from my uninvited guest. There he was in the self-same state. I now examined him steadily; but, instead of his being gifted with the faculties assigned to him by the fair authoress, I found he had only a talismanic existence – he was a mere automaton, a machine, a plant without the faculty of motion. His eyes – those yellow eyes so graphically depicted – rolled pendulously in their sunken sockets with a clicking sound not unlike that of a clock; there was a mechanical trepidation of all his fibres, and his whole frame had a convulsive motion, whilst his head moved from left to right and right to left, like that of a Chinese mandarin. As I gazed and gazed on the image before me, I pitied him, and said to myself, I will be a new Frankenstein, and a greater. Frankenstein has left his work imperfect; he has resuscitated a corpse: *I will give him a mind.*

A mind; yes, with a frantic joy I shouted, till the room re-echoed in loud vibrations, 'I will create a mind for you, and such a mind as man, till now, never possessed!' But, how to begin? Such an undertaking, till within the last twenty years, would have seemed preposterous and absurd. But, what were all the physicians and metaphysicians of old compared to the philosophers of the new school? There are only two sciences worth cultivating – phrenology and animal magnetism – and it was by their means that I hoped to accomplish the great *arcanum*.

All who know anything of craniology must be aware that genius depends on organisation, and organisation only – on the elevation and depression of certain gasses in the cerebrum. The cerebellum is another affair. With toil of mind that strengthens with its own fatigue, I made a discovery which, alone, in any other planet, would have immortalised me. I found out what neither Gall nor Spurzheim ever dreamed of; I learned intuitively, or, rather, by that sense which I need not name animal magnetism. I perceived, I say, that every one of those compartments, as laid down in the most approved charts of the head, contains a certain gas, though it has, like the nervous fluid circulating in that curious network of the frame, hitherto escaped analysis or detection. To this gas I have given the appellation of the 'cerebral afflatus', and now felt satisfied that the protuberances of the cranium, called 'brains', are derived from the action of this mental air pent up in its cells. Newton, when the laws of gravitation flashed upon his mind by the apple hitting the boss of mathematics, never experienced the proud gratification this sublime discovery gave me.

Ulysses, as all know, carried about with him the winds in bladders – a contrivance clever enough before the invention of glass; and the Usula of Don Cleophas bottled the lame devil Asmodeus. These hints were not lost upon me. I set, therefore, my mechanical genius to work, and fabricated a number of tubes, composed of a mixture of diverse metals, such as went to the formation of Perkins's Tractors.

These tubes had, at one end, tunnels; and to the other I attached phials, in the shape of balls communicating with them, and so contrived as to open and shut by means of screws, or vices, so that the fluid of which I was in search, once risen to the top, might be there imprisoned, and, once hermetically closed, could only escape at my option. These tubes were all of one size; but not so the globes, which I blew of a vast thickness, lest it should happen that the expansion of the confined air might endanger the security of my retorts, which, like steam-engines, did not admit of safety-valves.

Thus admirably provided, I locked up my treasure, as carefully as a miser does his gold, and issued, like a new Captain Cook, on a voyage of discovery much more interesting and important than the great navigator's.

The author of *Faust* was then at Weimar. Easily accessible to a man of genius like myself, and ignorant of my motives (which, if he had known, his familiar would doubtless have befriended me), Goethe was easily persuaded to submit himself to my manipulation. No patient I ever had was easier brought *en rapport*. From him it was that I sought to extract *Imagination*; and I reconciled myself to the theft, knowing that, however much I might appropriate to myself for the use of my protégé, Goethe might well spare it. Nor would it be long missed, considering that the working of his fertile brain would soon generate fresh gas to supply the vacuum. So abundant was the stream, or steam, that flowed from my fingers' ends, and thence conducted by my thumb into the tube, that my largest globe was, at the first sitting, almost filled to explosion, and as soon inescapably sealed.

Delighted with the success of my first experiment, I now deliberated which of my compatriots I should next put in requisition. Unhappily, Kant (that mighty mystic!) was gone to the land of shadows; but he had bequeathed his spirit to a worthy disciple, who, to the uninitiated, lectures in an unknown tongue.

Transcendentalism, owing to the habitude of my own organs, has always been to me a wonder and a mystery, but I was determined that it should not be so to my adopted son. The gaseous effluvium which I drew from the professor was of so extra-subtle and super-volatile a nature, that it was long before I could satisfy myself that I had obtained a *quantum sufficit in ullo vehiculo*, as the physicians say; but, by dint of pressure with my finger-pump, in a happy moment I heard a slight crackling, like that of confined air in a bottle of champagne. I would have given worlds for half an hour with Swedenborg, or Madame Grizon. As I could not resuscitate the dead, I passed in review the living, and bethought me of one who had, as they, a religion of his own. He was [here the narrator turned to me] a compatriot of yours.

Imperfect, indeed, would the accumulated fog of my phenomenon have been without this great essential; and, therefore, I crossed the Alps, and found Shelley at the baths of Lucca. The great poet's animal magnetic sensibility is well known, and it had been, if possible, increased by a late visit to the Prato Fiorito, where he had fainted with the excess of sweetness of the jonquils that carpet that enamelled mead. He was, at that moment, full of the conception of his *Ode to Intellectual Beauty*; and I extracted enough of that particular sort of devotion to form a recipe for my ideal citizen.

Passing through Bologna on my return, I tapped the Bibliotecario Mezzofanti for three hundred and sixty-five languages; which, strange to say, he had acquired without stirring out of his own library.

Travelling night and day, behold me now, as *'I stood tiptoe upon a little hill.'*

That little hill was Primrose Hill. I for a moment looked down on the mighty Babylon beneath me, and listened to the hum of the 'million-peopled city vast', itself hidden in a dense fog. Out of all the multitude, there was only one whom I sought: the eminent Coleridge. I found him at no great distance, in his own rural retreats of Highgate, and at that time taking 'his ease in his inn'. No man was more accessible. Talking was not the amusement, but the occupation of his life; and it must be confessed that he was an adept in the art, as should naturally have been a person whose tongue was employed for eighteen hours out of the twenty-four. For the first five of our interview, the clack of a water-mill, the wheels of a steamboat, the waves on a sea-shore, were poor comparisons to express the volubility of his organ. That coma, or trance, somnambulism, into which I had hoped to throw him, was transferred from the operated on to the operator. I called to mind the celebrated epigram:

> *'Safe from the syren's tuneful air*
> *The sage Ulysses fled;*
> *But had that man of prose been there,*
> *He would have talked him dead.'*

The mighty stream, 'without o'erflowing, full', rolled on, and carried all before it – even the floodgates of reason. He was the despair of the animal magnetist, and I almost began to doubt the efficacy, not of the system, but of my own powers, when he filled from a quart bottle a bumper of his favourite beverage, black-drop; and during its opiate influence I felt a vibration of the tube, like the string of a harp in concert-pitch, thrill through every fibre of my frame, to its utmost ramifications. *'Io triumphe!'* The victory was complete.

And now, behold me back to Manheim. No miser, gloating over his stores – no devotee, the possessor of some relic of her patron saint, not even Psyche herself, with her precious casket, felt half the raptures I enjoyed as I turned the key of my laboratory.

I found my *homuncio* (which means, I believe, a great ugly fellow, though not such did he seem to me) posted exactly where I had left him, with the same mechanical clicking of the eyes, the same oscillation of the frame. And now for my reward.

One by one did I carefully unvalve my phials, and apply the contents to the portals of the brain – the porticoes of my *innominato*, as the man-fiend is called in the *Promessi Sposi*. Scarcely had I discharged through the olfactory nerves the subtle fluids, when I perceived a strange confusion ensue, and it was easy to perceive that the late arrivals were dissatisfied with their new lodging, finding, doubtless, the apartments not to their taste. I was immediately reminded of Casti's *Caso di Coscunza*, in which the spirits of the hero and heroine – a priest and his housekeeper, removed simultaneously from the world – being called back by the prayers of the good peasants of Estramadura to reanimate their clay, by mistake enter the wrong bodies; so that the don finds himself no man, and the donna no woman. Thus happened it, I should conjecture, with some of the newly imported and imprisoned spirits in my *innominato*'s cranium. It was long before quiet was established in that 'dome of thought', and I waited, in an agony of impatience, to see the effect of my operation.

Motionless as the sculptor, or almost turned to stone as one who had seen Medusa, I stood, all eyes and ears intently fixed on my phenomenon. I saw the glassy and unmeaning glare of his eyes give place to the fire of intelligence; the jaundiced hue of his cheek disappear, like the grey of the morning at the uprising of the sun; and, as his lungs became inflated, I could distinctly hear the *a, w* – those sounds so expressive of inspiration and expiration – at measured intervals repeated. I now expected that his first impulse would be to fall down and worship me. But, far from this, what was my vexation and disappointment to mark the look of unutterable scorn and hate with which he regarded me.

I think I now hear the floor ringing with his heavy tread, as he paced it backwards and forwards to give circulation to his blood, or as though waiting for the chaos of his thoughts to be reduced to form, ere he attempted to give them utterance. At length, he found that distinguishing characteristic of man above all other animals – speech. His voice was hollow, hoarse, and unmodulated, resembling most a pair of asthmatic bellows, or a cracked bassoon, rather than aught human. At first, his utterance, like that of a newborn babe, consisted of inarticulate sounds; but, after running up and down the gamut of the vowels, he put together a variety of words, as by way of practice, and with a slow and laboured delivery, and a sort of telegraphic gestures, commenced a harangue.

It was composed of all languages, which he called into requisition to express more fully his meaning, or no meaning. I have said, that his delivery was at first slow and difficult, but as he proceeded his facility of pronunciation, his volubility, increased. From a fountain, a rivulet, a river, he poured forth at last a torrent of eloquence, which it was impossible to stop, or almost to make intelligible in words. His merciless imagination flew with the speed of thought from subject to subject, from topic to topic, in a perpetual flux and reflux. It was a labyrinth inextricable – an ill-linked chain of sentences the most involved, parentheses within parentheses, a complication of images and figures the most *outré*. In short, imagine to yourselves the mysticism of Kant, the transcendental philosophy of Coleridge, the metaphysics of Shelley and Goethe, the poetry of Lycophron, mingled and massed together in one jargon, compounded of Greek, Latin, Italian, French, Spanish, German, and English, not to mention tongues known and unknown, and you may form some idea of his style; but of his barbarous pronunciation I can give you none.

I now perceived, to my infinite sorrow, that I had done infinite mischief by this Phrengenesis. Its very creation weighed upon me like remorse upon the guilty. I had now the means of knowing that he had nothing to know, yet knew nothing.

Thus it was that I found out the Theosophs were right in separating entirely the mind from the soul, in considering them diametrically opposite relations – as different principles, as the physic and the phrenic. And I became satisfied that my paradox had no soul. What was to be done now? Should I leave the work imperfect, or endeavour to create one? Was it impious? I scarcely dared put the question. Was there any tradition on the earth, below the earth, or above the earth, of the Psycogenesis? The more I reflected, the more was I lost and confounded. In the lowest depths there was yet a lower depth of mystery.

Imagine yourself to have lost your way, benighted amid some inhospitable desert, some savage range of Alpine solitudes – far from a path, as you suppose, or the abode of man – and when you are about to lay yourself down and die, in your despair, hear all at once the bark of a house-dog, and see the light streaming from the window of a cottage; and, when you enter, find a cheerful fire blazing in the hearth, and a young girl, beautiful as the houris, who welcomes you with a voice tremulous with delight, and presents to your parched lips an exquisite and life-giving cordial.

Thus was it with me, when a scroll of vellum slowly unrolled itself. It was a palimpsest. The writing – the work of some falsely pious monk – that supplied the place of the original MSS, gradually became obliterated, and shewed beneath some characters, dim and indistinct, in a language long lost. It had been one of the hermetic books escaped from the burning of the Alexandrian Library, and once belonged to that of Ragusa, the last temple of the Greek and Roman muses. Oh, the marvellous power of somnambulism, that imparts wisdom to brutes, and furnishes a clue to all sciences and tongues! It was by its mysterious power that my eyes were opened, that I could decipher in the pictured language, above the rest, these words, *Thebes Adamite King*. Then came a sarcophagus, in which was traced in blood the mystical triangle, enclosed within a circle, the sacred emblem and diagram of the Magi and Brahmans.

Yes, said I, it was in Osiris that the Egyptians supposed to reside all living beings, the genii and the souls of men. To Egypt, then, there to unravel the mystery!

With my double, my second self, behold me journeying to Alexandria. We ascended the sacred stream of the Nile, and found ourselves among the ruins of ancient Thebes. At the further extremity of the tomb, I discovered, hollowed out of the rock, a subterranean passage, that seemed to descend into the very bowels of the earth. With a delight unutterable, I led the way down the perpendicular stairs, till we came to a lofty door, the entrance to the Necropolis. On each side of this door crouched two colossal sphynxes, as though they were the guardians of the place.

No human foot had for three thousand years profaned the sanctity of that City of the Dead, into which our venturous steps were treading.

The winding passage widened as we advanced, when, on a sudden, a light burst on my eyes that dimmed the glare of our torches. It proceeded from myriads of Naphtha lamps, held by gigantic figures, part-man part-beast, in combinations strange as that of the snake-man in the Inferno, in whom it was impossible to distinguish where the man began, and the reptile ended.

With an indefinable terror, that even stilled the eternal babble of my Caliban, we continued to pace those Hades, popular with the dead; and as the azure light flickered and quivered, like serpents' tongues, from the lamps of the colossi, my imagination gifted the vapours with shapes all differing from each other, floating light as the atoms in the sunbeams along the walls, even to the lofty roof.

And now, afar off, murmurs were heard. Was it the many voices of the dead? It became more distinct. 'Twas the Nile rushing above our heads, swollen with the Abyssinian rains. Still we passed on, till its echoes died away in distant music among the catacombs.

Should we sink to rest among these labyrinthian cells, stifled in that dust of centuries, which rose from our feet in volumes – such were some of the reflections that began to suggest themselves, when I was attracted by an illumination, rendered more brilliant than the rest by the impenetrable depth of pitchy darkness of a cavern at its back. This galaxy of light proceeded from lamps held by twelve figures of the natural size, so admirable as a work of art, that they might have been supposed from the chisel of Phydias or Praxiteles. Was this the sarcophagus of the mysterious scroll? Did it contain the sacred emblems? My heart beat audibly with hope. I approached, and leaned over the shoulder of one of the bearers. Yes! It was there – the sacred diagram! That most perfect of figures enclosed in its mystic circle, as I had seen it in my trance!

And now for the great *arcanum*! With hands trembling at the sacrilege I was about to commit, I proceeded to lift off the lid of the sarcophagus. It slowly yielded, lost its equilibrium, and fell with a heavy crash on the floor. The sound was like that of thunder, and vibrated through the pitchy cavern in long echoes, which, from their repetition, proved it to be of vast extent – perhaps the hades of the Egyptians.

There lay the undecaying corpse of the Adamite king. Like to life he was – the hues of life were yet upon his cheek-his eyes were open, and glared on me with more than mortal lustre; and, lit by that reflection, made more wan his lips, that moved and quivered, as though he was only waiting for me to address him, ere he replied in answer to my questions.

At that awful moment, the whole Necropolis rocked and shook, as though rent by an earthquake; and there arose on all sides, out of the ground, a multitude of hideous fiends, vibrating in their hands torches, from which the ruddy fire flew off in flakes. They came in crowds that seemed to thicken as they approached, and joining in one chorus. The words were these:

'Papai Satan, Papai Satan, Aleppe!'

At that moment all the tombs opened with one accord, and the dead that had slept for ages rose slowly out of them in their shrouds, pressing forward in throngs from the depths of the streets that branched out on every side. They advanced as to a festival; and the light from their eyes was like that of a distant world, whose ashes are burning after it is extinct.

As they came near, I felt a sort of numbing iciness emanate from their bodies, the poisonous effluvia of the grave, penetrating to my marrow like a thousand points of steel. Yet did my heart beat wildly, panting to respire the atmosphere of life, struggling between life and death, suffocated amid that dust of millennia, the flame of torches, the damp of the catacombs. And imagine to yourself, added to all this, the daemons of the night howling, roaring in my stunned ears all one chorus-those discordant and mysterious words of invocation:

'Papai Satan, Papai Satan, Aleppe!'

Then, too, the earth seemed to open beneath my feet, and a red spiral flame issued forth, which by degrees assumed a form, a shape. It was, yet it was not, my old tutor. Then I awoke, and found it was – A DREAM.

The Diamond Lens

FITZ-JAMES O'BRIEN (1858)

In science fiction, there is often very little distinction between being the object of a Mad Scientist's affections and the subject of his experiments. Fitz-James O'Brien's narcissistic, murderous, bigoted microbiologist Linley blends science and the occult to achieve his goals, with dire consequences for everyone around him, including the woman with whom he has fallen in love, unbeknownst to her. O'Brien is also known for his short story 'What Was It?' (1859), which features a similar blend of science and horror in its depiction of an invisible monster.

I

FROM A VERY EARLY PERIOD of my life the entire bent of my inclinations had been toward microscopic investigations. When I was not more than ten years old, a distant relative of our family, hoping to astonish my inexperience, constructed a simple microscope for me by drilling in a disk of copper a small hole in which a drop of pure water was sustained by capillary attraction. This very primitive apparatus, magnifying some fifty diameters, presented, it is true, only indistinct and imperfect forms, but still sufficiently wonderful to work up my imagination to a preternatural state of excitement.

Seeing me so interested in this rude instrument, my cousin explained to me all that he knew about the principles of the microscope, related to me a few of the wonders which had been accomplished through its agency, and ended by promising to send me one regularly constructed, immediately on his return to the city. I counted the days, the hours, the minutes that intervened between that promise and his departure.

Meantime, I was not idle. Every transparent substance that bore the remotest resemblance to a lens I eagerly seized upon, and employed in vain attempts to realise that instrument the theory of whose construction I as yet only vaguely comprehended. All panes of glass containing those oblate spheroidal knots familiarly known as 'bull's-eyes' were ruthlessly destroyed in the hope of obtaining lenses of marvellous power. I even went so far as to extract the crystalline humour from the eyes of fishes and animals, and endeavoured to press it into the microscopic service. I plead guilty to having stolen the glasses from my Aunt Agatha's spectacles, with a dim idea of grinding them into lenses of wondrous magnifying properties – in which attempt it is scarcely necessary to say that I totally failed.

At last the promised instrument came. It was of that order known as Field's Simple Microscope, and had cost perhaps about fifteen dollars. As far as educational purposes went, a better apparatus could not have been selected. Accompanying it was a small treatise on the microscope – its history, uses, and discoveries. I comprehended then for the first time the 'Arabian Nights' Entertainments'. The dull veil of ordinary existence that hung across the world seemed suddenly to roll away, and to lay bare a land of enchantments. I felt toward my companions as the seer might feel toward the ordinary masses of men. I held conversations with nature in a tongue which they could not understand. I was in daily communication with living wonders such as they never imagined in their wildest visions, I penetrated beyond the external portal of things, and roamed through the sanctuaries. Where they beheld only a drop of rain slowly rolling down the window-glass, I saw a universe of beings animated with all the passions common to physical life, and convulsing their minute sphere with struggles as fierce and protracted as those of men. In the common spots of mould, which my mother, good housekeeper that she was, fiercely scooped away from her jam-pots, there abode for me, under the name of mildew, enchanted gardens, filled with dells and avenues of the densest foliage and most astonishing verdure, while from the fantastic boughs of these microscopic forests hung strange fruits glittering with green and silver and gold.

It was no scientific thirst that at this time filled my mind. It was the pure enjoyment of a poet to whom a world of wonders has been disclosed. I talked of my solitary pleasures to none. Alone with my microscope, I dimmed my sight, day after day and night after night, poring over the marvels which it unfolded to me. I was like one who, having discovered the ancient Eden still existing in all its primitive glory, should resolve to enjoy it in solitude, and never betray to mortal the secret of its locality. The rod of my life was bent at this moment. I destined myself to be a microscopist.

Of course, like every novice, I fancied myself a discoverer. I was ignorant at the time of the thousands of acute intellects engaged in the same pursuit as myself, and with the advantage of instruments a thousand times more powerful than mine. The names of Leeuwenhoek, Williamson, Spencer, Ehrenberg, Schultz, Dujardin, Schact, and Schleiden were then entirely unknown to me, or, if known, I was ignorant of their patient and wonderful researches. In every fresh specimen of cryptogamia which I placed beneath my instrument I believed that I discovered wonders of which the world was as yet ignorant. I remember well the thrill of delight and admiration that shot through me the first time that I discovered the common wheel animalcule (*Rotifera vulgaris*) expanding and contracting its flexible spokes and seemingly rotating through the water. Alas! as I grew older, and obtained some works treating of my favourite study, I found that I was only on the threshold of a science to the investigation of which some of the greatest men of the age were devoting their lives and intellects.

As I grew up, my parents, who saw but little likelihood of anything practical resulting from the examination of bits of moss and drops of water through a brass tube and a piece of glass, were anxious that I should choose a profession.

It was their desire that I should enter the counting-house of my uncle, Ethan Blake, a prosperous merchant, who carried on business in New York. This suggestion I decisively combated. I had no taste for trade; I should only make a failure; in short, I refused to become a merchant.

But it was necessary for me to select some pursuit. My parents were staid New England people, who insisted on the necessity of labour, and therefore, although, thanks to the bequest of my poor Aunt Agatha, I should, on coming of age, inherit a small fortune sufficient to place me above want, it was decided that, instead of waiting for this, I should act the nobler part, and employ the intervening years in rendering myself independent.

After much cogitation, I complied with the wishes of my family, and selected a profession. I determined to study medicine at the New York Academy. This disposition of my future suited me. A removal from my relatives would enable me to dispose of my time as I pleased without fear of detection. As long as I paid my Academy fees, I might shirk attending the lectures if I chose; and, as I never had the remotest intention of standing an examination, there was no danger of my being 'plucked'. Besides, a metropolis was the place for me. There I could obtain excellent instruments, the newest publications, intimacy with men of pursuits kindred with my own – in short, all things necessary to ensure a profitable devotion of my life to my beloved science. I had an abundance of money, few desires that were not bounded by my illuminating mirror on one side and my object-glass on the other; what, therefore, was to prevent my becoming an illustrious investigator of the veiled worlds? It was with the most buoyant hope that I left my New England home and established myself in New York.

II

My first step, of course, was to find suitable apartments. These I obtained, after a couple of days' search, in Fourth Avenue; a very pretty second floor, unfurnished, containing sitting-room, bedroom, and a smaller apartment which I intended to fit up as a laboratory. I furnished my lodgings simply, but rather elegantly, and then devoted all my energies to the adornment of the temple of my worship. I visited Pike, the celebrated optician, and passed in review his splendid collection of microscopes: Field's Compound, Hingham's, Spencer's, Nachet's Binocular (that founded on the principles of the stereoscope), and at length fixed upon that form known as Spencer's Trunnion Microscope, as combining the greatest number of improvements with an almost perfect freedom from tremor. Along with this I purchased every possible accessory – draw-tubes, micrometers, a camera lucida, lever-stage, achromatic condensers, white cloud illuminators, prisms, parabolic condensers, polarising apparatus, forceps, aquatic boxes, fishing-tubes, with a host of other articles, all of which would have been useful in the hands of an experienced microscopist, but, as I afterward discovered, were not of the slightest present value to me. It takes years of practice to know how to use a complicated microscope. The optician looked suspiciously at me as I made these valuable purchases. He evidently was uncertain whether to set me down as some scientific celebrity or a madman. I think he was inclined to the latter belief. I suppose I was mad. Every great genius is mad upon the subject in which he is greatest. The unsuccessful madman is disgraced and called a lunatic.

Mad or not, I set myself to work with a zeal which few scientific students have ever equalled. I had everything to learn relative to the delicate study upon which I had embarked – a study involving the most earnest patience, the most rigid analytic powers, the steadiest hand, the most untiring eye, the most refined and subtle manipulation.

For a long time, half my apparatus lay inactively on the shelves of my laboratory, which was now most amply furnished with every possible contrivance for facilitating my investigations. The fact was that I did not know how to use some of my scientific implements – never having been taught microscopies – and those whose use I understood theoretically were of little avail until by practice I could attain the necessary delicacy of handling. Still, such was the fury of my ambition, such the untiring perseverance of my experiments, that, difficult of credit as it may be, in the course of one year I became theoretically and practically an accomplished microscopist.

During this period of my labours, in which I submitted specimens of every substance that came under my observation to the action of my lenses, I became a discoverer – in a small way, it is true, for I was very young, but still a discoverer. It was I who destroyed Ehrenberg's theory that the *Volvox globator* was an animal, and proved that his 'monads' with stomachs and eyes were merely phases of the formation of a vegetable cell, and were, when they reached their mature state, incapable of the act of conjugation, or any true generative act, without which no organism rising to any stage of life higher than vegetable can be said to be complete. It was I who resolved the singular problem of rotation in the cells and hairs of plants into ciliary attraction, in spite of the assertions of Wenham and others that my explanation was the result of an optical illusion.

But notwithstanding these discoveries, laboriously and painfully made as they were, I felt horribly dissatisfied. At every step I found myself stopped by the imperfections of my instruments. Like all active microscopists, I gave my imagination full play. Indeed, it is a common complaint against many such that they supply the defects of their instruments with the creations of their brains. I imagined depths beyond depths in nature which the limited power of my lenses prohibited me from exploring. I lay awake at night constructing imaginary microscopes of immeasurable power, with which I seemed to pierce through all the envelopes of matter down to its original atom. How I cursed those imperfect mediums which necessity through ignorance compelled me to use! How I longed to discover the secret of some perfect lens, whose magnifying power should be limited only by the resolvability of the object, and which at the same time should be free from spherical and chromatic aberrations – in short, from all the obstacles over which the poor microscopist finds himself continually stumbling! I felt convinced that the simple microscope, composed of a single lens of such vast yet perfect power, was possible of construction. To attempt to bring the compound microscope up to such a pitch would have been commencing at the wrong end; this latter being simply a partially successful endeavour to remedy those very defects of the simplest instrument which, if conquered, would leave nothing to be desired.

It was in this mood of mind that I became a constructive microscopist. After another year passed in this new pursuit, experimenting on every imaginable substance – glass, gems, flints, crystals, artificial crystals formed of the alloy of various vitreous materials – in short, having constructed as many varieties of lenses as Argus had eyes, I found myself precisely where I started, with nothing gained save an extensive knowledge of glass-making. I was almost dead with despair. My parents were surprised at my apparent want of progress in my medical studies (I had not attended one lecture since my arrival in the city), and the expenses of my mad pursuit had been so great as to embarrass me very seriously.

I was in this frame of mind one day, experimenting in my laboratory on a small diamond – that stone, from its great refracting power, having always occupied my attention more than any other – when a young Frenchman who lived on the floor above me, and who was in the habit of occasionally visiting me, entered the room.

I think that Jules Simon was a Jew. He had many traits of the Hebrew character: a love of jewellery, of dress, and of good living. There was something mysterious about him. He always had something to sell, and yet went into excellent society. When I say sell, I should perhaps have said peddle; for his operations were generally confined to the disposal of single articles – a picture, for instance, or a rare carving in ivory, or a pair of duelling-pistols, or the dress of a Mexican caballero. When I was first furnishing my rooms, he paid me a visit, which ended in my purchasing an antique silver lamp, which he assured me was a Cellini – it was handsome enough even for that – and some other knick-knacks for my sitting-room. Why Simon should pursue this petty trade I never could imagine. He apparently had plenty of money, and had the entrée of the best houses in the city – taking care, however, I suppose, to drive no bargains within the enchanted circle of the Upper Ten. I came at length to the conclusion that this peddling was but a mask to cover some greater object, and even went so far as to believe my young acquaintance to be implicated in the slave-trade. That, however, was none of my affair.

On the present occasion, Simon entered my room in a state of considerable excitement.

'Ah! *Mon ami!*' he cried, before I could even offer him the ordinary salutation. 'It has occurred to me to be the witness of the most astonishing things in the world. I promenade myself to the house of Madame … How does the little animal – *le renard* – name himself in the Latin?'

'*Vulpes,*' I answered.

'Ah! Yes – Vulpes. I promenade myself to the house of Madame Vulpes.'

'The spirit medium?'

'Yes, the great medium. Great heavens! What a woman! I write on a slip of paper many of questions concerning affairs of the most secret – affairs that conceal themselves in the abysses of my heart the most profound; and behold, by example, what occurs? This devil of a woman makes me replies the most truthful to all of them. She talks to me of things that I do not love to talk of to myself. What am I to think? I am fixed to the earth!'

'Am I to understand you, M. Simon, that this Mrs Vulpes replied to questions secretly written by you, which questions related to events known only to yourself?'

'Ah! more than that, more than that,' he answered, with an air of some alarm. 'She related to me things … But,' he added, after a pause, and suddenly changing his manner, 'why occupy ourselves with these follies? It was all the biology, without doubt. It goes without saying that it has not my credence. But why are we here, *mon ami*? It has occurred to me to discover the most beautiful thing as you can imagine – a vase with green lizards on it, composed by the great Bernard Palissy. It is in my apartment; let us mount. I go to show it to you.'

I followed Simon mechanically; but my thoughts were far from Palissy and his enamelled ware, although I, like him, was seeking in the dark a great discovery. This casual mention of the spiritualist, Madame Vulpes, set me on a new track. What if, through communication with more subtle organisms than my own, I could reach at a single bound the goal which perhaps a life of agonising mental toil would never enable me to attain?

While purchasing the Palissy vase from my friend Simon, I was mentally arranging a visit to Madame Vulpes.

III

Two evenings after this, thanks to an arrangement by letter and the promise of an ample fee, I found Madame Vulpes awaiting me at her residence alone. She was a coarse-featured woman, with keen and rather cruel dark eyes, and an exceedingly sensual expression about her mouth and under jaw. She received me in perfect silence, in an apartment on the ground floor, very sparsely furnished. In the centre of the room, close to where Mrs Vulpes sat, there was a common round mahogany table. If I had come for the purpose of sweeping her chimney, the woman could not have looked more indifferent to my appearance. There was no attempt to inspire the visitor with awe. Everything bore a simple and practical aspect. This intercourse with the spiritual world was evidently as familiar an occupation with Mrs Vulpes as eating her dinner or riding in an omnibus.

'You come for a communication, Mr Linley?' said the medium, in a dry, business-like tone of voice.

'By appointment – yes.'

'What sort of communication do you want – a written one?'

'Yes, I wish for a written one.'

'From any particular spirit?'

'Yes.'

'Have you ever known this spirit on this earth?'

'Never. He died long before I was born. I wish merely to obtain from him some information which he ought to be able to give better than any other.'

'Will you seat yourself at the table, Mr Linley,' said the medium, 'and place your hands upon it?'

I obeyed, Mrs Vulpes being seated opposite to me, with her hands also on the table. We remained thus for about a minute and a half, when a violent succession of raps came on the table, on the back of my chair, on the floor immediately under my feet, and even on the window-panes. Mrs Vulpes smiled composedly.

'They are very strong tonight,' she remarked. 'You are fortunate.' She then continued, 'Will the spirits communicate with this gentleman?'

Vigorous affirmative.

'Will the particular spirit he desires to speak with communicate?'

A very confused rapping followed this question.

'I know what they mean,' said Mrs Vulpes, addressing herself to me; 'they wish you to write down the name of the particular spirit that you desire to converse with. Is that so?' she added, speaking to her invisible guests.

That it was so was evident from the numerous affirmatory responses. While this was going on, I tore a slip from my pocket-book and scribbled a name under the table.

'Will this spirit communicate in writing with this gentleman?' asked the medium once more.

After a moment's pause, her hand seemed to be seized with a violent tremor, shaking so forcibly that the table vibrated. She said that a spirit had seized her hand and would write. I handed her some sheets of paper that were on the table and a pencil. The latter she held loosely in her hand, which presently began to move over the paper with a singular and seemingly involuntary motion.

After a few moments had elapsed, she handed me the paper, on which I found written, in a large, uncultivated hand, the words, 'He is not here, but has been sent for.' A pause of a minute or so ensued, during which Mrs Vulpes remained perfectly silent, but the raps continued at regular intervals. When the short period I mention had elapsed, the hand of the medium was again seized with its convulsive tremor, and she wrote, under this strange influence, a few words on the paper, which she handed to me. They were as follows:

'I am here. Question me.
Leeuwenhoek.'

I was astounded. The name was identical with that I had written beneath the table, and carefully kept concealed. Neither was it at all probable that an uncultivated woman like Mrs Vulpes should know even the name of the great father of microscopies. It may have been biology; but this theory was soon doomed to be destroyed. I wrote on my slip – still concealing it from Mrs Vulpes – a series of questions which, to avoid tediousness, I shall place with the responses, in the order in which they occurred:

I – Can the microscope be brought to perfection?
Spirit – Yes.
I – Am I destined to accomplish this great task?
Spirit – You are.
I – I wish to know how to proceed to attain this end. For the love which you bear to science, help me!
Spirit – A diamond of one hundred and forty carats, submitted to electro-magnetic currents for a long period, will experience a rearrangement of its atoms inter se *and from that stone you will form the universal lens.*
I – Will great discoveries result from the use of such a lens?

Spirit – So great that all that has gone before is as nothing.

I – But the refractive power of the diamond is so immense that the image will be formed within the lens. How is that difficulty to be surmounted?

Spirit – Pierce the lens through its axis, and the difficulty is obviated. The image will be formed in the pierced space, which will itself serve as a tube to look through. Now I am called. Good night.

I cannot at all describe the effect that these extraordinary communications had upon me. I felt completely bewildered. No biological theory could account for the discovery of the lens. The medium might, by means of biological rapport with my mind, have gone so far as to read my questions and reply to them coherently. But biology could not enable her to discover that magnetic currents would so alter the crystals of the diamond as to remedy its previous defects and admit of its being polished into a perfect lens. Some such theory may have passed through my head, it is true; but if so, I had forgotten it. In my excited condition of mind there was no course left but to become a convert, and it was in a state of the most painful nervous exaltation that I left the medium's house that evening. She accompanied me to the door, hoping that I was satisfied. The raps followed us as we went through the hall, sounding on the balusters, the flooring, and even the lintels of the door. I hastily expressed my satisfaction and escaped hurriedly into the cool night air. I walked home with but one thought possessing me – how to obtain a diamond of the immense size required. My entire means multiplied a hundred times over would have been inadequate to its purchase. Besides, such stones are rare, and become historical. I could find such only in the regalia of Eastern or European monarchs.

IV

There was a light in Simon's room as I entered my house. A vague impulse urged me to visit him. As I opened the door of his sitting-room unannounced, he was bending, with his back toward me, over a Carcel lamp, apparently engaged in minutely examining some object which he held in his hands. As I entered, he started suddenly, thrust his hand into his breast pocket, and turned to me with a face crimson with confusion.

'What!' I cried, 'poring over the miniature of some fair lady? Well, don't blush so much; I won't ask to see it.'

Simon laughed awkwardly enough, but made none of the negative protestations usual on such occasions. He asked me to take a seat.

'Simon,' said I, 'I have just come from Madame Vulpes.'

This time Simon turned as white as a sheet, and seemed stupefied, as if a sudden electric shock had smitten him. He babbled some incoherent words and went hastily to a small closet where he usually kept his liquors. Although astonished at his emotion, I was too preoccupied with my own idea to pay much attention to anything else.

'You say truly when you call Madame Vulpes a devil of a woman,' I continued. 'Simon, she told me wonderful things tonight, or rather was the means of telling me wonderful things. Ah! if I could only get a diamond that weighed one hundred and forty carats!'

Scarcely had the sigh with which I uttered this desire died upon my lips when Simon, with the aspect of a wild beast, glared at me savagely, and, rushing to the mantelpiece, where some foreign weapons hung on the wall, caught up a Malay *kris*, and brandished it furiously before him.

'No!' he cried in French, into which he always broke when excited. 'No! you shall not have it! You are perfidious! You have consulted with that demon, and desire my treasure! But I will die first! Me, I am brave! You cannot make me fear!'

All this, uttered in a loud voice, trembling with excitement, astounded me. I saw at a glance that I had accidentally trodden upon the edges of Simon's secret, whatever it was. It was necessary to reassure him.

'My dear Simon,' I said, 'I am entirely at a loss to know what you mean. I went to Madame Vulpes to consult with her on a scientific problem, to the solution of which I discovered that a diamond of the size I just mentioned was necessary. You were never alluded to during the evening, nor, so far as I was concerned, even thought of. What can be the meaning of this outburst? If you happen to have a set of valuable diamonds in your possession, you need fear nothing from me. The diamond which I require you could not possess; or, if you did possess it, you would not be living here.'

Something in my tone must have completely reassured him, for his expression immediately changed to a sort of constrained merriment, combined, however, with a certain suspicious attention to my movements. He laughed, and said that I must bear with him; that he was at certain moments subject to a species of vertigo, which betrayed itself in incoherent speeches, and that the attacks passed off as rapidly as they came.

He put his weapon aside while making this explanation, and endeavoured, with some success, to assume a more cheerful air.

All this did not impose on me in the least. I was too much accustomed to analytical labours to be baffled by so flimsy a veil. I determined to probe the mystery to the bottom.

'Simon,' I said gayly, 'let us forget all this over a bottle of Burgundy. I have a case of Lausseure's Clos Vougeot downstairs, fragrant with the odours and ruddy with the sunlight of the Côte d'Or. Let us have up a couple of bottles. What say you?'

'With all my heart,' answered Simon smilingly.

I produced the wine and we seated ourselves to drink. It was of a famous vintage, that of 1848, a year when war and wine throve together, and its pure but powerful juice seemed to impart renewed vitality to the system. By the time we had half-finished the second bottle, Simon's head, which I knew was a weak one, had begun to yield, while I remained calm as ever, only that every draught seemed to send a flush of vigour through my limbs. Simon's utterance became more and more indistinct. He took to singing French chansons of a not very moral tendency. I rose suddenly from the table just at the conclusion of one of those incoherent verses, and, fixing my eyes on him with a quiet smile, said, 'Simon, I have deceived you. I learned your secret this evening. You may as well be frank with me. Mrs Vulpes – or rather, one of her spirits – told me all.'

He started with horror. His intoxication seemed for the moment to fade away, and he made a movement toward the weapon that he had a short time before laid down. I stopped him with my hand.

'Monster!' he cried passionately, 'I am ruined! What shall I do? You shall never have it! I swear by my mother!'

'I don't want it,' I said; 'rest secure, but be frank with me. Tell me all about it.'

The drunkenness began to return. He protested with maudlin earnestness that I was entirely mistaken, that I was intoxicated; then asked me to swear eternal secrecy, and promised to disclose the mystery to me. I pledged myself, of course, to all. With an uneasy look in his eyes, and hands unsteady with drink and nervousness, he drew a small case from his breast and opened it. Heavens! How the mild lamplight was shivered into a thousand prismatic arrows as it fell upon a vast rose-diamond that glittered in the case! I was no judge of diamonds, but I saw at a glance that this was a gem of rare size and purity. I looked at Simon with wonder and – must I confess it? – with envy. How could he have obtained this treasure? In reply to my questions, I could just gather from his drunken statements (of which, I fancy, half the incoherence was affected) that he had been superintending a gang of slaves engaged in diamond-washing in Brazil; that he had seen one of them secrete a diamond, but, instead of informing his employers, had quietly watched the man until he saw him bury his treasure; that he had dug it up and fled with it, but that as yet he was afraid to attempt to dispose of it publicly – so valuable a gem being almost certain to attract too much attention to its owner's antecedents – and he had not been able to discover any of those obscure channels by which such matters are conveyed away safely. He added that, in accordance with oriental practice, he had named his diamond with the fanciful title of 'The Eye of Morning'.

While Simon was relating this to me, I regarded the great diamond attentively. Never had I beheld anything so beautiful. All the glories of light ever imagined or described seemed to pulsate in its crystalline chambers. Its weight, as I learned from Simon, was exactly one hundred and forty carats. Here was an amazing coincidence. The hand of destiny seemed in it. On the very evening when the spirit of Leeuwenhoek communicates to me the great secret of the microscope, the priceless means which he directs me to employ start up within my easy reach! I determined, with the most perfect deliberation, to possess myself of Simon's diamond.

I sat opposite to him while he nodded over his glass, and calmly revolved the whole affair. I did not for an instant contemplate so foolish an act as a common theft, which would of course be discovered, or at least necessitate flight and concealment, all of which must interfere with my scientific plans. There was but one step to be taken – to kill Simon. After all, what was the life of a little peddling Jew in comparison with the interests of science? Human beings are taken every day from the condemned prisons to be experimented on by surgeons. This man, Simon, was by his own confession a criminal, a robber, and I believed on my soul a murderer. He deserved death quite as much as any felon condemned by the laws: why should I not, like government, contrive that his punishment should contribute to the progress of human knowledge?

The means for accomplishing everything I desired lay within my reach. There stood upon the mantelpiece a bottle half-full of French laudanum. Simon was so occupied with his diamond, which I had just restored to him, that it was an affair of no difficulty to drug his glass. In a quarter of an hour he was in a profound sleep.

I now opened his waistcoat, took the diamond from the inner pocket in which he had placed it, and removed him to the bed, on which I laid him so that his feet hung down over the edge. I had possessed myself of the Malay *kris*, which I held in my right hand, while with the other I discovered as accurately as I could by pulsation the exact locality of the heart. It was essential that all the aspects of his death should lead to the surmise of self-murder. I calculated the exact angle at which it was probable that the weapon, if levelled by Simon's own hand, would enter his breast; then with one powerful blow I thrust it up to the hilt in the very spot which I desired to penetrate. A convulsive thrill ran through Simon's limbs. I heard a smothered sound issue from his throat, precisely like the bursting of a large air-bubble sent up by a diver when it reaches the surface of the water; he turned half round on his side, and, as if to assist my plans more effectually, his right hand, moved by some mere spasmodic impulse, clasped the handle of the *kris*, which it remained holding with extraordinary muscular tenacity. Beyond this there was no apparent struggle. The laudanum, I presume, paralyzed the usual nervous action. He must have died instantly.

There was yet something to be done. To make it certain that all suspicion of the act should be diverted from any inhabitant of the house to Simon himself, it was necessary that the door should be found in the morning locked on the inside. How to do this, and afterward escape myself? Not by the window; that was a physical impossibility. Besides, I was determined that the windows also should be found bolted. The solution was simple enough. I descended softly to my own room for a peculiar instrument which I had used for holding small slippery substances, such as minute spheres of glass, etc. This instrument was nothing more than a long, slender hand-vice, with a very powerful grip and a considerable leverage, which last was accidentally owing to the shape of the handle. Nothing was simpler than, when the key was in the lock, to seize the end of its stem in this vice, through the keyhole, from the outside, and so lock the door. Previously, however, to doing this, I burned a number of papers on Simon's hearth. Suicides almost always burn papers before they destroy themselves. I also emptied some more laudanum into Simon's glass – having first removed from it all traces of wine – cleaned the other wine-glass, and brought the bottles away with me. If traces of two persons drinking had been found in the room, the question naturally would have arisen, who was the second? Besides, the wine-bottles might have been identified as belonging to me. The laudanum I poured out to account for its presence in his stomach, in case of a post-mortem examination. The theory naturally would be that he first intended to poison himself, but, after swallowing a little of the drug, was either disgusted with its taste, or changed his mind from other motives, and chose the dagger. These arrangements made, I walked out, leaving the gas burning, locked the door with my vice, and went to bed.

Simon's death was not discovered until nearly three in the afternoon. The servant, astonished at seeing the gas burning – the light streaming on the dark landing from under the door – peeped through the keyhole and saw Simon on the bed.

She gave the alarm. The door was burst open, and the neighbourhood was in a fever of excitement.

Everyone in the house was arrested, myself included. There was an inquest; but no clue to his death beyond that of suicide could be obtained. Curiously enough, he had made several speeches to his friends the preceding week that seemed to point to self-destruction. One gentleman swore that Simon had said in his presence that 'he was tired of life'. His landlord affirmed that Simon, when paying him his last month's rent, remarked that 'he should not pay him rent much longer'. All the other evidence corresponded: the door locked inside, the position of the corpse, the burned papers. As I anticipated, no one knew of the possession of the diamond by Simon, so that no motive was suggested for his murder. The jury, after a prolonged examination, brought in the usual verdict, and the neighbourhood once more settled down to its accustomed quiet.

V

The three months succeeding Simon's catastrophe I devoted night and day to my diamond lens. I had constructed a vast galvanic battery, composed of nearly two thousand pairs of plates: a higher power I dared not use, lest the diamond should be calcined. By means of this enormous engine I was enabled to send a powerful current of electricity continually through my great diamond, which it seemed to me gained in lustre every day. At the expiration of a month I commenced the grinding and polishing of the lens, a work of intense toil and exquisite delicacy. The great density of the stone, and the care required to be taken with the curvatures of the surfaces of the lens, rendered the labour the severest and most harassing that I had yet undergone.

At last the eventful moment came; the lens was completed. I stood trembling on the threshold of new worlds. I had the realisation of Alexander's famous wish before me. The lens lay on the table, ready to be placed upon its platform. My hand fairly shook as I enveloped a drop of water with a thin coating of oil of turpentine, preparatory to its examination, a process necessary in order to prevent the rapid evaporation of the water. I now placed the drop on a thin slip of glass under the lens, and throwing upon it, by the combined aid of a prism and a mirror, a powerful stream of light, I approached my eye to the minute hole drilled through the axis of the lens. For an instant I saw nothing save what seemed to be an illuminated chaos, a vast, luminous abyss. A pure white light, cloudless and serene, and seemingly limitless as space itself, was my first impression. Gently, and with the greatest care, I depressed the lens a few hairbreadths. The wondrous illumination still continued, but as the lens approached the object a scene of indescribable beauty was unfolded to my view.

I seemed to gaze upon a vast space, the limits of which extended far beyond my vision. An atmosphere of magical luminousness permeated the entire field of view. I was amazed to see no trace of animalculous life. Not a living thing, apparently, inhabited that dazzling expanse. I comprehended instantly that, by the wondrous power of my lens, I had penetrated beyond the grosser particles of aqueous matter, beyond the realms of infusoria and protozoa, down to the original gaseous globule, into whose luminous interior I was gazing as into an almost boundless dome filled with a supernatural radiance.

It was, however, no brilliant void into which I looked. On every side I beheld beautiful inorganic forms, of unknown texture, and coloured with the most enchanting hues. These forms presented the appearance of what might be called, for want of a more specific definition, foliated clouds of the highest rarity – that is, they undulated and broke into vegetable formations, and were tinged with splendours compared with which the gilding of our autumn woodlands is as dross compared with gold. Far away into the illimitable distance stretched long avenues of these gaseous forests, dimly transparent, and painted with prismatic hues of unimaginable brilliancy. The pendent branches waved along the fluid glades until every vista seemed to break through half-lucent ranks of many-coloured drooping silken pennons. What seemed to be either fruits or flowers, pied with a thousand hues, lustrous and ever-varying, bubbled from the crowns of this fairy foliage. No hills, no lakes, no rivers, no forms animate or inanimate, were to be seen, save those vast auroral copses that floated serenely in the luminous stillness, with leaves and fruits and flowers gleaming with unknown fires, unrealisable by mere imagination.

How strange, I thought, that this sphere should be thus condemned to solitude! I had hoped, at least, to discover some new form of animal life, perhaps of a lower class than any with which we are at present acquainted, but still some living organism. I found my newly discovered world, if I may so speak, a beautiful chromatic desert.

While I was speculating on the singular arrangements of the internal economy of Nature, with which she so frequently splinters into atoms our most compact theories, I thought I beheld a form moving slowly through the glades of one of the prismatic forests. I looked more attentively, and found that I was not mistaken. Words cannot depict the anxiety with which I awaited the nearer approach of this mysterious object. Was it merely some inanimate substance, held in suspense in the attenuated atmosphere of the globule, or was it an animal endowed with vitality and motion? It approached, flitting behind the gauzy, coloured veils of cloud-foliage, for seconds dimly revealed, then vanishing. At last the violet pennons that trailed nearest to me vibrated; they were gently pushed aside, and the form floated out into the broad light.

It was a female human shape. When I say human, I mean it possessed the outlines of humanity; but there the analogy ends. Its adorable beauty lifted it illimitable heights beyond the loveliest daughter of Adam.

I cannot, I dare not, attempt to inventory the charms of this divine revelation of perfect beauty. Those eyes of mystic violet, dewy and serene, evade my words. Her long, lustrous hair following her glorious head in a golden wake, like the track sown in heaven by a falling star, seems to quench my most burning phrases with its splendours. If all the bees of Hybla nestled upon my lips, they would still sing but hoarsely the wondrous harmonies of outline that enclosed her form.

She swept out from between the rainbow-curtains of the cloud-trees into the broad sea of light that lay beyond. Her motions were those of some graceful naiad, cleaving, by a mere effort of her will, the clear, unruffled waters that fill the chambers of the sea. She floated forth with the serene grace of a frail bubble ascending through the still atmosphere of a June day. The perfect roundness of her limbs formed suave and enchanting curves. It was like listening to the most spiritual symphony of Beethoven the divine, to watch the harmonious flow of lines. This, indeed was a pleasure cheaply purchased at any price. What cared I if I had waded to the portal of this wonder through another's blood? I would have given my own to enjoy one such moment of intoxication and delight.

Breathless with gazing on this lovely wonder, and forgetful for an instant of everything save her presence, I withdrew my eye from the microscope eagerly. Alas! as my gaze fell on the thin slide that lay beneath my instrument, the bright light from mirror and from prism sparkled on a colourless drop of water! There, in that tiny bead of dew, this beautiful being was forever imprisoned. The planet Neptune was not more distant from me than she. I hastened once more to apply my eye to the microscope.

Animula (let me now call her by that dear name which I subsequently bestowed on her) had changed her position. She had again approached the wondrous forest, and was gazing earnestly upward. Presently one of the trees – as I must call them – unfolded a long ciliary process, with which it seized one of the gleaming fruits that glittered on its summit, and, sweeping slowly down, held it within reach of Animula. The sylph took it in her delicate hand and began to eat. My attention was so entirely absorbed by her that I could not apply myself to the task of determining whether this singular plant was or was not instinct with volition.

I watched her, as she made her repast, with the most profound attention. The suppleness of her motions sent a thrill of delight through my frame; my heart beat madly as she turned her beautiful eyes in the direction of the spot in which I stood. What would I not have given to have had the power to precipitate myself into that luminous ocean and float with her through those grooves of purple and gold! While I was thus breathlessly following her every movement, she suddenly started, seemed to listen for a moment, and then cleaving the brilliant ether in which she was floating, like a flash of light, pierced through the opaline forest and disappeared.

Instantly a series of the most singular sensations attacked me. It seemed as if I had suddenly gone blind. The luminous sphere was still before me, but my daylight had vanished. What caused this sudden disappearance? Had she a lover or a husband? Yes, that was the solution! Some signal from a happy fellow-being had vibrated through the avenues of the forest, and she had obeyed the summons.

The agony of my sensations, as I arrived at this conclusion, startled me. I tried to reject the conviction that my reason forced upon me. I battled against the fatal conclusion, but in vain. It was so. I had no escape from it. I loved an animalcule.

It is true that, thanks to the marvellous power of my microscope, she appeared of human proportions. Instead of presenting the revolting aspect of the coarser creatures, that live and struggle and die, in the more easily resolvable portions of the water-drop, she was fair and delicate and of surpassing beauty. But of what account was all that? Every time that my eye was withdrawn from the instrument it fell on a miserable drop of water, within which, I must be content to know, dwelt all that could make my life lovely.

Could she but see me once! Could I for one moment pierce the mystical walls that so inexorably rose to separate us, and whisper all that filled my soul, I might consent to be satisfied for the rest of my life with the knowledge of her remote sympathy.

It would be something to have established even the faintest personal link to bind us together – to know that at times, when roaming through these enchanted glades, she might think of the wonderful stranger who had broken the monotony of her life with his presence and left a gentle memory in her heart!

But it could not be. No invention of which human intellect was capable could break down the barriers that nature had erected. I might feast my soul upon her wondrous beauty, yet she must always remain ignorant of the adoring eyes that day and night gazed upon her, and, even when closed, beheld her in dreams. With a bitter cry of anguish, I fled from the room, and flinging myself on my bed, sobbed myself to sleep like a child.

VI

I arose the next morning almost at daybreak, and rushed to my microscope. I trembled as I sought the luminous world in miniature that contained my all. Animula was there. I had left the gas-lamp, surrounded by its moderators, burning when I went to bed the night before. I found the sylph bathing, as it were, with an expression of pleasure animating her features, in the brilliant light which surrounded her. She tossed her lustrous golden hair over her shoulders with innocent coquetry. She lay at full length in the transparent medium, in which she supported herself with ease, and gambolled with the enchanting grace that the nymph Salmacis might have exhibited when she sought to conquer the modest Hermaphroditus. I tried an experiment to satisfy myself if her powers of reflection were developed. I lessened the lamplight considerably. By the dim light that remained, I could see an expression of pain flit across her face. She looked upward suddenly, and her brows contracted. I flooded the stage of the microscope again with a full stream of light, and her whole expression changed. She sprang forward like some substance deprived of all weight. Her eyes sparkled, and her lips moved. Ah! if science had only the means of conducting and reduplicating sounds, as it does rays of light, what carols of happiness would then have entranced my ears! what jubilant hymns to Adonais would have thrilled the illumined air!

I now comprehended how it was that the Count de Cabalis peopled his mystic world with sylphs – beautiful beings whose breath of life was lambent fire, and who sported forever in regions of purest ether and purest light. The Rosicrucian had anticipated the wonder that I had practically realised.

How long this worship of my strange divinity went on thus I scarcely know. I lost all note of time. All day from early dawn, and far into the night, I was to be found peering through that wonderful lens. I saw no one, went nowhere, and scarce allowed myself sufficient time for my meals. My whole life was absorbed in contemplation as rapt as that of any of the Romish saints. Every hour that I gazed upon the divine form strengthened my passion – a passion that was always overshadowed by the maddening conviction that, although I could gaze on her at will, she never, never could behold me!

At length I grew so pale and emaciated, from want of rest and continual brooding over my insane love and its cruel conditions, that I determined to make some effort to wean myself from it. 'Come,' I said, 'this is at best but a fantasy. Your imagination has bestowed on Animula charms which in reality she does not possess. Seclusion from female society has produced this morbid condition of mind. Compare her with the beautiful women of your own world, and this false enchantment will vanish.'

I looked over the newspapers by chance. There I beheld the advertisement of a celebrated danseuse who appeared nightly at Niblo's. The Signorina Caradolce had the reputation of being the most beautiful as well as the most graceful woman in the world. I instantly dressed and went to the theatre.

The curtain drew up. The usual semicircle of fairies in white muslin were standing on the right toe around the enamelled flower-bank of green canvas, on which the belated prince was sleeping. Suddenly a flute is heard. The fairies start. The trees open, the fairies all stand on the left toe, and the queen enters. It was the Signorina. She bounded forward amid thunders of applause, and, lighting on one foot, remained poised in the air. Heavens! was this the great enchantress that had drawn monarchs at her chariot-wheels? Those heavy, muscular limbs, those thick ankles, those cavernous eyes, that stereotyped smile, those crudely painted cheeks! Where were the vermeil blooms, the liquid, expressive eyes, the harmonious limbs of Animula?

The Signorina danced. What gross, discordant movements! The play of her limbs was all false and artificial. Her bounds were painful athletic efforts; her poses were angular and distressed the eye. I could bear it no longer; with an exclamation of disgust that drew every eye upon me, I rose from my seat in the very middle of the Signorina's pas-de-fascination and abruptly quitted the house.

I hastened home to feast my eyes once more on the lovely form of my sylph. I felt that henceforth to combat this passion would be impossible. I applied my eyes to the lens. Animula was there, but what could have happened? Some terrible change seemed to have taken place during my absence. Some secret grief seemed to cloud the lovely features of her I gazed upon. Her face had grown thin and haggard; her limbs trailed heavily; the wondrous lustre of her golden hair had faded. She was ill – ill, and I could not assist her! I believe at that moment I would have forfeited all claims to my human birth right if I could only have been dwarfed to the size of an animalcule, and permitted to console her from whom fate had forever divided me.

I racked my brain for the solution of this mystery. What was it that afflicted the sylph? She seemed to suffer intense pain. Her features contracted, and she even writhed, as if with some internal agony. The wondrous forests appeared also to have lost half their beauty. Their hues were dim, and in some places faded away altogether. I watched Animula for hours with a breaking heart, and she seemed absolutely to wither away under my very eye. Suddenly I remembered that I had not looked at the water-drop for several days. In fact, I hated to see it; for it reminded me of the natural barrier between Animula and myself. I hurriedly looked down on the stage of the microscope. The slide was still there – but, great heavens, the water drop had vanished! The awful truth burst upon me; it had evaporated, until it had become so minute as to be invisible to the naked eye; I had been gazing on its last atom, the one that contained Animula – and she was dying!

I rushed again to the front of the lens and looked through. Alas! the last agony had seized her. The rainbow-hued forests had all melted away, and Animula lay struggling feebly in what seemed to be a spot of dim light. Ah! the sight was horrible: the limbs once so round and lovely shrivelling up into nothings; the eyes – those eyes that shone like heaven – being quenched into black dust; the lustrous golden hair now lank and discoloured. The last throe came. I beheld that final struggle of the blackening form, and I fainted.

When I awoke out of a trance of many hours, I found myself lying amid the wreck of my instrument, myself as shattered in mind and body as it. I crawled feebly to my bed, from which I did not rise for many months.

They say now that I am mad; but they are mistaken. I am poor, for I have neither the heart nor the will to work; all my money is spent, and I live on charity. Young men's associations that love a joke invite me to lecture on optics before them, for which they pay me, and laugh at me while I lecture. 'Linley, the mad microscopist' is the name I go by. I suppose that I talk incoherently while I lecture. Who could talk sense when his brain is haunted by such ghastly memories, while ever and anon among the shapes of death I behold the radiant form of my lost Animula!

The Age of Science

FRANCES POWER COBBE (1877)

Satirical extracts from future newspapers almost constituted a subgenre of their own in the nineteenth and early twentieth centuries, and few of them carried glad tidings of things to come. The following abridged novella by Frances Power Cobbe is similarly pessimistic, but it stands out from the crowd in the way that it communicates the author's worries about women's civil rights and cruelty to animals with irony and dark humour. In Cobbe's imaginary future, reactionaries use the language of science and rationality as they try to reverse social advancement; thus, scholarly apes aside, this piece seems oddly prescient.

THE GREATEST DISCOVERY ever achieved by man is beyond all question that which it is now our privilege to announce, namely, that of the new *Prospective Telegraph*. By this truly wonderful invention (exquisitely simple in its machinery, yet of surpassing power) the obstacle of Time is as effectually conquered as that of Space has been for the last generation by the Electric Telegraph; and future years – even, it is anticipated, future centuries – will be made to respond to our call as promptly and completely as do now the uttermost parts of the earth wherewith the magic wire has placed us in communication.

For obvious reasons the particulars of this most marvellous invention, and the name of its author, must be withheld from the public till the patents (and the enormous profits) be secured to the Company which is invited to undertake to work it (with limited liability). We are only permitted by special favour to hint that the natural Force relied on to set the machinery in action is neither Electric, Magnetic, nor Galvanic; nor yet any combination of these; but that other great correlated imponderable agency, whose existence has been for some time suspected by many intelligent inquirers, called the Psychic Force. That no scepticism may linger in the minds of our readers, we desire to add that we have at this moment in our hands a complete transcript of a newspaper dated January 1st, 1977. As the printed matter of this gigantic periodical equals at least in bulk the whole of Gibbon's History, or Mr Jowett's edition of Plato, we cannot attempt to do more than offer our readers a few brief extracts.

The name of this journal (which, we conclude, may be considered the *Times* of the twentieth century) is THE AGE OF SCIENCE, and obviously refers with pride to the consciousness of its readers that they live in a period of the world's history when Science reigns supreme over human affairs, having triumphed over such things as War, the Chase, Literature, Art, and Religion. This appropriate title is printed, we may remark, in the largest and clearest possible Roman type: judging from the opticians' advertisements of 'Spectacles for Infants', 'Spectacles for Elementary Schools by the gross', and 'Cautions to Mothers' against allowing babies to use their eyes, it would appear that unassisted vision has become rare, if not unknown. There are ten columns on each page, each ten times as long as it is broad, and there are a hundred pages in the journal, proving that the decimal system has been thoroughly adopted even in such details.

Spread out open, the *Age of Science* would cover the floor of a very large hall. The familiarity of the contributors with all substances of chemistry, all the bones of all the beasts, birds, and fishes, alive or dead, and all the diseases incidental to humanity, speaks volumes for the superiority of their scientific education over our own. At the same time, on two or three occasions when illustrations have been chosen from past History or Poetry, the writers betray that their studies have not been much extended in the direction of Literature. One gentleman thinks that Mr Gladstone wrote the *Iliad* on hints afforded by Dr Schliemann, and that Milton was the author of the Book of Genesis. Another refers to the period when Rome was founded by Romeo and Juliet, while a third mentions the 'once-celebrated *Divina Commedia* by Molière', and regrets that 'so curious a specimen of archaic Japanese art as Titian's *Assumption* should not have been spared from the pile in which the *Transfiguration* of Phidias and the *Last Supper* of Praxiteles were destroyed by order of the Committee of the Royal Academy, to stop the propagation of bad aesthetic taste'.

The first page is rationally devoted to Telegraphic Intelligence, which everyone may be supposed to desire first to read. However, since the invention of the 'Army Exterminator' forty years prior, followed up so rapidly by the invention of the 'Fleet Annihilator', international policy has necessarily undergone a great modification. As war has become impossible as an *ultima ratio* in any case, and the principle of Arbitration, on which such hopes were founded, has proved ineffective, a permanent state of discord between nations seems to have become established. The foreign news of the hour is somewhat unsatisfactory. In consequence of the generally lawless condition of the Southern Russian Republics, the great corn districts of those regions have for some years been falling out of cultivation; and no hopes are entertained that any more grain shall be imported from Odessa, or indeed from any quarter of the world.

Despite these developments, instead of political news these telegrams consist mainly of minute verbatim reports of the proceedings of over ninety Scientific Congresses, which seem to be taking place at the same time in Europe, Asia, America, Australia, and Africa. It would occupy more space than the whole of this volume to offer even the briefest condensation of these reports, as they are carried on in terms quite unintelligible to us, and refer to scientific disputes to which we do not possess a clue. Following this is a Report of the Assembly of Convocation – a topic which we were surprised to find possessed such prominent interest, till we discovered that the Convocation of 1977 will consist exclusively of Medical men. The Upper House seems to be formed of Physicians and Surgeons who have obtained titles of Nobility, and the Lower House to be a representative body elected by medical graduates throughout the kingdom.

After the Report of Convocation, the *Age of Science* contains one column of Stocks and Shares, not possessing any special interest for readers of the present day, but appearing to prove, strangely enough, that investments are much fewer than in our time, and cannot be made in any Foreign securities. It seems the dream of Free Trade has been exploded; following the example of the American Empire (which ceased to be a Republic decades beforehand), prohibitive duties are placed on each state's own exports and the imports of other countries, meaning that commerce is considerably hampered. The restored native rulers of what was formerly called Britain's Indian Empire, and China after its brief occupation, have adopted American and European ideas as to placing for this next year such duties on rice and tea as will almost prohibit the importation of those articles into the English market, while they have positively forbidden the introduction of English cotton or iron into their respective States. The bad and deceptive quality of the goods furnished by British manufacturers is the alleged cause of these unfortunate regulations.

After these, in lieu both of Naval and Military Intelligence, and of the Church, five columns are devoted to Medical Appointments and Promotions. After all these we find twenty columns devoted to Latest Intelligence, in short paragraphs, of which we cull a few of the most interesting.

'OCCASIONAL NOTES. The magnificent Joss House now in process of erection by the Chinese of London forms a striking ornament to Regent Street, standing as it does on the site of the old deserted Langham Chapel. It will, we imagine, be the only place dedicated to religion's purposes which has been built during the last twenty years in the metropolis, and almost the only one in actual use. Although we cannot, as a Scientific nation, formally join in the worship of Buddha, we must all regard with sympathy and satisfaction the honours paid to that great Teacher by the very important section of our community, the Chinese, of whom it is said more than half a million have contributed to the erection and adornment of this Temple. The statue of Buddha is a noble work of modern sculpture by Mr Merino. The traditional pose of the crossed legs is slightly altered to bring them within the rules of scientific anatomy, and the Sage is obviously pondering those profound lessons of Pessimism (that it is a bad world we live in, and that we need not expect a better) which have justly secured for him the reverence of cultivated Europe.'

'An Accident of the ordinary sort occurred last night to the new Magnetic train, which was at the moment passing under the Channel, about ten miles from Dover. It appears that the engineers have been again at fault in the construction of the roof of the tunnel, and that the sea was rushing in with such violence that little hopes were entertained of bringing the train to the next watertight compartment; it must he assumed that the unfortunate passengers – numbering, it is supposed, about 800 – have been drowned like so many rats in a trap. The accident is unfortunate for the proprietors of Submarine Tunnel Stock, and also for several Insurance Companies, as extensive repairs will be required; but Science teaches us to regard these occurrences with composure, as serving to check the increase of a superabundant population.'

'The Simian Educational Institute (on Frobel's system), for members of the Ape family, continues to attract the strongest interest. In testing the educability of the Simian tribe, we are solving one of the most important problems of Science, and hitherto everything seems to promise the triumphant success of the experiment. There are now three Chimpanzees among the pupils at the Institute, whose grandfathers and grandmothers have all been well-educated monkeys; so that the set of the brain of these young people is already marked towards progress and civilisation. It is needless to observe that all the students are required to wash and dress themselves every morning in the becoming male and female habiliments provided by the taste of the Governors of the Institute. Great pains are also taken with their manners at meal times, and, to avoid temptation, nuts are not admitted at dessert.

'One of the young gentlemen (Joseph Macacus Silenus, Esq., generally known by his intimates as "Joe") is said to exhibit extraordinary talents, and to be able to answer any question in elementary science by means of an alphabet and a system of knocks – the best substitute for a spoken language, having been formerly invented by an ingenious race of impostors named Mediums, who flourished in the obscurity of the Victorian age. The plan adopted in France to employ the anthropoid apes as domestic servants has proved, we are informed, altogether successful in several families. Madame Le Singe, a fine specimen of the Gorilla tribe, has acted for some months as confidential Nurse in the family of M. Gobemouche, and is said to maintain discipline among her charges excellently well. It is an instructive spectacle to see Madame Le Singe walking on a fine day with the children, and pushing a perambulator in the Gardens of the Tuileries. The more ordinary employment found, however, for domestic Apes is that of cooks, when it is observed they occasionally call in the services of the household cat to assist them as kitchen-maid, especially when roast chestnuts form part of the entertainment.'

'The absolute prohibition to Women to read or write – even in cases where they may have formerly acquired those arts (now recognised as so unsuitable to their sex) – will, we apprehend, tell importantly on the health of infants, and of course eventually on that of the community. So long as females indulged in no more deleterious practices than dancing in hot rooms all night, unclothing their necks and chests, wearing thin slippers which exposed their feet to deadly chills, and tightening their waists till their ribs were crushed inwards, the Medical Profession very properly left them to follow their own devices with but little public remonstrance. The case was altered, however, when, three or four generations ago, a considerable movement was made for what was then called the Higher Education of women. The feeble brains of young females were taxed to study the now forgotten Greek and Latin languages, and even Mathematics and such Natural Science as was then understood.

'The result was truly alarming; for these poor creatures flung themselves with such energy into the pursuits opened to them, that, as one of their critics remarked, they resembled "the palm-er-worm and the canker-worm – they devoured every green thing", and not seldom surpassed their masculine competitors. At length they began to aim at entering the learned Professions – the Legal, and even the Medical. Our readers may be inclined to doubt the latter fact, which seems to involve actual absurdity, but there is evidence that there once existed two or three Lady

Doctors in London, who, like Pope Joan in Rome, foisted themselves surreptitiously into an exalted position from which Nature should have debarred them.

'Of course, it was the solemn duty of the Medical Profession to put a stop at once to an error which might lead to such a catastrophe, and numerous books were immediately written proving (what we all now acknowledge) that the culture of the brains of women is highly detrimental to their proper functions in the community; and, in short, that the more ignorant a woman may be, the more delightful she is as a wife, and the better qualified to fulfil the duties of a mother. Since Science has thoroughly gained the upper hand over Religious and other prejudices, the position of women, we are happy to say, has been steadily sinking, and the dream of a Higher Education has been replaced by the abolition of even Elementary Schools for girls, and now by the final Act of last Session, which renders it penal for any woman to read a book or newspaper, or to write a letter. We anticipate the very happiest results from this thoroughly sound and manly legislation.'

'The cheerful ceremony of opening the new Incineration Hall was performed an hour ago in Manchester by the Lord Doctor of Manchester, attended by the Mayor. It is a magnificent building, with a furnace capable of reducing twelve bodies at a time to ashes, which, after a certain period, will be used in the manufacture of water-filters for the drinking-fountains of the town. It is especially fortunate that the Hall can be employed at once, since the number of persons despatched by Euthanasia has been so great during the past week all over the country that the other Cremation establishments have proved inadequate to dispose of the corpses with sufficient rapidity.'

'An Important addition has been made to that instructive place of public amusement, the Zoological Gardens in Regent's Park: a department to contain those species of animals which are rapidly dying out in Europe. Among these are the Ass, the Fox, the Dog, the Hare, the Pheasant, and Partridge. In this age of Science it is, of course, impossible to go on employing a creature like the Donkey, proverbial for its intellectual deficiency, and we have no regret that only two pair of animals of the species (both in the Regent's Park collection) now survive in England, though a few are said to linger in Egypt. Connected with the dog there are so many traditional records of sagacity, having a certain scientific interest in connection with the form and size of its brain, that we should have been glad if a more complete collection of the varieties could have been preserved. However, the Foxhound, the Greyhound, Setter, and Pointer, seem all to have become extinct within about thirty years of the repeal of the Game Laws and the consequent cessation of field sports; and several of the more favoured kinds of dogs – Italian Greyhounds, Toy Terriers, Pomeranians, and Poodles – were, it is said, privately destroyed by the hundreds by their owners, who disgracefully sought to withdraw them from the researches of physiologists.

'The remaining kinds have been perhaps rather recklessly used by vivisectors, whose ardour in the noble cause of science has caused them to experiment, on an average, on about 14,000 dogs apiece, and the result has been that we only find at present twelve animals surviving, of whom nine belong to the class Mongrel. One noble old Newfoundland, who would have greatly graced the collection, was drowned by his owner last year under interesting circumstances. After rescuing a physiologist's son from drowning, the animal itself was so exhausted that its breathing and other symptoms suggested to the physiologist the scientific interest in watching it slowly drowning in a suitable vessel, where all the conditions of that death could be accurately investigated on so large a scale as that of a full-sized dog. The learned gentleman accordingly drowned the animal in a tub in his physiological laboratory as soon as his son was sufficiently recovered to witness the instructive and entertaining spectacle. The dog, when withdrawn half dead for a moment from the water, attempted to lick the boy's face; the child was weak enough to implore his father to spare it, but the learned gentleman of course pointed out to the boy the folly of such a request, and the experiment was completed. We trust to see this young gentleman hereafter as sound and eminent a physiologist as his distinguished father.'

After some five columns more of similar Intelligence, the *Age of Science* proceeds to give its readers a few Reviews of Books. The brevity of the remarks vouchsafed to these productions seems to indicate that no great importance is attached to Literature properly so called, but only to treatises on Physical Science. The Notices run as follow:

'REVIEWS. We do not usually in the *Age of Science* intrude on the province of the sixteen leading daily Scientific Newspapers devoted to critical notices of the books which pour from the press on Electrology, Physiology, Astronomy, Geology, &c. We are tempted to depart from our rule, however, so far as to offer our need of applause and congratulation on the publication of the last of the six splendid volumes forming the magnificent monograph on Cheese-mites, and the still more costly and exhaustive treatise on the great mystery of the Formation of Dust in Disused Apartments.

'In the inferior non-scientific walks of Literature we find that no Histories have been published during the last twelvemonth, and only one Historical Essay, namely *The Fall of the Church of England*, by the late (and last) Dean of Westminster. The author of this book composed it, we are informed, during his retirement in the Isle of Anglesea, whither, like most of the clergy, and the Druids in former ages, he retreated after the great victory gained by Science, when the Cathedrals and Churches were made over by Parliament to the Medical Profession. The Dean traces the fall of the Anglican Establishment to the folly of a party in the Church, who, in an age of doubt and transition, when religion needed to be presented in its most spiritual shape, made it appear by their practices a matter of rites and forms altogether childish. We are persuaded, however, that the abolition of the Churches was due to a deeper and more widespread cause – namely, the growth of that sound philosophy which recognises Matter as containing itself the germ and potency of every form of life, and, of course, dismisses the dream of a Soul in man, which might enjoy existence after death. As soon as this great truth had had time to penetrate the minds of the masses, the collapse of Religion obviously became imminent.

'FICTION. *The Precession of the Equinox, and other Tales*, by Wilkinson Collinson, Esq.: This is a highly sensational story, and will sell like wildfire at the bookstalls. The interest of the plot turns on the phenomenon in question, but embraces subsidiary problems respecting the sun's path through the Zodiac. *Daniel Allround*, by George Evans: The chief attraction of this book lies in the abstruse technical terminology which the author has employed to illustrate profound observations of men and things, but too much space is lost by delineations of characters without tracing them to the laws of heredity. *Edwin and Angelina*, By J. Fitzparnell: The author of this charming novel has afforded his readers a perfect study of the effects of each of the passions – Pity, Sympathy, Regret, Disappointment, Hope, and Love – on the various glands which they respectively affect. The lucid explanation of the physiological reasons why Mothers love their children is particularly valuable, as calculated to explode the last stronghold of the superstitious reverence which was once paid to parents among semi-civilised nations.'

After these critical Notices of Books, the *Age of Science* proceeds to offer the following remarks on the Theatre:

'At this season in former times, when boys were foolishly allowed to leave school for the holidays, the theatres (as some of us are old enough to remember) were much frequented, and were principally used for a silly kind of entertainment called *Pantomimes.* Of the three theatres in London which continue to be devoted to some sort of dramatic performance, and have not been transferred into Lecture Halls, one only (the Gaiety) seems successful this winter. Crowds attend every night to witness *School,* a piece in which there is no folly of love-making, but the anxieties of a Competitive Examination for Honours in Science are finely realised. A tragic interest is imparted to the plot by making the hero become insane just as he has achieved the object of his ambition.

'At the Haymarket there has been a failure which we fear will result in the ruin of the lessee. This enterprising gentleman imagined it might be possible to revive in these days an interest in some of the old plays once popular in this country, and after (it appears) long consultation and deliberation, determined to bring *The Merchant of Venice* upon the boards. It was hoped that the proposal of one of the characters of the piece, named Shylock, to cut a pound of flesh from another, and the discussion whether this could be done without the effusion of blood, would excite the interest of the spectators. Unfortunately, as the author of the drama (Shakespeare, we are informed) stops short at the very crisis of the physiological experiment, and allows the intended subject to escape, the audience not unnaturally have exhibited disappointment, and the piece has been pronounced a failure.'

In the *Age of Science*, there are no less than fifty pages devoted to announcements and puffs of the most astonishing variety, including hundreds of articles whose names and uses are at present quite unknown. Of advertisements of servants and other persons requiring employment we have not found a single instance, but there were at least twenty columns of invitations to 'Ladies and Gentlemen' to act in the capacity of housekeeper, steward, super-intendent of the house, or some equally well-sounding office, the remuneration offered being at the lowest, it would seem, about £200 a year, with 'the use of a steam carriage', and 'every other luxury desired'. We must, however, leave the columns of Advertisements for future examination, and proceed to give an account of the more important Law and Police Reports.

It seems that, by 1977, it had become necessary to hold assizes in at least twenty towns and villages in every county; and that the judges were incessantly occupied with cases of robbery, garrot-ting, arson, rape, stabbing, poisoning, and a number of offences with new names, of whose nature we can merely guess, such as 'Debarrassing', 'Morbifying', 'Disbraining', 'Petroleumisation', 'Electroding' and 'Mesmeraciding'. For all these crimes the same class of penalties are allotted; the convicted persons are invar-iably sentenced by the presiding judge to so many weeks' or months' detention – not in prison, but in the Penal Hospitals of their respective towns or villages. The principle on which crime is thus visited appears from the addresses of several of the magistrates, who remark that the 'diseased minds' of criminals 'obviously require careful medical treatment'. In numerous cases, as the offenders have been sentenced many times previously, the judge speaks of their crime as exhibiting 'an intermittent fever' of homicidal rage, or of covetousness. Extradition treaties have apparently been abandoned, and thanks to the invention of the aero-magnetic propeller, criminals of every country routinely take refuge in the neighbouring state to escape detention in the Penal Hospitals.

A very different method of treatment, however, is adopted towards another class of offenders, whom it would appear the authorities in the *Age of Science* are determined to put down in grim earnest. That our readers may not suppose we mistake the sense of the amazing paragraphs in which these new features of English legislation appear, we quote them as they stand in the *Age of Science*, pp. 63 and 64:

'POLICE. At the Mansion House this morning, 79 men and 140 women were summoned for the non-attendance of their boys under two years old at the Public Infants' Science Classes in the new kindergarten in the Tower. Various pleas were, as usual, put forth by the defendants, purporting to prove in some cases that the children were ill with small-pox and scarlet fever, and in several instances that they were dying or dead. Mr Alderman Busby remarked that "if they were to listen to such pleas, children would grow up to three or four years old without learning even the rudiments of astronomy or palaeontology". He ordered all the fathers to be publicly flogged, and the mothers to receive each a dozen stripes of the birch privately. [Similar judgments are recorded at several other police-courts in London and the provincial towns.]

'Considerable excitement prevails just now in many of our large towns in consequence of the needful, but somewhat troublesome, formalities required by law before any trade or handicraft may be exercised. Blacksmiths' apprentices, we are told, very generally resent the necessity of passing their proper examinations in Metallurgy before they are qualified to shoe a horse; and the Artificial Flower Makers constantly evade attendance at the lectures on Botany, given expressly for their benefit. The candidates for licenses as Cabdrivers have more than once exhibited signs of discontent, when rejected on the grounds that they failed to answer some of the simplest examination questions on the principles of Mechanics applied to Traction, and on the correlation of Heat and Motion.

'A strike (it is even rumoured) is impending among the stone-masons and bricklayers and slaters in a certain large city, because the Police, at the order of the Magistrates, having brought up several members of those trade-unions to the Local Examining Board for inquiry, it was elicited that none of them had acquired a competent knowledge of Geology in general, nor even of the formation of the strata of rocks wherewith their proper business is concerned. These difficulties were to be anticipated in the progress of Scientific knowledge among the masses, and we earnestly hope that no proposal to relax the late very wise legislation will be made in Parliament, but rather to reinforce the existing Acts by severer penalties upon ignorance and inattention. Who can for a moment think, for example, of allowing his shirt to be washed by a person who knows nothing of the chemistry of soap, blue, and starch? Or his dinner cooked by a man who (however skilled in the mere kitchen art of sending up appetising dishes) is totally ignorant of how much albumen, salts, and alkalies go to the formation of vegetable and animal diet?'

These citations now complete, we must conclude this imperfect but thoroughly reliable account of the remarkable journal of 1977, whose discovery has been the glorious first-fruits of the *Prospective Telegraph*. Nevertheless, it would ill become any of us who have the privilege to live in this enlightened age to entertain a shadow of a doubt that our Scientific method is the right one, and that by-and-by (while we respectfully wait the results of their experiments) our great medical men will discover the proper remedies for murder, rape, and robbery. For our own part, it is superfluous to assure our readers, we retain unwavering, unbounded faith in the resources of Science to provide a perfect substitute for Religion, for Conscience, and for Honour.

The Story of a Star

Æ (GEORGE WILLIAM RUSSELL) (1894)

Religion and mysticism, though at first glance incompatible with the supposed 'rationality' of science fiction, have always informed the genre to one degree or another, in stories that directly engage with spiritual conundrums, make use of religious imagery, or rely upon moral codes derived from religious doctrine. A follower of the teachings of Russian mystic Helena Blavatsky, Irish author and artist Æ(George William Russell) believed that each solar system was the expression of a governing spirit, and with recourse to hypothesised powers of the mind, he allows his narrator to witness these spirits' life cycles.

THE EMOTIONS THAT HAUNTED ME in that little cathedral town would be most difficult to describe. After the hurry, rattle, and fever of the city, the rare weeks spent here were infinitely peaceful. They were full of a quaint sense of childhood, with sometimes a deeper chord touched – the giant and spiritual things childhood has dreams of. The little room I slept in had opposite its window the great grey cathedral wall; it was only in the evening that the sunlight crept round it and appeared in the room strained through the faded green blind. It must have been this silvery quietness of colour which in some subtle way affected me with the feeling of a continual Sabbath; and this was strengthened by the bells chiming hour after hour. The pathos, penitence, and hope expressed by the flying notes coloured the intervals with faint and delicate memories. They haunted my dreams, and I heard with unutterable longing the dreamy chimes pealing from some dim and vast cathedral of the cosmic memory, until the peace they tolled became almost a nightmare, and I longed for utter oblivion or forgetfulness of their reverberations.

More remarkable were the strange lapses into other worlds and times. Almost as frequent as the changing of the bells were the changes from state to state. I realised what is meant by the Indian philosophy of Maya. Truly my days were full of Mayas, and my work-a-day city life was no more real to me than one of those bright, brief glimpses of things long past. I talk of the past, and yet these moments taught me how false our ideas of time are. In the Ever-living yesterday, today, and tomorrow are words of no meaning. I know I fell into what we call the past and the things I counted as dead for ever were the things I had yet to endure. Out of the old age of earth I stepped into its childhood, and received once more the primal blessing of youth, ecstasy, and beauty. But these things are too vast and vague to speak of, the words we use today cannot tell their story. Nearer to our time is the legend that follows.

I was, I thought, one of the Magi of old Persia, inheritor of its unforgotten lore, and using some of its powers. I tried to pierce through the great veil of nature, and feel the life that quickened it within. I tried to comprehend the birth and growth of planets, and to do this I rose spiritually and passed beyond earth's confines into that seeming void which is the Matrix where they germinate. On one of these journeys I was struck by the phantasm, so it seemed, of a planet I had not observed before. I could not then observe closer, and coming again on another occasion it had disappeared. After the lapse of many months I saw it once more, brilliant with fiery beauty. Its motion was slow, revolving around some invisible centre. I pondered over it, and seemed to know that the invisible centre was its primordial spiritual state, from which it emerged a little while and into which it then withdrew. Short was its day; its shining faded into a glimmer, and then into darkness in a few months. I learned its time and cycles; I made preparations and determined to await its coming.

THE BIRTH OF A PLANET

At first silence and then an inner music, and then the sounds of song throughout the vastness of its orbit grew as many in number as there were stars at gaze. Avenues and vistas of sound! They reeled to and fro. They poured from a universal stillness quick with unheard things. They rushed forth and broke into a myriad voices gay with childhood. From age and the eternal, they rushed forth into youth. They filled the void with revelling and exultation. In rebellion they then returned and entered the dreadful Fountain. Again they came forth, and the sounds faded into whispers; they rejoiced once again, and again died into silence.

And now all around glowed a vast twilight; it filled the cradle of the planet with colourless fire. I felt a rippling motion which impelled me away from the centre to the circumference. At that centre a still flame began to lighten; a new change took place, and space began to curdle, a milky and nebulous substance rocked to and fro. At every motion the pulsation of its rhythm carried it farther and farther away from the centre; it grew darker, and a great purple shadow covered it so that I could see it no longer. I was now on the outer verge, where the twilight still continued to encircle the planet with zones of clear transparent light.

As night after night I rose up to visit it they grew many-coloured and brighter. I saw the imagination of nature visibly at work. I wandered through shadowy immaterial forests, a titanic vegetation built up of light and colour; I saw it growing denser, hung with festoons and trailers of fire, and spotted with the light of myriad flowers such as earth never knew. Coincident with the appearance of these things I felt within myself, as if in harmonious movement, a sense of joyousness, an increase of self-consciousness: I felt full of gladness, youth, and the mystery of the new. I felt that greater powers were about to appear, those who had thrown outwards this world and erected it as a place in space.

I could not tell half the wonder of this strange race. I could not myself comprehend more than a little of the mystery of their being. They recognised my presence there, and communicated with me in such a way that I can only describe it by saying that they seemed to enter into my soul, breathing a fiery life; yet I knew that the highest I could reach to was but the outer verge of their spiritual nature, and to tell you but a little I have many times to translate it; for in the first unity with their thought I touched on an almost universal sphere of life, I peered into the ancient heart that beats throughout time; and this knowledge became changed in me, first into a vast and nebulous symbology, and so down through many degrees of human thought into words which hold not at all the pristine and magical beauty.

I stood before one of this race, and I thought, 'What is the meaning and end of life here?' Within me I felt the answering ecstasy that illuminated with vistas of dawn and rest. It seemed to say:

'Our spring and our summer are an unfolding into light and form, and our autumn and winter are a fading into the infinite soul.'

I questioned in my heart, 'To what end is this life poured forth and withdrawn?'

He came nearer and touched me; once more I felt the thrill of being that changed itself into vision.

'The end is creation, and creation is joy. The One awakens out of quiescence as we come forth, and knows itself in us; as we return we enter it in gladness, knowing ourselves. After long cycles the world you live in will become like ours; it will be poured forth and withdrawn; a mystic breath, a mirror to glass your being.'

He disappeared while I wondered what cyclic changes would transmute our ball of mud into the subtle substance of thought.

In that world I dared not stay during its period of withdrawal; having entered a little into its life, I became subject to its laws; the Powers on its return would have dissolved my being utterly. I felt with a wild terror its clutch upon me, and I withdrew from the departing glory, from the greatness that was my destiny – but not yet.

From such dreams I would be aroused, perhaps, by a gentle knock at my door, and my little cousin Margaret's quaint face would peep in with a 'Cousin Robert, are you not coming down to supper?'

Of these visions in the light of after thought I would speak a little. All this was but symbol, requiring to be thrice sublimed in interpretation ere its true meaning can be grasped. I do not know whether worlds are heralded by such glad songs, or whether any have such a fleeting existence, for the mind that reflects truth is deluded with strange phantasies of time and place in which seconds are rolled out into centuries and long cycles are reflected in an instant of time. There is within us a little space through which all the threads of the universe are drawn; and, surrounding that incomprehensible centre, the mind of man sometimes catches glimpses of things which are true only in those glimpses; when we record them the true has vanished, and a shadowy story – such as this – alone remains. Yet, perhaps, the time is not altogether wasted in considering legends like these, for they reveal, though but in phantasy and symbol, a greatness we are heirs to, a destiny which is ours though it be yet far away.

Mercia, the Astronomer Royal

AMELIA GARLAND MEARS (1895)

Though the resurrection of Early Modern English and the persistence of 'empire' seem anachronistic, in this abridged novel extract Amelia Garland Mears extrapolates how new inventions (such as the tape recorder) and discoveries (such as psychic powers) might be incorporated into the legal infrastructure of a future society. In Mears's imagined year 2000, the promise of gender equality is largely fulfilled in a legal sense, but sexist attitudes and sexual harassment linger; like Frances Power Cobbe, she warns the reader that advances in social equality will have to be defended.

THE ROYAL OBSERVATORY was a stately building close to the old building in Greenwich Park. The lower apartments of the new building were occupied by Mercia and her household, while the upper rooms were devoted to the purposes of her profession. In a spacious apartment on the third floor was Mercia, surrounded by curious astroscopes, stellar-spectroscopes, and wonderfully constructed cameras. She was seated at her desk making some mathematical calculations of the celestial depths, and was so completely engrossed in her labours that the entrance of her fellow-worker, Geometrus, went unheeded. At length, she finished, raised her head and smiled.

'Ah, Geometrus, is it thou? I have finished the measurement of our new star.'

By this time, English was the commercial language of the whole world, but the ancient style was reverted to in the matter of the personal pronoun; the substitution of the plural 'you' for its singular 'thou' was once again considered ungrammatical.

'You say "our", my mistress,' replied the young man. 'It is thou alone who hast done the work.'

'I made the observations and calculations, but it was thy cunning which formed the instrument. Take thy due, my friend, and be not over-modest; some base imitator may someday defraud thee of thine invention, unless thou wilt consent to acknowledge it openly.'

No sooner had Mercia made this observation than she heard some unusual noise going on outside, and stepping to the window, she saw several gentlemen assembled near the Observatory, among whom she discerned the Emperor Felicitas himself.

'Here's a pretty surprise for thee, Mistress Mercia,' exclaimed Geometrus. 'None other than the Emperor! It is not I he seeks, but thou, Mistress Mercia; I will then away.'

'Stay, Geometrus!' exclaimed Mercia quickly, 'I would prefer thy company when I receive the Emperor. I will now retire and change into something more suitable for so honourable a visitor.'

But before she could leave the room, a messenger was at the door desiring an audience for his royal master. Mercia silently bowed her assent; and a moment later the monarch entered her studio. As he did so, she rose from her seat at the large table – which was covered with charts and maps of the celestial regions, all of her own making – but the Emperor quickly said, 'Stay, lady, keep thy seat, for it is meet that monarchs should serve thee, who art so full of knowledge and wisdom.'

'What is thy wish, Sire, wherefore am I honoured by this visit?'

'I would know, fair Mercia, the cause of this change of temperature throughout the world. For three successive years an extreme cold has prevailed each season. I fain would learn the reason.'

'Some serious internal changes are taking place within the body of our sun. Great caverns, about one-fourth of the sun's diameter, have discovered themselves in his centre. We are not the only planet-dwellers suffering from cold at this time, for a difference will be experienced throughout the whole of the solar system. But it is only a temporary inconvenience; from close observation I find that our sun is absorbing numerous meteoric bodies, of which there are billions wandering in interstellar space. I conclude therefore that there is no cause for alarm. Interstellar hydrogen is pressed into our sun's service and a constant heat sustained, which may last for thousands of years to come.'

'Of all the stars, thou art the brightest, Mercia. Thou art as fair as thou art far-seeing. Thy words give comfort to the world, and thy beauty brings thy Sovereign much delight.'

While Felicitas was uttering these pleasant gallantries, he was gradually edging his chair nearer and nearer to that of Mercia.

Mercia's countenance at once assumed a more serious expression; hastily glancing towards that part of the room where Geometrus was seated, she found he had slipped out unobserved, doubtless with the intention of leaving them quietly to their discussion on the sun's condition.

'Truly, it is most kind of thee, Sire, to show such appreciation; but I seek no flatteries, or compliments,' she answered with downcast eyes.

'Why, what harm is there in speaking a truth, Mercia? I do affirm that thy beauty only exceeds thy knowledge, or thy knowledge thy beauty, I know not which.'

'Be it so, then, Sire. It is nothing to my credit if I be beautiful; I had no part in the making.'

'Ah, Mercia, why spoil those eyes more beautiful than the brightest star in gazing into unknown regions day and night; year in, year out? Thou knowest no enjoyment – thou hast no pleasure of life, as other women; thine existence is lonely, colourless. Drink of the draught of love as nature wills it, and let the study of the stars stand over for a space.'

The voice of Felicitas as he uttered these words was low and full of passion; but Mercia, owing to the confusion that covered her, did not notice the change of tone. She was dumb, tongue-tied; at this inopportune moment a knock was heard at the door, and the Emperor himself touched the button and gave admittance to another visitor.

It was Geometrus, who had returned for a part of an instrument he was making, which he had inadvertently left behind. His entrance put a prompt stop to the Emperor's wooing. Mercia, hardly knowing what she was doing, rose from her seat and turned to leave the apartment. Observing her intention, the Emperor concluded that it was time to withdraw.

'Farewell, mistress,' he said as he made her a bow, 'I will come again, ere long, and learn of the sun's condition which is so necessary to be acquainted with.'

Mercia made her way into her most private apartment, and shutting herself within, she sank upon the silken couch. Was the Emperor putting her probity to the test, or was it only a random shot on his part, made for mere amusement? Had some person, envious of her position, told some tale to Felicitas with a view of bringing about her downfall? If so, who could it be?

Then the thought crossed her mind of the possibility that the Emperor might have been giving voice to his true feelings, but she dismissed this possibility, for Felicitas was already married, and to offer Mercia an illicit love would be an unparalleled presumption – even from an Emperor.

It was, indeed, a bold step for the Emperor to take with one so high-minded, so self-controlled as she. But her very unattainability made her more desirable in his eyes: the more he dwelt on the futility of his wish the more his passion raged within him.

'I must have Mercia!' he exclaimed to himself as he lay awake dwelling on her beauty, her goodness, and her extraordinary abilities. 'I will go to her again. I will risk all, and tell her of my love. If she refuses to become mine secretly, I will wed her openly, and get rid of that flat-faced Russian woman whom my ministers talked me into marrying.'

Mercia, meanwhile, was somewhat settled in her mind regarding the course she ought to take with the Emperor. If Felicitas should chance not to make mention of the subject of love, which was a forbidden one to her, owing to her position, she made up her mind to forbear making inquiries concerning his motive for introducing it.

Quite alone, and unattended by any member of his suite, Felicitas set off to pay Mercia his promised visit; she gave him a pleasant welcome. In her heart, she hoped that the interpretation of his words would prove favourable. After all, could he not influence his ministers to do away with this absurd marriage objection?

It so happened that Geometrus on that day had business in the city, which detained him several hours, and as the Emperor was being driven, he saw Geometrus enter a machine warehouse, or shop, where electrical household machines were vended.

'Ah,' thought the Emperor, 'thou art there, my friend: pray make no hurry on my account.'

When arrived at his destination, the Emperor entered the Observatory with a firm resolution to make good use of the opportunity with which fortune had favoured him. Now, Mercia, with the same motive in her mind, received him very cordially, for she desired to make a favourable impression, with a view of obtaining his royal clemency in the matter of matrimony, even though it was not certain that she would at any time change her present condition.

Neither of them noticed the presence of an old man named Sadbag, a leading Radical politician, reformist, anti-monarchist and fervent Republican, seated behind a screen in one corner of the room; he had been awaiting an audience with Mercia, and had fallen asleep while reading. He was soon roused, however, by the Emperor's voice.

'Ah, Mistress Mercia,' he exclaimed, 'what cheerful looks thou dost carry today, methinks thy face betokens much content – hast thou taken my words to heart, fair lady?'

'Sire, thou said something concerning the sun – thou didst talk of coming to learn more of his condition, I believe,' answered Mercia.

'True,' he replied with a laugh, 'I would know more of the sun's late vagaries, but it would please me better to learn something of thyself: dost thou never feel lonely?'

'Often enough, Sire; the hours speed away at times very quickly when I am hard at work.'

'Art thou then tired of this occupation? It is indeed, too much for thee. Rest a while, sweet Mercia, and let the stars take care of themselves for a season.'

'Oh, that would spoil all my calculations; the work of years would be as naught were I to stay my hand now.'

'Health, and Love, sweet Mercia, go hand in hand together. I know it; for thine eyes were made for the conquest of man's heart, rather than star-gazing. Cease to disregard the designs of Nature when she formed thee, and yield thyself to the pleasure of love.'

Mercia essayed to answer him, but her tongue refused her utterance, so great was her confusion. 'Sire, I know not what answer to give in this matter.'

'Hast thou not felt the want of companionship, dear Mercia? It is good to be loved, fair one, to realise how much thy womanhood means: hast thou never felt its joys – its pains?'

'Sire, I cannot break my bond, signed by my own hand, to forswear love and marriage: no one but thyself can relieve me of this obligation.'

'I heartily relieve thee, then, my good Mercia,' replied the delighted monarch. 'I care not for the bond one iota, if that's all that's in thy way. Keep thy post, and enjoy the delights of love at the same time.' Then, forgetting all his caution and self-restraint, he caught her in his arms, and in a perfect frenzy of rapture commenced to shower hot kisses on her brow, her cheeks, her lips.

Mercia was so taken aback by this that her brain reeled for a moment; then, recovering her senses, she wrenched herself out of his arms. Gazing on him with blanched face, she cried in a voice gasping with pain and indignation –

'What means the Emperor by this unheard-of liberty? What have I done that I should be treated as a courtesan by my Sovereign?'

'A courtesan!' he repeated. 'Why Mercia, I would give thee a crown if I could! Thy queenly brow was truly made for one; and by the stars, thou shalt have it yet!'

'Surely, Sire, thou hast gone mad!'

'Yes, truly, I am mad – mad with love for thee, and thou knowest it, Mercia, else wouldst thou have kissed my hand in acknowledgment of it?'

'It was not so!' she answered in strong indignant tones. 'Thy love never entered my thought.'

'Dost thou place that poltroon Geometrus before me? Am I to be flouted for him? Mercia, Mercia, give me thy love!' he cried. 'Take me, my beloved, spurn me no longer, for without thee I am as one dead!'

For an instant Mercia paused, and passed her hand across her brow, as if to recover her senses; then she said in a deliberate and dignified voice:

'Felicitas, the Emperor hath no crown to offer his subject, Mercia, for it sits already on the brow of his royal spouse; neither has he love to offer his servant, Mercia, for it is sworn to his Empress for ever. It is an insult to me, thine offer of illicit love, and I refuse to longer remain in thy service.'

Upon hearing these words, the heat of the Emperor's temper cooled; he saw he had not only ruined his cause with the lady, but he was bringing upon himself public dishonour, for the reason of the resignation of their gifted and enthusiastic astronomer would be demanded by both ministers and nation alike.

As she turned to leave the apartment, for she disdained having further converse with him, he caught her by the dress, with a view of detaining her.

'Stay, Mercia, stay, and listen to me! Listen to one word more, I beseech thee. Thou shalt, for indeed I will not let thee go!' He shouted, for she was wrenching herself out of his grasp.

'Touch me not,' she exclaimed, 'or I will kill thee as thou standest!' From her girdle she took a small ebony stick, electrically charged, which she wore as a kind of life-preserver, in accordance with the custom of ladies who worked, or walked out a good deal alone.

She had reached the door and opened it, when who should rush upon the scene but Geometrus.

'Mercia insulted, and by the Emperor! What is the meaning of this?'

'I am not insulting her,' the Emperor replied. 'She has disobeyed my commands respecting some important astronomical information I required, and is endeavouring to shield her own shortcomings by getting into a rage: 'tis a woman's way, but I'll have none of it.'

Then Mercia, drawing herself up to her full height, exclaimed in indignant voice –

'Liar, I despise thee! Bid thine Empress come hither, for I have something to tell her. As for me, I shall never receive thee here again! Get some other to fill my place, for I shall quit it forthwith.'

Then she turned away with haughty mien and left the apartment.

'It shall not end in this way,' said Geometrus. 'I shall see that this matter is not hushed up!'

'I will have no more of this,' responded Felicitas, who, looking very uncomfortable, made for the door. 'I will have thee indicted for a revolutionist and a maker of mischief in my realms, and pay thee well for all these insults.'

So perfect was the system of communication throughout the globe that two hours later, the news was in every part of the world. From the commoner to the crowned head of every country, almost, the story of the Emperor of the Teutonic Empire and his astronomer was discussed. In the cottage, the castle, the street corner, the court and the club, it became at once the leading subject of conversation.

Meanwhile, Felicitas was relating his own version of events, in which his powers of imagination had been considerably called upon, to his Prime Minister.

'At the very least,' urged the Emperor, 'these newspapers ought to be indicted for conspiring to undermine my reputation, and thereby bring me into my people's disfavour.'

'What about thy two astronomers? Does thy Majesty desire to include them in the indictment?'

'Certainly,' replied the Emperor. 'Did not Mistress Mercia threaten my life, and hath not Geometrus taken her part?'

'Would it not be far wiser to require them to apologise for their ill-behaviour?'

'That they will never do, I am assured! Their looks and language betrayed their evil designs towards me. Get a warrant sent quickly, and put them in prison without delay.'

When Mercia retired to her private apartment she hardly knew whither she was going. In a few moments, however, she recovered herself, and began to consider her situation, or rather her loss of situation, for she had thrown it up in the heat of her anger with the Emperor.

'I have refused, perhaps, the crown of an Empress to take the lowly condition of a poor scholar out of place; but I have remained true to myself, and to my sex, and before all things have kept my heart and hands clean.'

How a man could express the most profound attachment for her at one moment, and seek her destruction at the next, seemed to her pure mind so monstrous and unnatural that its possibility in her case was altogether out of the question. That Felicitas would go the lengths of formally making such an infamous accusation she could not bring herself to believe.

When the constables entered, they did so in a somewhat hesitating manner. Evidently, they did not at all relish their work.

'Why this intrusion on a lady in her private apartment?' demanded Geometrus.

'What is your wish?' inquired Mercia in quiet tones.

'Mistress, very unwillingly, I confess, I call upon thee in the Emperor's name to surrender thyself – here is my authority,' and he held out the warrant for her perusal. When she had finished, she stood for a moment thinking, whereupon he stepped forward to lead her away, when Mercia falling back a little, drew herself up and exclaimed –

'Touch me not, fellow; I will leave this house of mine own accord when I am fully prepared. I must attire myself suitably before going into the night air, and my carriage must be made ready for me.'

'We have brought the ordinary police van by special order of the Emperor,' said another officer. 'We dare not let any other be used.'

'The police-van for me!' repeated Mercia. 'And by the Emperor's orders too! What has the Emperor to do with the administration of the law? I refuse to obey such an order.'

'And rightly so,' interjected Geometrus. 'This lady goes with you in her own carriage, or not at all.'

'What is that to thee?' returned the sergeant of police. 'A pretty person to lay down conditions to us, and dictate how we are to perform our duty, seeing thou art in the same boat thyself. Here is the warrant for thy apprehension; and get thee ready quickly.'

Nevertheless, Mercia's carriage was soon in readiness, and Geometrus watched the light barouche roll along the smooth macadamised roadway.

Of all the persons who laid claim to the gift of thought-reading there was none so sensitive as the great Anglo-Indian, Dayanand Swami. It was said of him that he almost lived upon a wonderful elixir of his own manufacture, the preparation of which had been handed down to him from his Mahatma forefather some generations back. Being in the possession of all the accumulated knowledge of successive generations of Yogis, he was filled with wonderful wisdom. Moreover, his powers were considerably strengthened by reason of his advanced culture, aided by his natural gift of psychic energy.

It was no uncommon occurrence for a fair Duchess to find out where her noble husband was spending his evenings; the Duke in question, guessing that she would do so, would beforehand try to bribe Swami to keep the secret. Or an over-anxious wife would worry herself concerning the safety of her husband who had taken a journey across the Atlantic in his flying machine; or a young man striving to obtain a Government appointment would seek to learn if his lady friend, of whom he was in mortal fear, would bowl him out in the coming examination. No matter of what the difficulty consisted, this Anglo-Indian sage solved it satisfactorily.

One soft spring afternoon, there came rolling up to his residence the royal carriage, carrying the Emperor Felicitas himself. The Swami received the monarch with that easy and gentle courtesy he extended to everybody.

'What doth his Majesty require of me?' he asked.

'Indeed,' cried the Emperor, 'I wish my crown anywhere but on my head! What good is power if it leaves one craving for that which he most desires? I want that which I am denied, Swami, and which my heart is bursting for – the love of a woman! If thou hast magic power, as I am told, tell me how I can attain this?'

'Is she so perverse?'

'Perverse isn't the word for it – she is ice, immovable as a rock! Yes,' returned the Emperor, 'she is as cold as she is beautiful; and I have put her in prison! Believe me, Swami, I cannot sleep, eat, or work, for I am intensely, hopelessly miserable.'

'I am truly sorry to see thy Majesty in such a plight,' remarked Swami. 'But why didst thou place the lady thou lovest in a prison? It seems a high-handed way of dealing with a subject; truly a mighty strange method of inducing her love?'

'I was put in a quandary,' replied Felicitas, for he knew there was no good gained by attempting to deceive the thought-reader. 'I was suddenly surprised by visitors as I was attempting to detain her, when a craven spirit entered me, and I denounced her as a would-be murderer.'

'Did she endeavour to harm thee?' inquired Swami.

'Yes, truly she raised her life-preserver to strike me if I touched her.'

'But she did it in self-defence, evidently,' retorted Swami, while a bright light illumined his dreamy eyes. 'Besides, those ebony trifles that ladies sometimes carry do not kill, they do but temporarily paralyse the part they touch.'

'Oh, it matters little now, what they do. I wish she had killed me outright; anything but this dreadful torture of doubt to go through. This frightful fear nearly drives me mad – I wish it were all over.'

'What?' inquired Swami, wishful to obtain a clear command from the king in so many words, for his thoughts were in a state of the wildest confusion.

'The trial, the trial! I dread it. I wish I had never sent that warrant. The Crown Prosecutor has got the case in hand, and, Swami, I am ashamed of it. Help me, I pray thee, and tell me how it will all end, and I will well reward thee.'

Swami soon perceived wherein the Emperor's chief trouble lay. 'I see by the brainwaves emanating from thee that the woman thou lovest is in confinement in the first-class misdemeanants' quarters, in the Metropolitan Prison. Now that will do; I know enough.'

Then the Emperor, remembering that the real object of his visit was not yet accomplished, blurted out – 'I desire to learn the issue of the trial, that is my chief care at present.'

'Of that I am aware, Sire,' replied Swami. 'Thou desirest to learn the issue of the trial on thine own account. I perfectly understand it. In the meantime, I would advise that Mercia be allowed her liberty, subject to her own recognisances. It will be more advisable from every point of view, lest thy subjects deem thee harsh and unjust towards her.'

'Ha, Sorcerer, thou knowest her name! Who told it thee?' exclaimed Felicitas in much surprise.

'Thyself,' replied the Soul-Reader. 'I read it on thy brain. Moreover, fear, more than love, predominates within thy bosom. Thy Majesty doth dread the testimony of the witnesses arrayed against thee.'

'I do not deny it,' returned Felicitas, for he was subdued by the two-fold influence of anxiety concerning the impending case, and awe of the Soul-reader's power to divine his thought. 'But I must own it gives me more uneasiness the testimony of Mercia herself, for none will doubt her word.'

'Then, let me advise thy Majesty to withdraw the charge and set the lady at liberty forthwith.'

Felicitas, looking ill at ease, endeavoured to take the implied rebuke lightly. 'The law still holds good that "a king can do no wrong". But Swami,' he continued in a pleading tone, 'thine advice is good if my way be not: tell me first what the issue of the trial will be, and I will then accommodate myself to circumstances.'

'Be it so,' answered Swami, rising from his seat and conducting the Emperor into his library. From thence he led him into an inner room, which having no window was in a state of complete darkness.

'Presently,' explained Swami, 'I will illumine the sensitive plate on which the scene is projected from my brain, and show to thy Majesty three pictures of the scenes which will certainly be enacted at the court, during the coming trial. For I find that the case will come off independently of thy action. I can only now advise what course thy Majesty can best take concerning it.'

Then Swami, having all the results in readiness of his wonderful instrument – the psycho-register – touched a spring, and forthwith an immense illuminated picture appeared, filling one side of the room and representing a scene in the Great Hall of the

Court, almost dazzling in its brilliancy of colouring. So complete was Felicitas' surprise that he started back, for the strange vividness of the scene made him nervous; but Swami, accustomed to finding his visitors startled, reassured him.

'Sire,' said he, 'be not alarmed, there is nothing to hurt thy Majesty.'

It proved, in truth, a most wonderful and striking picture of the Great Justice Hall in the Metropolitan Court. Tiers of seats were filled to overflowing with the elite of Great Britain, and Ireland, Berlin, Paris, and most of the European Continent; nobles and great dames, and even several crowned heads, had assembled from all parts to see the cause celebre.

In the dock was seated Mercia, looking calm, beautiful, and self-possessed. Innumerable opera glasses were being levelled at her by both sexes; while busy barristers in their black gowns and white wigs scanned their note-books. The place set apart for newspaper reporters was filled with representatives of the press setting in order their respective phonographs, which were to register the whole proceedings of the case.

On his feet stood the Crown Prosecutor, stating his case, while Geometrus was seated at one side, but no Emperor Felicitas could be discovered anywhere: indeed, he was conspicuous by his absence, seeing he was the only witness in his own case.

Felicitas gazed in amazement at the immense group photographed there; exclaiming from time to time, as he recognised each member of the nobility with whom he was acquainted, from the Duke of Northumberland to Nicholas of Russia and Louis of France.

'Well, I must say, they're all most excellent likenesses – they look, indeed, like living pictures. What a treat they are getting! An Emperor in a witness-box isn't an every-day occurrence, to be sure! And, oh, there's Mercia, how pale, how beautiful, how sad she appears! Ah, Swami, I have no heart to go on with this prosecution. I love her – I would die for her – canst thou not exercise thy magic and make her love me?'

'I possess no power over the human heart,' returned Swami. 'My work is to make known futurity to a slight extent.'

'Would she marry me if I were free?'

'She is destined for another, far beneath thy Majesty in social position; but who can give her a heart wholly devoted to her.'

'I am aware that Mercia is in love already. That fellow Geometrus desires her, and she loves him; at all events, she told me as much. I suppose thy prophecy refers to him. Turn on the next scene, if it be ready, for I would learn all with as great a speed as possible.'

Upon hearing this request Swami pressed another button, and the room was enveloped in darkness, and the picture vanished altogether from sight. The next picture which appeared upon the crystal plate portrayed the court with the same visitors in similar order as before, but with this difference. The serious expression which the countenances of all present wore in the first instance was now changed to that of intense excitement in some, while the greater part of the audience seemed bursting with merriment.

Mercia, on her part, was blushing; Geometrus was scowling, while all the barristers were endeavouring to conceal their merriment by fluttering their pocket-handkerchiefs under the pretence of blowing their noses. Mercia's counsel wore an air of happy triumph, which appeared to indicate complete satisfaction with his own good management of the case. Felicitas was absent, as before, but his Empress was among the audience, looking as flushed and angered as an injured wife might well be.

'What the deuce is everybody laughing at?' queried the Emperor, while a deep frown crossed his face.

'Canst not thy Majesty comprehend the situation?'

'No, I do not,' answered Felicitas. 'Tell me the meaning of it all.'

'Time alone will show the full development. There is sufficient pictured to give thy Majesty ample warning.'

'It is easy enough to see that I shall be made a pretty laughing-stock for the whole world. They have worked some vile trick upon me – that is very evident. Strange that thou art unable to explain what it is!'

'We have had enough of this,' observed Swami, as he pressed the extinguishing button, producing perfect darkness. 'We will now show the closing scene and dismiss the matter for tonight. Thine hour of trial is at hand. But see, here is Mercia's hour of triumph, mark how everybody is showing her honour, and offering their congratulations.'

However striking these photo-crystal pictures had appeared, this last, without doubt, displayed the most stirring scene. It represented the intense joy of a great multitude, who were offering their congratulations, and testifying their admiration of one who had gone through a severe ordeal, out of which she had come victorious.

'’Tis the want of this that's brought my trouble,' murmured Felicitas. 'If I had Mercia's love, then wouldst thou see how pious I could be.'

'Is a child contented wholly when one desire is satisfied? No, he cries hourly for new toys and new delights. Thy Majesty would weary in course of time with the beauteous Mercia, as thou hast wearied of thy spouse. Sire, be content; as thou hast made thy bed, so must thou lie upon it.'

The Emperor fell silent for a moment, and then nodded. 'This night urgent affairs of state shall summon me to Berlin. Good-bye, Swami, for the present. We shall see whether thy Soul-reading crystal plate has discovered to us the false or the true.'

'How convenient to be a king, and know naught of the penalties of wrong-doing,' thought Swami, as he conducted the monarch to the great doors, outside which his carriage stood in readiness.

In consequence of Swami's advice, the Emperor at the proper quarters intimated his desire to bestow the royal pardon on the Mercia; which command being as quickly carried out as officialism would admit, she was made acquainted with her position with little delay. When the governor of the prison read the document to Mercia which contained the so-called 'pardon', an indignant flush rose to her cheeks.

'Ah!' she cried, 'the Emperor generously sends me a pardon before it is solicited, for a crime I have never committed! His clemency oppresses me – it is really more than I can accept.'

'It is certainly most unparalleled in prison records,' remarked the governor, who looked mystified. 'I don't know of a similar instance in all my experience. The pardon should be accorded after the sentence is passed, should the prisoner be found guilty. I understand that his Gracious Majesty being himself the prosecutor, departs from the ordinary routine observed in such matters. He desires to set thee at liberty without further delay.'

'I cannot accept his Majesty's clemency,' repeated Mercia after a pause. 'The case is in readiness, my counsel informs me, and witnesses are fully prepared to establish my innocence. I will therefore remain here.'

The Great Justice Hall, as it was named, was large enough to hold several thousands of persons, who on this occasion of unprecedented interest availed themselves of it without delay. A long line of carriages containing the elite of society awaited the opening of the great door with that admirable spirit of patience which the aristocracy display on great occasions. A few of these vehicles were drawn by horses, but most were impelled by electric motive force.

By the time the Court was opened every available seat was filled, not only by the elite of the Empire, but by members of the Continental aristocracy also, including two Crowned Heads among their number. It was not every day that an Emperor appeared in the witness box, and on such an unparalleled occasion it was necessary to make an effort and not miss such a rare treat.

Of course, the newspapers circulating in the Teutonic Empire were much too circumspect to hint at the true aspect of the affair. To have anticipated evidence; or to have expressed an opinion on a case still pending would have led to serious difficulties, proving most embarrassing to the proprietors. A distracting shade of mystery surrounded the coming trial, making it particularly attractive to everybody.

'What glorious fun!' cried the young sprig of nobility. 'Felicitas falling out with his lady Astronomer. I wouldn't miss it for worlds!'

'What a disgraceful episode in the annals of Royalty!' remarked the elderly prude, who was as anxious as anyone to listen to the forthcoming details.

'I wouldn't be Mercia for millions!' exclaimed the serious young lady. 'It is altogether frightful to have such dealings with a man!' She showed her abhorrence of such indecency by bringing her opera glasses to scan the scene more critically.

'This comes of the preposterous advancement of women,' observed a failed scientist of the male sex. 'Had the Astronomer Royal been a man such a scene could not have occurred.'

'If it be a political intrigue, how can sex affect her loyalty? The same might have happened with a variation, had the Astronomer Royal been male,' returned his neighbour.

'It is a love-intrigue, ending with the usual quarrel,' whispered an elderly Solomon, wise in the knowledge of the world's weakness.

'I thought Mercia incapable of love-intrigues, or any other, being a perfect model of all the virtues,' answered his neighbour.

'All women are "perfect" till they're tried,' uttered the same cynic.

'It will be sinfully disappointing if the case is hushed up,' whispered one man to his neighbour, in another part of the Hall. 'The Emperor is *non est*: he has bunked!'

'What! Has he fled? Impossible! He dares not do so. He threw the gauntlet, and must abide the issue. He cannot run away!'

'All the same, he is off, gone to Berlin on important State affairs, leaving word that the trial could be abandoned altogether, or take its chance without him.'

'I hope it won't be permitted to fall through. It would be monstrous after all this fuss and preparation.'

Just before half-past ten, disengaged barristers, who came to see and hear for the sake of gaining experience, took their appointed seats. Counsel engaged in the case, arrayed in gown and wig, appeared also, whose capabilities were freely discussed by the onlookers.

But when Mercia entered the Hall, escorted by the renowned Swami, so universal was the feeling in her favour, that a great burst of applause greeted her appearance. Mercia smiled and bowed her head in acknowledgment of the sympathy accorded her, while attendant ushers vainly called for silence. While this commotion was going on, the three Judges, attired as in days of old, took their seats with suitable solemnity; the Court opened with the same formularies as had been in use for hundreds of years, for the Courts of Law more than any other institution cling to the ancient order of things with tenacity.

After a short delay the auditory was startled by hearing the charge delivered:

'Mercia Montgomery, you are charged with feloniously attempting the life of His Imperial Majesty, Albert Felicitas, Supreme Ruler and Governor of Great Britain and Ireland, Emperor of the Teutonic, Indian, and African Empires, which murderous attempt is accounted High Treason by the law of these Realms. Do you plead Guilty or not Guilty?'

Before the accused had time to give her answer, the Public Prosecutor interfered.

'I am empowered to convey to the prisoner the favour of his Imperial Majesty's clemency. Taking into consideration the prisoner's long and valuable service rendered to her country, also the great loyalty she has ever evinced towards her Sovereign during that period of faithful service, the Emperor has decided to overlook the sudden outburst of passion made by his otherwise faithful subject, and illustrious Astronomer, and has therefore conveyed to her his Royal Pardon, in proper form, forthwith.'

Mercia, motioning her counsel to keep his seat a moment longer, and rising to her full height, replied, 'Being altogether innocent of the crime of which I am charged, I am unable to accept the clemency offered by his Most Gracious Majesty. It will be soon enough to pray for pardon when I am proved guilty. I will leave this Court with my name unsullied, or hide my head in shame forever.'

When everybody had quieted down, Mercia's counsel stood up and requested that the Public Prosecutor should state his case, to which demand the Judges agreed. Thereupon, the Emperor's counsel made his charge according to the way he had been instructed, but having no witnesses to produce, he concluded quickly, and the Defence was commenced without delay.

Rising to his feet, Mercia's counsel proceeded with his speech.

'Today I am placed in a position as painful to me as a subject, as it is unique in the annals of a Law Court: I shall have to accuse my Sovereign of conduct so base that the meanest subject of his Realms would blush to be found guilty of the like.

'I am in a position to show that the Emperor's visits to his Astronomer were not made either in the interests of science, or those of his subjects. On the contrary, these interviews were made with the intention of corrupting her pure mind, and of beguiling her away from her duty.

'By his artful insinuations, he endeavoured to lead her to disregard her vows of abstention from Love, or Marriage, with a view of paving the way for his own purposes. Like the Eastern fable of Eve and the Serpent, she listened to the voice of the Tempter without knowing he was planning her downfall. But luckier than our First Mother, Mercia discovered her mistake before touching the forbidden fruit.

'At length, mortified and indignant, she essayed to leave him, when he endeavoured to forcibly detain her; upon which she raised her ebony life-preserver to warn him from trespassing on her person.

'At this juncture he was surprised by Geometrus, who was amazed at a scene so unexpected. Embarrassed at being caught at such a moment, he tried to explain away the difficulty, and turned the tables upon the lady, by accusing her of some failure in duty; at this moment, who should emerge from a corner of the apartment, which was partially concealed by a large screen, but Mr Sadbag.

'It appears that this gentleman, having just purchased a new-fangled phonograph as a gift for one of his grandchildren, carried it to Mistress Mercia with a view to recording her conversation, which he expected would prove instructive and interesting to his grandchild.

'I will now call upon Mr Sadbag to open his instrument, and give us the dialogue that was so unintentionally recorded therein; but which I am afraid will prove more interesting to the company present, than edifying or instructive to that gentleman's progeny.'

Mr Sadbag sprang to his feet, and taking up the mysterious parcel proceeded to the witness box, when he requested a few moments' grace to adjust the mechanism of his unique witness; after which was heard in the most natural tones the voices of the Emperor and Mercia.

'Isn't that machine playing it low on the lady?' whispered Prince Osbert to Louis, his neighbour, as the phonograph reeled off all it had recorded.

'Hush,' returned the French Emperor, 'there's a volley of kisses going off – be quiet, pray!'

All eyes regarded the beautiful culprit seated in the witness box with increased interest. *'Oh, thou guilty creature – think shame to thyself!'* the ladies' looks said as plainly as possible.

'He's having a good time of it!' whispered one spectator to his neighbour.

'She's no better than she should be, after all!' muttered another.

'Such pretty lips were made for kissing!' remarked another.

'Oh, the hussy!' said one woman to her husband. 'Don't look at her. What a cheek, to face it out like this!'

These various remarks, and many more besides, occupied but a few seconds for delivery, for the Usher calling out silence, on hearing the low murmur of voices, the machine began talking again.

As the instrument gave utterance to the rest of the story, only one feeling prevailed throughout that great assembly – admiration for the noble character of the woman sitting there before them, whose flushed cheek and lowered eyelids evidenced her modesty. When the excitement had somewhat subsided, she rose to her feet, and turning her gaze with an air of modest dignity upon the people, she addressed them.

'Dear friends; my Lords,' she said, 'it is true that this instrument has been instrumental in rendering undeniable testimony of the value of the evidence placed before you. Nevertheless, had I been aware that such was Mr Sadbag's intention, my place at this justice bar would never have been filled.'

'That will do, Mr Sadbag,' said the senior Judge. 'We have heard quite enough to enable us to arrive at a decision. The prisoner – I mean, the accused – is found Not Guilty of the charge against her. The lady will now leave the Court without a stain on her character. This case ought never to have come before the Court at all.'

As soon as the trial was concluded, the reporters rushed out *en masse* to send their respective recordings to the editors of the various journals they represented. Never before had they such a titbit to offer their employers as was now their good luck to possess. A love scene between their Emperor and his astronomer, delivered in a dialogue wherein the actual voices were reproduced, was a treat not to be met with every day.

At least a hundred delicate voice-recorders had caught the sound-waves from Sadbag's phonograph, and borrowing the tones of Felicitas and Mercia in their never-to-be-forgotten colloquy gave them a value unprecedented in all time. As soon as it got abroad that their proprietors were in possession of these treasures, hundreds of speculators offered enormous prices for their purchase, with a view of reeling out their contents to admiring and appreciative audiences throughout the globe. Before long, all the homage due to a great hero was rendered unto Mercia, just as Felicitas had seen pictured in the psycho-development the day before.

'I thought to bring her low – to humiliate her,' muttered Felicitas bitterly, as he read the story in Berlin, 'but alas, I have only brought about a public triumph for her, and public dishonour to myself. What good is it looking into futurity? I cannot control the current of events; all will take place exactly as if I had known nothing.'

And so it did, as the cry spreading itself through every quarter of the vast Empire was caught up in wild delight – *Long live Mercia, our Empress!* – being echoed from every part, by people of every caste and every creed.

The Professor's Experiment

MARGARET WOLFE HUNGERFORD (1895)

The limits of the human lifespan pose a problem for authors keen to cross the gulfs of time and space, necessitating the invention of some way to keep one's narrator alive indefinitely. During the nineteenth century, there was something of a trend for stories of suspended animation; as in the following extract by Margaret Wolfe Hungerford, the potions that allowed for such hibernation were often attributed to Native American herbalism and traditional medicine. Once more, a young woman becomes the subject of a Mad Scientist's experiments, though this time she does so willingly, and the unexpected outcome works in her favour.

THE LAMP WAS BEGINNING to burn low; so was the fire. But neither of the two people in the room seemed to notice anything. The Professor had got upon his discovery again, and once there, no man living could check him. He had flung his arms across the table towards his companion, and the hands, with the palms turned upwards, marked every word as he uttered it, thumping the knuckles on the table here, shaking some imaginary disbeliever there, and never for a moment quiet.

He was talking eagerly, as though the words flowed to him faster than he could utter them. This invention of his, this supreme discovery, would make a revolution in the world of science.

The young man looking back at him from the other side of the table listened intently. He was a tall man of about eight-and-twenty, and if not exactly handsome, very close to it. Wyndham was a barrister, and a rising one – a man who loved his profession for its own sake, and strove and fought to make a name in it, though no such struggle was needful for his existence, as from his cradle his lines had fallen to him in pleasant places.

The Professor had been his tutor years ago, and the affection that existed between them in those far-off years had survived the changes of time and circumstance. Wyndham had never known a father; the Professor came as near as any parent could, and in this new wild theory of the old man's he placed implicit faith. It sounded wild, no doubt – it was wild – but there was not in all Ireland a cleverer man than the Professor, and who was to say but it might have some grand new meaning in it?

'You are sure of it?' he said, looking at the Professor with anxious but admiring eyes.

'Sure! I have gone into it, I have studied it for twenty years, I tell you. What, man, d'ye think I'd speak of it even to you, if I weren't sure? I tell ye … I tell ye' – he grew agitated and intensely Irish here – 'it will shake the world!'

The phrase seemed to please him; he drew his arms off the table and lay back in his chair as if revelling in it. He saw in his mind a day when in that old college of his over there, only a few streets away – in Trinity College – he should rise, and be greeted by his old chums and his new pupils, and the whole world of Dublin, with cheers and acclamations. Nay! it would be more than that: there would be London, and Vienna, and Berlin. He put Berlin last because, perhaps, he longed most of all for its applause; but in these dreamings he came back always to old Trinity, and found the greatest sweetness in the laurels to be gained there.

'There can't be a mistake,' he went on, more now as if reasoning with himself than with his visitor, who was watching him, and was growing a little uneasy at the pallor that was showing itself round his nose and mouth – a pallor he had noticed very often of late when the old man was unduly excited or interested. 'I have gone through it again and again. There is nothing new, of course,

under the sun, and there can be little doubt but that it is an anaesthetic known to the Indians of Southern America years ago, and
the Peruvians. There are records, but nothing sufficient to betray
the secret. It was by the merest accident, as I have told you, that
I stumbled on it. I have made many experiments. I have gone
cautiously step by step, until now all is sure. So much for one hour.
So much for six, so much for twenty-four, so much' – his voice
rose almost to a scream, and he thumped his hand violently on
the table – 'for seven days ... for seven *months!*'

His voice broke off, and he sank back in his chair. The young
man went quickly to a cupboard and poured out a glass of some
white cordial.

'Thank you,' said the Professor, swallowing the nauseous
mixture hurriedly, as though regretting the waste of time it took
to drink it.

'Why talk any more tonight?' said the young man anxiously. 'I
can come again to see you tomorrow. It is late.' He glanced at the
clock, which pointed to ten minutes past eleven. The movement
he made in pointing pushed aside his overcoat and showed that
he was in evening dress. He had evidently been dining out, and
had dropped in to see the Professor on his way home.

'I must talk while I can,' said the Professor, smiling. The cordial,
whatever it was, had revived him, and he sat up and looked again
at his companion with eyes that were brilliant. 'As for this pain
here,' he said, touching his side, 'it is nothing. What I want to say,
Paul, is this: if I could send a human creature to sleep for seven
months, then why not for seven years – or *forever?*'

Wyndham looked at him incredulously. 'But the last time ...'

'The last time, I had not quite perfected my discovery. But
since then some of my experiments have led me to think – to be
absolutely certain – that life can be sustained, with all the appearance of death upon the subject, for a full week at all events.'

'And when consciousness returns?'

'The subject treated wakes to life again in exactly the same condition as when he or she fell asleep, without loss of brain or body power.'

'Seven days! A long time!' The young man smiled. 'You bring back old thoughts and dreams. Are you a second Friar Laurence? Even though he could make the fair Juliet sleep till all believed her dead, he could not prolong it beyond a certain limit. "And in this borrowed likeness of shrunk death/Thou shalt continue two-and-forty hours." Less than two days; and yet, you conjurer' – he slapped the Professor's arm gaily – 'you would talk of keeping one in death's bonds for years!'

'Ay, years!' The Professor looked back at him, and his eyes shone. Old age seemed to slip from him, and for the moment a transient youth was his again. 'This is but a beginning – a mere start; but if it succeeds – if life can be sustained by means of this drug alone for seven days, why not for months and years?'

'You forget one thing,' said the young man. 'Who would care for it? Why should one care to lie asleep for years?'

'Many!' said the Professor slowly.

He ceased, and a strange gloom shadowed his face. His thoughts had evidently gone backward into a long-dead past. 'Have you no imagination?' he said at last reproachfully. 'Think, boy – think! When affliction falls on one, when a grievous sorrow tears the heart, who would not wish for an oblivion that would be longer than a sleeping-draught could give, and less pernicious than suicide?'

'The same refusal in both cases to meet and face one's doom,' said the young man. 'You would create a new generation of cowards.'

'Pshaw! There will be cowards without me,' said the Professor. 'But here, again, take another case. A man, we will say, has had his leg cut off: let him sleep until the leg is well, and he will escape all the twinges, the agonising pains of the recovery. This is but one instance; all surgical cases could be treated so, and so much pain saved in this most painful world. To see the blossom of my labour bear fruit – that is my sole, my last demand from life. I have so short a time to live that I would hasten the fulfilment of my hopes.'

'You mean ...'

'That I want to see the drug used on a human being. I have approached the matter with some of the authorities at Kilmainham, with a view to getting a condemned criminal to experiment upon; but I have been refused, and in such a presumptuous manner as leads me to fear I shall never receive a better answer. Surely a man respited for seven days, as has been the case occasionally, might as well risk those seven days in the cause of science.'

Wyndham shrugged his shoulders. 'I have never met that man,' said he. But the Professor did not hear him.

'The most humane people in the world,' said he, 'refuse help to the man who has devoted twenty years of his life to the cause of humanity. Such an anaesthetic as mine would work a revolution in the world of medicine. As I have told you, a man might not only be unconscious whilst a limb was being lopped off, but might remain so until the wound was healed, and then, made free of pain and perfectly well, be able to take his part in the world again.'

'It sounds like a fairy-tale,' said Wyndham, smiling. 'You have, I suppose, made many experiments?'

'On animals, yes – and of late without a single failure; but on a human body, no. As yet, no opportunity has been afforded me. Either jealousy or fear has stopped my march, which I feel would be a triumphal one were the road made clear. I tell you I have addressed many leading men of science on the subject. I have asked them to be present. I would have everything above board, as you who know me can testify. I would have all men look on and bear witness to the splendour of my discovery.' Here again the Professor's strange deep eyes grew brilliant, once again that queer flash of a youth long ago departed was his. 'I would have it shown to all the world in a blaze of light. But no man will take heed or listen. They laugh. They scoff. They will not countenance the chance of my killing someone; as if the loss of one poor human life was to be counted, when the relief of millions is in the balance.'

He sank back as if exhausted, and then went on, his tone hard, yet excited:

'Now it has come to this. If the chance were given me of trying my discovery on man, woman, or child, I should take it, without the sanction of the authorities, and with it that other chance of being hanged afterwards if the experiment failed.'

'You feel so sure as that?' questioned Wyndham. The old man's enthusiasm had caught him. He too was looking eager and excited.

'Sure!' The Professor rose, gaunt, haggard, and with eyes that flashed fire beneath the pent brows that overhung them. 'I would stake my soul – nay, more, my reputation – on the success of my discovery. Oh, for a chance to prove it!'

At this moment there was a low knock at the door.

The door opened with a considerable amount of caution, and presently a man's head appeared. The servant looked eagerly first at the younger man, who was his master, and then at the Professor, and then back again at Wyndham.

'Well, Denis?' said the latter, a little impatiently.

'If ye please, sir, there's an unfortunate young female on the steps below.'

'If she is noisy or troublesome, you had better call a policeman,' Wyndham said indifferently.

'Noisy! Divil a sound out of her,' said Denis. 'She looks for all the world as if there wasn't a spark o' life left in her.'

'I had better see to this,' said the young man, rising. He left the room, followed by Denis, and went down to the cold, bare hall below.

The light from the solitary gas-lamp scarcely lit it, but Wyndham saw the figure of a young and very slight girl. She was lying on the ground, her back supported against a chair, with the Professor's coat under her head. Lifting her quickly in his arms, he carried her upstairs to the room he had just left, where the Professor sat lost in fresh dreams of the experiment. He had already forgotten why the young man had left the room.

'She seems very ill,' said Wyndham.

The Professor came nearer and stared down at her. She was very young – hardly eighteen – but already Misery or Want, or both, had seized and laid their cruel hands upon her, dabbing in dark bistre shades beneath her eyes, and making sad hollows in her pallid cheeks. The face was so young, so free of hardness, vice, or taint of any kind, that Wyndham's very heart bled for her. Misery alone seemed to mark it. That was deeply stamped. Looking at her, he almost hoped that she would never wake again; but even as this thought crossed his mind, she stirred, sighed softly, and opened her eyes.

For a while she gazed at them, and then with a sharp, quick movement she released herself from the arm Wyndham had placed round her, raising herself to a sitting posture. There was such terror in her eyes as she did this that the younger man hastened to reassure her.

'You are quite safe here,' he said kindly.

The girl looked at him, then cast a frightened glance past him, and over his shoulder, as though looking fearfully for some dreaded object.

'My man found you on the steps outside. You were ill – fainting, he said – so he brought you in here to this gentleman's house.'

The girl looked anxiously at the Professor, who nodded as if duty bound, but who seemed unmistakably bored, for all that, and angry enough to frighten her afresh.

'If you will tell us where you live,' said Wyndham gently, 'we shall see that you are taken back there.'

The girl shrank visibly, then lifted her heavy eyes to his. 'I shall not go back,' she said. Her tone was low, but defiant, and very firm.

'But where, then, are you going?' asked Wyndham impulsively.

'I don't know.' She drew her breath slowly, heavily. It was hardly a sigh. There was enough misery in it for ten sighs, but her passion was all gone, and a terrible indifference had taken its place. 'I wish,' said she, with a forlorn look, 'that I had the courage to die.'

The Professor had begun to study her. He was always studying people, and now a curious expression had crept into his face. He leaned forward and peered at her. There was no compassion in the glance, no interest whatever in her as a suffering human, but there was a sudden sharp interest in her as a means to a desired end.

'Then why live?' he asked. 'Death is easy.'

'No, it is hard,' she said. 'And I am afraid of pain.'

'If there were no pain, you would risk it then?'

To Wyndham, waiting, watching, it occurred that the Professor was like a spider creeping towards its prey. He shuddered, took the Professor by the shoulders and pushed him gently backwards and out of hearing.

'If this drug of yours possesses the life-giving properties you claim, why speak to her of death? Do you honestly believe in this experiment? Or do you fear it – when you suggest this sort of suicide to her?'

'I fear nothing,' said the old man. 'But we are all mortal. We can all err, even in our surest judgments. The experiment – though I do not believe it – might fail. For all that, I shall not lose this chance,' said the Professor shortly. He turned and went back to the girl.

She was sitting in the same attitude as when he left her – her hands clenched upon her knees, her eyes staring into the fire. God alone knew what she saw there. She did not change her position, but sat like that, immovable as a statue, as the Professor expounded his experiment to her, and then asked her the cold, unsympathetic question as to whether, now she knew what the risk was, she would accept it. It might mean death, but if not, it would mean safety and protection in the future.

When he had finished, she turned her sombre eyes on his. 'I will take the risk,' she said.

Wyndham made a movement as if to speak, but the Professor checked him.

'Of course, if the experiment is successful,' he said, 'I shall provide for you for life.'

'I hope you will not have to provide for me,' she said.

Wyndham started, his voice vibrating with horror. 'No, no!' he cried. 'She does not understand, and neither do you. If this thing fails, it will mean murder. Think, I entreat you, before it is too late to think. Look at her!' His voice shook. 'Many a happier girl at her age would still be in her schoolroom. She is so young that, whatever her wrongs, her sorrows may be, she has still time before her to conquer or live them down. Professor, I implore you, do not go on with this.'

The Professor rested a contemptuous glance on him for a moment, then addressed the girl.

'You are willing?'

'Yes.' She spoke quite firmly, but she was looking at Wyndham.

It was a strange look, made up of surprise and some other feeling hardly defined.

'For God's sake, Professor, think yet a moment!' said the younger man, holding him in his grasp. 'She is young – so young! To take a life like that!'

'I am going to take no life. I see now that you never had any faith in me at all.'

'I believe in you as no other man does,' said Wyndham. 'But to try so deadly an experiment here, at midnight – with no witnesses, as it were – great heavens! You must see the pitfall you are laying for yourself. If this experiment fails—'

'It will not fail,' said the Professor coldly. 'In the meantime – if you are afraid of being called as a witness – it is still open to you to avoid such a disagreeability.' He pointed to the door.

Wyndham said nothing.

'Stay, then,' said the Professor. He went into an inner room and returned with a phial and glass, and advanced towards the girl with an almost buoyant step. There was, indeed, an exhilaration in his whole air, that amounted almost to madness. He looked wild – spectral, indeed – in the dim light of the solitary lamp, with his white hair thrown back and his eyes shining fiercely beneath the rugged brows.

The Professor poured some of the pale fluid from the phial into the glass with a hand that never faltered, and the girl took it with a hand that faltered quite as little; but before she could raise it to her lips, Wyndham caught her arm.

'Stop!' cried he, as if choking. 'Have you thought – have you considered that there is no certainty in this drug?'

Her eyes rested for a moment on his. 'I thought there was a certainty,' she said.

'A certainty of death, perhaps,' said he, poignant fear in his tone. 'At this last moment I appeal to you, for your own sake.

Don't take it. If you do, it is doubtful whether you will ever come back to life again.'

She looked at him steadily. 'I hope there is no doubt,' she said. She raised the glass and drank its contents to the dregs.

As she did so, some clock in the silent city outside struck the midnight hour.

She sank into a slumber so profound, so representative of death, that Wyndham uttered an exclamation of despair. As he stood watching the Professor, a sound smote upon his ear. One! Again, the city clock was tolling the hour. The Professor rose; his face was ghastly. One, two, three, four, five, six!

Could it be unreal? Wyndham rose once and bent over her. No faintest breath came from her lips or nostrils; the whole face had taken the pinched, ashen appearance of one who had lain for a full day dead. The hands were waxen, and the forehead too. He shuddered and drew back. At that moment he told himself that she was dead, and that he had undoubtedly assisted at a form of murder.

He turned to the Professor, who was sitting watch in hand, count-ing the moments. He would have spoken, but the old man's grim face forbade him. He was waiting. At twelve o'clock the girl had sunk into a slumber so profound, so representative of death, that Wyndham had uttered an exclamation of despair, and had told himself she was indeed struck down by the Destroyer. Six o'clock was about to strike – the hour when she ought to have risen from her strange slumbers, if the Professor's drug possessed the powerful properties he attributed to it.

As Wyndham stood watching the Professor, a sound smote upon his ear. One! Again the city clock was tolling the hour. The Professor rose, his face ghastly. One, two, three, four, five, six!

Six! The Professor bent down over the girl, and Wyndham went near to him, to be ready to help him when the moment came – when the truth was made clear to him that his discovery had failed. Wyndham himself had long ago given up hope, but he feared for the old man, to whom his discovery had been more than life or love for over twenty years.

The Professor still stood peering into the calm face. Six, and no sign, no change!

Already the sun's rays were beginning to peep sharply through the window; there was a slight stir in the street below. Six-thirty, and still the Professor stood gazing on the quiet figure, as motionless as it. Seven o'clock, and still no movement. The face, now lovely in its calm, was as marble, and the limbs lay rigid, the fingers lightly locked. Death ... death alone could look like that!

Half-past seven! As the remorseless clock recorded the time, the Professor suddenly threw up his arms.

'She is dead!' he said. 'Oh, my God!'

He reeled forward, and the young man caught him. He was almost insensible, and was gasping for breath. Wyndham carried him into an adjoining room and laid him on a bed, and, finding him cold, covered him with blankets. This, so far as it went, was well enough for the moment, but what was the next step to be? The old man lay gasping, and evidently there was but a short step between his state and that of his victim outside. Yet how to send for a doctor with that victim outside? To the Professor, whose hours were numbered, it would mean little or nothing; but to Wyndham, it would mean, if not death, eternal disgrace. He drew a long breath and bent over the Professor, who was now sensible again.

'Shall I send for Marks or Drewd?' he asked, naming two of the leading physicians in Dublin.

The Professor grasped his arm; his face grew frightful.

'No one! No one!' he gasped. 'Are you mad? Do you think I would betray my failure to the world? To have them laugh, deride—' He fell back, gasping still, but menacing the young man with his eye. By degrees the fury of his glance relaxed, and he fell into a sort of slumber, always holding Wyndham's arm, however, as if fearing he should go. He seemed stronger, and Wyndham knelt by the bed, wondering vaguely what was going to be the end of it all, and whether it would be possible to remove the corpse outside without detection. There was Denis; Denis was faithful, and could be trusted.

Presently the Professor roused from his fit of unconsciousness. He looked up at the young man, and his expression was terrible. Despair in its worse form disfigured his features. The dream of a life had been extinguished. He tried to speak, but at first words failed him, then, 'All the years – all the years!' he mumbled. Wyndham understood, and his heart bled. The old man had given the best years of his life to his discovery, and now ...

'I have killed her!'

'Science has killed her,' said Wyndham.

'No; I, with my cursed pride of belief in myself – I have killed her,' persisted the old man. 'I would to God it were not so!' He did not believe in anything but science, yet he appealed to the Creator occasionally, as some moderns still do to Jove. His lean fingers beat feebly on the blankets. 'A failure ... a failure,' he kept muttering, his eyes vacant. 'I go to my grave a failure! I set my soul on it. I believed in it, and it was naught.' He fell into a violent fit of shivering, and Wyndham gently laid him back in his bed, and covered him again with the blankets, where he lay sullen, powerless.

'Try not to think,' implored the young man.

'Think? Think! what else is left to me? Oh, Paul!' He stretched out his arm and caught Wyndham. 'That it should be a failure after all. I wish ...' He paused, and then went on: 'I wish I had not tried it upon her. She was like ... someone ...'

He broke off.

'She was a mere waif and stray,' said Wyndham, trying to harden his voice.

'She was no waif or stray of the sort you mean,' said the Professor. 'Her face was not like that. There – go; look on her for yourself, and read the truth of what I say.'

'It is not necessary,' said the young man, with a slight shudder. And again, a silence fell between them. It was again broken by the Professor.

'She was full of life,' he said, 'and I took it.'

Wyndham roused himself with an effort from his horrible thoughts, and made a faint effort to withdraw his hand from the Professor's. After a little while the Professor's grasp relaxed, and Wyndham rose to his feet. A shrinking from entering the room beyond was combated by a wild desire to go there and look once again upon the girl lying in death's sweet repose upon her couch. He went to the door, hesitated involuntarily for a second or two, and then entered.

He looked at her long and earnestly, and all at once it came to him that she was beautiful. It struck him as strange: that pinched look about the features that he had noticed an hour ago was gone now. The mouth was soft, the rounded chin curved as if in life. Almost there seemed a little bloom upon the pale, cold cheeks.

With a heavy sigh he turned away, and, leaning his arm upon the mantelshelf, gave himself up as prey to miserable thought. The fire had died out long ago, and the morning was cold and raw, and from under the ill-fitting door a little harsh wind was rushing.

What was to be done? The Professor would have to see a doctor, even if the medical man were brought in without his knowledge. Would it be possible to remove the – that girl, and arrange for her removal to … To where? Again, he lost himself in a sea of agonised doubt and uncertainty.

He fell back upon all the old methods of concealing dead bodies he had ever heard of, but everything seemed impossible.

What fools all those others must have been! Well, he could give himself up and explain matters; but then the Professor – to have his great discovery derided and held up to ridicule! The old man's look, as he saw it a little while ago, seemed to forbid any betrayal of his defeat. Great heavens! what was to be done?

He drew himself up with a heavy sigh, and turned to go back to the inner room to see if the Professor was still sleeping. As he went he tried to avoid glancing at the couch where the dead form lay, but when he got close, some force stronger than his will compelled him to look at it. And as he looked he felt turned into stone. He seemed frozen to the spot on which he stood; his eyes refused to remove themselves from what they saw.

Staring like one benumbed, he told himself at last that he was going mad. How otherwise could he see this thing? Sweat broke out on his forehead, and a cry escaped him.

The corpse was looking at him!

Very intently, too, and as if surprised or trying to remember. Her large eyes seemed singularly brilliant, and for a while the only thing living about her. But all at once, as though memory had returned, she sprang to her feet and stood, strong, and utterly without support, and questioned him with those eyes silently but eloquently. The queerest thing about it all to Wyndham was that, instead of being enfeebled by the strange draught she had drunk, she looked younger, more vigorous, and altogether another person from the forlorn, poor child of eight hours ago; the drug had, beyond doubt, a property that even the Professor had never dreamt of; it gave not only rest, but renewed health and life to those who drank it.

Seeing Wyndham did not or could not speak, she did.

'I am alive – alive!' she cried, with young and happy exultation. Where was the desire for death that lay so heavily on her only a few hours ago? Her voice rang through the room fresh and clear, filling it with music of a hope renewed, and so penetrating that it even pierced into the room beyond. And as it reached it, another cry broke forth – a cry this time old and feeble.

Wyndham rushed to answer it. The Professor was sitting up in bed, a mere wreck, but with expectation on every feature. He was trembling visibly. Wyndham knelt down beside him, and took his hand in his.

'That girl from last night ... She lives, sir. Your experiment has not failed, after all.'

The Professor silenced him by a gesture. He was evidently in the midst of a quick calculation now.

'The hour she woke?' he asked presently, with such a vigorous ring in his tone that Wyndham rose to his feet astonished.

'Two minutes ago.'

'Hah!' The Professor went back to his calculations. Presently a shout broke from him. 'I see it now!' he cried victoriously. 'I see where the mistake lay! Fool that I was not to have seen it before! It was a miscalculation, but one easy to be rectified. An hour or two will do it. Here, help me up, Paul.'

'But Professor, you must rest; you—'

'Not another moment, not one, I tell you!' cried the Professor furiously. He lunged out of bed. 'This thing must be seen to at once. What time can any man be sure of, that he should waste it? The discovery must be assured. And what time have I—'

He fell forward; he had fainted.

The doctors, when they came, could do nothing for him. The Professor, though hardly an old man, had so burnt out his candle at both ends that all the science in Europe could not have kept him alive for another twenty-four hours. A spice of gruesome mirth seemed to fall into the situation when their declaration was laid bare and one thought of the great discovery.

'Why doesn't she speak now?' asked the Professor. 'They said she was dead.'

'Who was dead?' asked Wyndham.

The Professor had not known Wyndham's voice the first time, but now he did, and he turned and looked at him; and presently consciousness once more grew within his eyes.

'It is you, boy. And where is she?'

'She? The girl, you mean?'

'You are a good boy. But your Greek, boy, your Greek is bad … You must mend – you must mend—'

His dying eyes tried to take the old stern look as they rested on Wyndham, the look he used to give the boy when his Greek or his Latin verses were hardly up to the mark, but presently it changed and softened into a wider light. 'The boy', in the last of all moments, was forgotten for the love that was strongest of all.

'She was very like my wife,' he gasped faintly, and fell back and died.

With a heavy heart Wyndham, assisted by a physician of great note, had gone through the Professor's papers. There were few of them, and with regard to the experiment only a few useless notes here and there, principally written on the backs of envelopes. There was nothing that could be used. The Professor, it seemed, had been in the habit of writing on his brain, and on that only. There was nothing left wherewith to carry on the great discovery.

Wyndham abandoned his search with a sigh. There was no doubt now that the wonderful experiment was lost to all time.

An Advance Sheet

JANE BARLOW (1898)

Sci-fi has thrived on the philosophical problems inherent in the potential existence of intelligent life on other planets. In the novel *History of a World of Immortals Without a God* (1891), written either by Jane Barlow or her father (or both, in collaboration) under the pseudonym Antares Skorpios, the forbidding immensity of outer space is conquered by the mysterious powers of the human mind, and a philosophical puzzle is answered – but at a terrible cost. This story follows a similar thread, but instead of a misanthropic Earthman inflicting his nihilism on a peaceful alien civilisation, here the psychic voyage reveals the terrible truth to a hapless human dreamer.

MANY YEARS AGO, I lived for some time in the neighbourhood of a private lunatic asylum, kept by my old fellow-student, Dr Warden, and, having always been disposed to specialise in the subject of mental disease, I often visited and studied the various cases placed under his charge. In one among these, that of a patient whom I will call John Lynn, I came to feel a peculiar interest. He was a young man of about twenty-five, of pleasant looks and manners, and to a superficial observer apparently quite free from any symptoms of his malady. His intellectual powers were far above the average, and had been highly trained; in fact, the strain of preparing for a brilliantly successful university examination had proved the cause of a brain fever, followed by a long period of depression, culminating in more than one determined attempt at suicide, which had made it necessary to place him under surveillance.

When I first met him, he had spent six months at Greystones House, and was, in Dr Warden's opinion, making satisfactory progress towards complete recovery. His mind seemed to be gradually regaining its balance, and the only unfavourable feature in his case was his strong taste for abstruse metaphysical studies, which he could not be prevented from occasionally indulging. But a spell of Kant and Hartmann, Comte and Hamilton, was so invariably followed by a retrograde period of excitement and dejection, that Dr Warden and I tried very hard to keep his thoughts from those pernicious volumes, and quite often we succeeded. My acquaintance with him was several months old, when, one fine mid-summer day, I called at Greystones House after an unusually long absence of a week or more.

The main object of my visit was to borrow a book from John Lynn, and accordingly, after a short conversation with Dr Warden, I asked whether I could see him. 'Oh, certainly,' said the Doctor. 'I'm afraid, though, that you won't find him over-flourishing. He's been at that confounded stuff, *Skleegel* and *Ficty* and *Skuppenhoor*' – my friend is no German scholar, and his eccentric pronunciation seemed to accentuate his scorn – 'hammer and tongs ever since last Monday, and you know what that means. Today, however, he was talking about you at luncheon, which I thought rather a good sign; so perhaps he may come round this time without much trouble.'

Having reached John Lynn's apartments, however, I did not share the Doctor's optimism. For though he appeared composed and collected – epithets which, indeed, always sound a warning note – there was a restlessness in the young man's glance, and a repressed enthusiasm in his tone. Moreover, I found it quite impossible to steer our conversation out of the channel in which his thoughts were setting – the atomic theory. I did my best for some time, but to no purpose at all. The atoms and molecules drifted into everything, through the most improbable crevices, like the dust of an Australian whirlwind. They got into sport, and politics, and parochial gossip, and the latest novel of the season.

So at length, abandoning the struggle, I resolved to let him say his say, and the consequence was that, after some half-hour's discourse, which I will not tempt the reader to skip, I found myself meekly assenting to the propositions of the infinitude of the material universe, and the aggregation and vibration of innumerable homogeneous atoms as the origin of all things, from matter to emotion, from the four-inch brick to the poet's dream of the Unknown.

'Now, what has always struck me as strange,' quoth John Lynn, who at this point leaned forward towards me, and held me with a glittering eye (which to my mind sub-consciously suggested sedatives), 'what strikes me as strange is the manner in which scientists practically ignore an exceedingly important implication of the theory – one, too, that has been pointed out very distinctly by Lucretius, not to go farther back. I refer to the fact that such a limitless atomic universe necessarily involves the existence, the simultaneous existence, of innumerable solar systems absolutely similar to our own, each repeating it in every detail, from the willow-leaves in the sun to the petals on that geranium-plant in the window, while in each of them history has been identically the same, from the condensation of gaseous nebulae down to stock prices in London at noon today. A minute's rational reflection shows that the admission is inevitable. Even if the requisite combination doesn't occur more than once in a tract of a billion trillion quintillions of square miles, what's that, even squared and cubed, when we have infinite space to draw upon?

'But, of course, this isn't all. For it follows from the same considerations that we must recognise the present existence, not only of inconceivably numerous Earths contemporaneous with our own, but also of as many more, older and younger, now exhibiting each successive state, past and future, through which ours has already proceeded, or at which it is destined to arrive.

For example, there are some still in the Palaeolithic period, and others where our ancestors are driving their cattle westward over the Asiatic steppes. The battle of Marathon's going on in one set, and Shakespeare's writing *Hamlet* in another. Here they've just finished the general election of eighteen hundred and ninety-something, and here they're in the middle of the next big European war, and here they're beginning to get over the effects of the submergence of Africa, and the resurrection of Atlantis – and so on to infinity. To make a more personal application, there's a series of Earths where you at the present moment are playing marbles in a bib, and another where people are coming back from my funeral.'

'Oh well,' I said, in a studiously bored way, 'perhaps these speculations may be interesting enough. But what do they all come to? It seems to me quite easy to understand why scientists ignore them. They've so much more promising material on hand. Why should they waste their time over such hopeless hypotheses – or facts, whichever you like?'

'Then, conceding them to be facts, you consider that they can have no practical significance for science?' said John Lynn, with a kind of triumph in his tone.

'Not a bit of it,' I replied. 'Supposing that this world is merely one in a crop, all as much alike as the cabbages in a row, and supposing that I am merely one in a bushel of Tom Harlowes, what's the odds so long as these doubles – or rather infinitibles – are kept separate by those massive distances? If they were to run into each other, I grant that the effect might be slightly confusing and monotonous, but it seems that this is just not possible.'

'But I believe you're quite mistaken there, Dr Harlowe,' he said, still with the suppressed eagerness of a speaker who is clearing the approaches to a sensational disclosure; 'or would you think a fact had no scientific value, if it went a long way towards accounting for those mysterious phenomena of clairvoyance? For, if what I've said is factually true, the explanation is simply this: the clairvoyant has somehow got a glimpse into one of these facsimile worlds, which happens to be a few years ahead of ours in point of time, and has seen how things are going on there.'

'Really, my good fellow,' I interposed, 'considering the billions and quintillions of miles which you were talking about just now, the explanation is hardly as "simple" as you say it is.'

'It's still a better one than any that has hitherto been put forward,' he persisted, with unabated confidence. 'Why, nowadays, there's surely no great difficulty in imagining very summary methods of dealing with space. Contrast it with the other difficulty of supposing somebody to have seen something which actually does not exist, and you'll see that the two are altogether disparate. In short, the whole thing seems clear enough to me on *a priori* grounds; but, no doubt, that may partly be because I am to a certain extent independent of them, as I've lately had an opportunity of visiting a planet which differs from this one solely in having had a small start of it – five years, I should say, or thereabouts.'

Knowing that to reinforce a delusion is always dangerous, I asked, 'What on earth do you mean, Lynn? Am I to understand that you are meditating a trifling excursion through the depths of space, or has it already come off?'

'It has,' he answered.

'May I ask when?' I asked, with elaborate sarcasm.

'Yesterday. I'd like to give you an account of it – and if you'd take a cigar, perhaps you'd look less like a preposterous know-it-all. You really don't on the present occasion, and it is absurd, not to say exasperating,' quoth John Lynn, handing me the case, with a good-humoured laugh. I took one, feeling somewhat perplexed at his cheerfulness, as his attacks had hitherto been invariably attended by despondency and gloom; and he resumed his statement as follows:

'It happened yesterday morning. I was sitting up here, reading a bit of *De Natura Rerum*, when suddenly I discovered that I was really standing in a very sandy lane, and looking over a low gate into a sort of lawn or pleasure-grounds. Before you say it, I hadn't fallen asleep. The lawn ran up a slope to the back of a house, all gables, and queer-shaped windows, and tall chimney-stacks, covered with ivy and other creepers – clematis, I think. At any rate, there were sheets of white blossom against the dark green. It's a place I never saw before, that I'm certain of; there are some points about it that I'd have been likely to remember if I had. For instance, the long semi-circular flights of turf steps to left and right, and the flower-beds cut out of the grass between them into the shape of little ships and boats, a whole fleet, with sails and oars and flags, which struck me as a quaint device. Then in one corner there was a huge puzzle-monkey nearly blocking up a turnstile in the bank; I remember thinking it might be awkward for anyone coming that way in the dark. Looking back down the lane, which was only a few yards of cart-track, there were the beach and the sea close by; a flattish shore with the sand-hills, covered with bent and furze, zig-zagging in and out nearer to and farther from high-water mark. There are miles of that sort of thing along the east coast, and, as a matter of fact, I ultimately found out that it can have been no great distance from Lowestoft – from what corresponds with our Lowestoft, of course, I mean.

'And I may observe that I never have been in that part of the world, at least, not nearer than Norwich.

'Well, as you may suppose, such an abrupt change of scene is a rather startling experience; and I must frankly confess that I haven't the wildest idea how it happened—'

'Hear, hear,' said I.

'But the strange feeling wore off before long, and I began to make observations. As for the time of day, one could see by the shadows and dew on the grass that it was morning, a much earlier hour than it had been here, and the trees and flowers showed that it was early summer. Nobody was visible about the place, but I heard the scraping of a rake upon gravel somewhere near. I set out to find this unseen gardener, and I framed several questions ingeniously designed to extract as much information as possible without betraying my own state of bewildered ignorance.

'But when I tried to carry out this plan, it proved impossible. The gate at which I stood was unlatched and the banks on either hand were low and easily scalable, but I could not reach those pleasure-grounds. My attempts to do so were repulsed, in a manner which I am totally unable to describe; some strange force, invisible and irresistible as gravity, arrested every movement in that direction, almost before it had been telegraphed from brain to muscle. A few experiments revealed that while I could proceed unchecked to right or left along the shore, I was absolutely prohibited from taking a single step farther inland. I discovered that the water's edge did not bring me to the end of my tether, but naturally, I did not investigate how far into the sea I could go.

'I next thought of trying to make my presence audible. This experiment, however, failed even more promptly than the other; I couldn't utter a sound. I picked up a stone and knocked on the gate; I continued the process for some time before it dawned upon me that my hammering produced no noise whatever. It is true that soon afterwards a ridiculous-looking small terrier came trotting round the corner; but his bored and indifferent air only too plainly proved his arrival to be *non propter hoc*. I vainly endeavoured to attract his attention, whistling phantom whistles, and slapping my knees, and even going to the length of flour-ishing defiant legs; he paid no attention to me, and instead saw fit to bark himself hoarse at a flock of sparrows. Altogether it seemed sufficiently obvious that in these new scenes, where and whatever they might be, I was to play the part merely of a spectator, invisible, inaudible, intangible.

'What happened next was that a glass door in the house opened, and out of it came two ladies, one of whom I recognised as my eldest sister, Elizabeth. There was nothing in her appearance to make me for a moment doubt her identity, though it did strike me that she looked unusually grave and, yes, decidedly older. I was then inclined to attribute this impression to the old-fashioned dress she wore; but I must now suppose her attire to have been whatever *is to be the* latest novelty for that particular summer. The other girl puzzled me much more, for although there was certainly something familiar about her, I couldn't fit any name to her; and it wasn't until I heard my sister call her "Nellie" that I realised she was Helen Ronaldson. She, you know, is a sort of cousin of ours, and my mother's ward, and has lived with us most of her life; so, there was nothing surprising in finding her and Elizabeth together. The strange thing was that whereas I saw her a few months ago in the guise of an angular, inky-fingered school-girl of fifteen or sixteen at most, yesterday she had shot up to twenty or thereabouts, had grown several inches, and had undoubtedly turned into a young lady.

'They came down the path, running along inside the boundary-bank, and sat down on a garden seat, behind which I found no difficulty in taking up a position well within eavesdropping distance. I'd begun by this time to suspect how matters stood, and was consequently rather uneasy in my mind. One can't find oneself suddenly plumped down five years or so ahead of yesterday, without speculating as to how things – and people – have gone on in the meantime. So much may happen in five years. The situation produces the same sort of feeling that I fancy one might have upon finding oneself intact after a railway accident, and proceeding to investigate who among one's fellow passengers have held together, what number of limbs they still can muster, and so on. Of course, I was not sure that I would learn anything from their conversation; they might have talked for an hour without saying a word to enlighten me; but, as good luck would have it, they were discussing a batch of letters received that morning from various members of the family, about whom I was thus enabled to pick up many more or less disconnected facts. It appeared, for instance, that my sister Maud was married, and living in South Kensington. My brother Dick, who has just got a naval cadetship, was in command of a gunboat somewhere off the Chinese coast. Walter seemed to be doing well on the horse-ranch in the Rockies, which he's hankering after at present – all satisfactory enough. The only thing that made me uneasy was that for some time neither of them mentioned my mother, and it really was an immense relief to my mind when at last Elizabeth said, "We haven't got any sweet-pea, and mother always likes a bit for her table."

"We must get some before we go in. Her cold seems to be much better this morning," Nellie replied.

"Oh yes, nearly gone. There's no fear that she won't be able to appear on Thursday. That would be indeed unlucky; why, a wedding without a mother-in-law would be nearly as bad as one without a bridegroom, wouldn't it?"

Nellie laughed and blushed, but expressed no opinion, and Elizabeth went on:

"Talking of that, do you expect Vincent this morning?"

"I don't know. He wasn't sure whether his leave would begin today or tomorrow. He said that if he got it today, he would look in here on his way to Lowestoft."

"That's rather a roundabout way from Norwich, isn't it? You know, Nellie, I'm glad that you'll be in York next winter.

There's much more going on there, and you can ask me to stay with you!"

'From these last remarks I inferred two facts respecting Vincent, my youngest brother, neither of which would I have been at all inclined to predict: that he had entered the army, though he has so far displayed no leanings towards a military career; and that he was about to marry Helen Ronaldson. Why, the idea's absurd! I remember that in the days of their infancy, being nearly contemporaries, they used to squabble a good deal, and at present I believe they regard one another with a feeling of happy indifference. In Vincent's last letter to me he said he was afraid that he would find the house awfully overrun with girls when he went home, which was, if I'm not mistaken, a graceful allusion to the circumstance that Nellie's holidays coincide with his own.

'However, likely or unlikely, I had soon conclusive proof that such was actually the case, as Vincent himself arrived, not easily recognisable, indeed, having developed into a remarkably good-looking young fellow. The discreet way in which Elizabeth presently detached herself from the group and went to gather sweet-pea, would alone have led me to suspect the state of affairs, even if the demeanour of the other two had not made it so very plain before they walked round a corner beyond the range of my observations. But they were scarcely out of sight when there appeared upon the scene a fourth person who took me utterly by surprise, though, of course, if I had considered a little, it was natural enough that I – I mean he – should be there.

'All the same, it gives one an uncommonly uncanny sensation, I can tell you, to see oneself walk out of a door some way off, stand looking about for a minute or two, and then come sauntering towards one with his hands in your pockets – I'm afraid my pronouns are rather mixed, but I don't know how else to describe it. I'm not sure whether in such cases we see ourselves as others see us: I should fancy so, for I noticed that I looked extremely – I must hope abnormally – grumpy; I don't think I was improved either by the short beard he had set up, not to mention several streaks of grey in my hair. Just then I saw Elizabeth crossing the grass to speak to me – I don't mean to myself, you know, but to him – and I heard her say: "You're a very unfeeling relative! Have you forgotten that this is my birthday?" This, by the way, fixes the date exactly: it must have been the twenty-third of June, five years ahead from tomorrow. I regret to say that in reply he only gave a sort of grunt, and muttered something about anniversaries being a great bore; and I remember thinking that if I were she I'd leave him to get out of his bad temper myself – I say, these pronouns are really getting quite too many for me …'

'Your own name is rather a convenient length, why not use it?' I observed. Lynn considered and adopted the suggestion.

'Well, then, Elizabeth and John Lynn strolled aimlessly about for a while, but soon went into the house, and after that I saw nobody else, except occasionally the gardener, for what seemed a very long period. I had nothing at all to do, and the time dragged considerably. The strip of beach on which I could move about was hot and glaring, and disagreeably deep in soft sand; yet, for want of better occupation, in the course of the afternoon, I walked more than a mile along it in a northerly direction, until I came to a dilapidated-looking old boat-house, built in a recess between two sandhills, and just beyond the line I couldn't cross.

'Having reached this point, and seeing nothing else of interest, I slowly retraced my steps towards the pleasure-grounds' gate. By this time, it must have been four or five o'clock, and the weather, hitherto bright and clear, showed a change for the worse. An ugly livid-hued cloud was spreading like a bruise over the sky to the southeast, and sudden gusts began to ruffle up the long, bent grasses of the sand-hills on my right hand.

'When I came near the gate, several people were standing at it, apparently watching two men who were doing something to a small sailing-boat, which lay off a little pier close by. Elizabeth and Nellie, and my other sister Juliet, were there, and Elizabeth was explaining to an elderly man, whom I have never succeeded in identifying, that Jack and Vincent intended to sail across to Graston Spit – she pointed over the water to a low tongue of land at no great distance – which would be Vincent's shortest way to Lowestoft. "In that case," said he, "the sooner they're off the better, for it looks as if we might have a squall before very long, and the glass is by no means steady today." The women debated among themselves about whether the short trip was advisable, eventually concluding that the two men should give up the idea. John Lynn, whose temper seemed to have somewhat improved, asserted that they would have a splendid breeze, and that he would be back again in an hour or so. Accordingly, they hurried over their adieux, and lost no time in getting off, taking nobody else with them.

'They had been gone perhaps three-quarters of an hour, when the "splendid breeze" appeared in the shape of a furious squall, hissing and howling on with remarkable suddenness and violence, and brought the girls, who were still out-of-doors, running with dismayed countenances to look over the gate to the sea. The sweeping gusts bore to me fitful snatches of anxious colloquies, the general drift of which, however, seemed to be towards the conclusion that the boat must have got over before the wind sprang up, and that Jack would, of course, wait there until it went down. As the blasts moderated a little, they were accompanied by driving sheets of large-dropped rain, which again sent the girls scurrying indoors, and I was left alone. I thought much upon the boat and its occupants, who must, I thought, be having a rather nasty time of it, unless they had really landed before the squall; for both wind and tide were against them, and a surprising sea had got up already. I consider myself to know something about the management of a boat, and I supposed that my strange double or "fetch"[1] might be credited with an equal amount of skill; Vincent, however, has had little or no experience of nautical matters.

'I reviewed the situation, standing where the shallow foam-slides seethed to my feet, and I found myself contemplating a catastrophe to that John Lynn with a feeling which I can't either describe or explain. After a while, I began to pace up and down the beach as the light was thickening, when, on turning a corner, I again came in sight of the old boat-house again. Almost at the same moment, my eye was caught by some dark object on the sea, elusively disappearing and reappearing between the folds of grey vapour drifting low upon the water. A longer rift soon showed me plainly that it was a small boat in sorry plight, filling and settling down so fast, that her final disappearance would evidently be a question of a very few minutes. There was nobody in her, and I thought to myself that if anyone had gone overboard in that sea, he must assuredly have preceded her to the bottom. And I felt equally convinced that she was no other than the boat in which I had seen the two Lynns embark.

'This proved to be both right and wrong: she was the Lynns' boat, but the Lynns had not gone to the bottom. I now became aware of a human form, which, at not many yards' distance, was making slow and struggling progress through the swirling surf towards the water's edge, and had already reached a place shallow enough to admit of wading. As I ran forward, not to assist – having long since ascertained that I could by no means demonstrate my presence – but merely to investigate; it turned out to be John Lynn, half-carrying, and half-dragging along Vincent,

1. Editor's note: a 'fetch' is the Irish folkloric equivalent of a doppelgänger; it is the double of a person who is still alive, and its appearance heralds the death of the person it mimics.

who was apparently insensible. I had an awful scare, I can tell you, for he flopped down on the sand when I – when *John* let him go, in such a lifeless, limp sort of way, that I thought at first the lad had really come to grief. However, I suppose he had only been slightly stunned; at any rate, in a minute or two he sat up, and seemed none the worse. But when he got to his feet, it was evident that he had somehow damaged one of his ankles, and he could hardly attempt the feeblest hobble. All this time the rain was coming down in torrents, and it was blowing so hard that you could scarcely hear yourself speak.

"It's a good step – more than a mile," I heard the other John Lynn say. "Do you think you could get as far as the old boat-house? Then you'd be under shelter, while I run back and find some means of getting you home."

'They made their way haltingly to the boathouse, which, judging by the cobwebby creaking of the door, had not been entered for many a long day, and into which I was, of course, unable to follow them. Presently, John Lynn came out alone, and set off running towards the house at a very creditable pace, considering the depth of the sand and the weight of his drenched garments. I had found a tolerably sheltered station under the lee of a sand-bank, and I decided to wait where I was for his return; but I had to wait much longer than one might have expected. The twilight turned into dusk, and the wind dropped, and the sky cleared, and a large full-moon came out, all in a leisurely way, but there was no sign of anybody coming near us. I couldn't account for the delay, and abused John Lynn a good deal in consequence of it. I know my wits sometimes go wool-gathering, but I'm certain I should never have been such an ass as to leave another fellow sitting wet through for a couple of hours. Vincent, too, was evidently getting impatient, for I heard him shout "Jack" once or twice, and whistle at intervals in a way which I knew betokened exasperation.

'At last John Lynn came posting round the corner, apparently in no end of a hurry, but not a soul with him, though he'd been away long enough to have collected half the county. As he ran up to the boat-house, I saw him taking out of his pocket something which gleamed in the moonlight, and was, I'm pretty sure, the top of a flask, so he'd at any rate had the sense to bring some spirits. I wanted to find out whether any more people were on their way, and forgetting for the moment that the boat-house wasn't in my reach, I went after him to the door. And there two queer things happened.

'In the first place, I got a glimpse, just for an instant, but quite distinctly, of *you*, Dr Harlowe; and immediately afterwards an extraordinary feeling of horror came over me, and I began to rush away, I don't know why or where, but on, on, until the air suddenly turned into a solid black wall, and I went smash against it, and somehow seemed to wake up – sitting here at this table.'

'That's the first sensible remark you've made today,' I said, in the most soothingly matter-of-fact tone that I could assume. 'Only why do you say "seemed"? I should think it was perfectly obvious that you did really wake up – or is there more to follow?'

'Then I dreamt it all?' said he.

'All of it that you haven't elaborated since then, just by thinking it over,' I replied.

'Oh, well,' said my young friend with a certain air of forbearing superiority, 'as it happens, I dreamt it no more than you did. But if you prefer it, we'll call it a dream. At any rate, it wasn't a bad one. I should feel rather uncomfortable now if it had ended disastrously; however, as far as one can see, nothing worse seemed likely to come of it than Nellie's being obliged either to postpone her wedding for a week, or to put up with a hobbling bridegroom. Then, as to those disagreeable sensations at the conclusion, I dare say they could have been caused by the process by which one is conveyed back and forward; some phase, no doubt, of disintegration of matter. But you said, didn't you, that you wanted to borrow *Walt Whitman*? Here he is – mad Martin Tupper flavoured with dirt, in my judgment; however, you may like him better.'

During the remainder of our interview, John Lynn was so composed and rational that I began to think less seriously of his relapse. After all, many thoroughly sane people had been overcome by vivid and coherent dreams, and I felt no doubt that in his case the impression would wear off in a day or two. As I went out, I communicated these views to Dr Warden, who agreed with my assessment.

This proved to be my last conversation with John Lynn. That very evening I was unexpectedly called away by business, which obliged me to spend several months in America. Upon returning, I found that he had left Greystones House cured, and had gone abroad for a long tour. After which, I heard nothing more about him; as time went by, I thought of him less and less.

In the early summer, five years later – my diary fixes all dates – I happened to be wandering along the eastern coast, and arrived one evening at a remote little seaside place in Norfolk. The next morning, the twenty-third of June, was brilliantly fine, and tempted me out with my photographing gear. My negatives turned out better than usual, and as it was a new fad with me, I became so deeply absorbed in my attempts that I allowed myself to be overtaken, a good way from home, by a violent storm of wind and rain. I had an extremely unpleasant walk home with my unwieldy camera and other paraphernalia; having got into dry clothes, and ascertained that several of my most promising plates had been destroyed, I did not feel enthusiastically benevolent when the landlord appeared in my room.

A young man, he told me, had just come over in the dogcart from Sandford Lodge – Mrs Lynn's place below – to fetch a doctor for the old lady, who had taken a turn for the worse; the local doctor, however, was on a call several miles away and could not be reached. 'And so, sir,' proceeded my landlord, 'believin' as you be a medical gentleman, I made bold to mention the suckumstance to you, in case as how you might think on doin' summat for her.'

Common humanity, of course, compelled me so to go, and I at once set out again through the rain, which still fell thickly. The young man in the dogcart explained as much of the situation as he could along the way. The family, he said, had been at Sandford Lodge for about a couple of years, and were well liked in the neighbourhood. Two gentlemen from the house had been out sailing that afternoon, and had either been caught in the squall, or run into a rock, but had gone down 'clever and clean' one way or the other. Mr Jack managed to swim ashore, but there was no sign of his brother, Mr Vincent, who was supposed to be getting married in two days' time. After the awful news was delivered, they'd found the mistress of the house lying unconscious on the landing and couldn't rouse her.

The young man drove a few hundred yards down a deep-rutted, sandy lane, and pulled up next to an iron gate. 'There's a turnstile in the bank to your left, sir,' he said, as I alighted, 'and then if you go straight on up the lawn, you'll find the porch-door open, and there's safe to be someone about.'

I followed his instructions, feeling a curiously strong impression of familiarity with the place at which I had arrived – the sandy bank, the gate, the slope running up to the creeper-draped gabled house, standing out darkly against the struggling moon-beams. A common enough illusion, I reflected, but it was now without doubt unusually powerful and persistent. It was not dispelled even by my pricking my hand severely in brushing past a puzzle-monkey, which brandished its spiny arms in front of the turnstile. At the door I was met by two girls, who looked stunned and scared, but who reported that their mother had recovered from the long fainting-fit which had so much alarmed them.

They brought me upstairs to the room where she was sitting, and the first sight of her miserable face brought further latent memories to the surface, for she reminded me of someone I had met before, but I couldn't remember who – even though I knew I was speaking to a Mrs Lynn.

I found the interview dreary and embarrassing. Mrs Lynn was so far recovered that her health called for but little professional discourse, and yet I feared to appear unsympathetic if I hastened away abruptly. At length I decided to end the conversation by producing a visiting-card, which I handed to Mrs Lynn, murmuring something about a hope that if I could at any time be of any service to her she would— But before I was half through my sentence, she started, and uttered an exclamation, with her eyes fixed upon the name and address. 'Harlowe – Greystones,' she said; 'you're the one who was so kind to poor Jack when he was with Dr Warden!'

As she spoke, a ray of recognition shot into my mind. It could be no one but John Lynn's mother; of course I remembered John Lynn. Indeed, there was as strong a likeness between her and her son as there can be between an elderly lady and a young man. I was, however, still unable to recall the occasion upon which he had, as I now began to feel dimly aware, described this place to me.

Mrs Lynn appeared to be strangely agitated by her discovery of my identity. She sat for a minute or two glancing from the card to me, and said, 'Dr Harlowe, I must tell you something that has been upon my mind for a long time.' She continued, speaking low and rapidly, with many nervous glances towards the door. 'Perhaps you may have heard that my youngest son Vincent is going to be married. Their wedding was to have been the day after tomorrow, his and Helen Ronaldson's. She's my ward, who has lived with us all her life; and they've been engaged for nearly a year. Well, Dr Harlowe, my son Jack – you know Jack – has been at home, too, for three or four years, and some time ago I began to suspect a feeling on his part of attachment towards Nellie. I hoped at first that I was mistaken, but lately I've realised I'm not. I believe he never realised it himself until the time of his brother's engagement. And I fear he has at times, just occasionally, shown some jealousy towards Vincent. Not often at all, and nothing serious, you know; indeed, it may be only my own imagination.'

'Very true,' I said, because she looked at me as if wishing for assent.

'But that's not what I want to tell you,' she hurried on. 'Tonight, soon after he came back from that miserable boat, I was in here, when I heard Jack running upstairs, and I went to the door to speak to him, but before I could stop him, he had passed, and gone into his room. Just outside it he dropped something, and I picked it up. It was this!' She took out of her pocket a small gold horseshoe-shaped locket with an inch or so of broken chain attached to it. One side of its case had been wrenched off at the hinge, showing that it contained a tiny photograph – a girl's face, dark-eyed and delicately featured.

'That's Nellie,' said Mrs Lynn, 'and it belongs to Vincent; he always wore it on his watch-chain. So if he had really been washed away, as they said, I don't understand how Jack came to have it with him. Do you, Dr Harlowe?' This poor mother leaned forward and laid a hand on my sleeve, in her eagerness for an answer.

'He might have been trying to rescue his brother – to pull him ashore, or into the boat, and have accidentally caught hold of it in that way,' I suggested. 'It looks as if it had been torn off by a strong grip.'

'Do you think that may be how it was?' she said with what seemed to me an odd mingling of relief and disappointment in her tone. 'When I had picked it up, I waited about outside Jack's door, and thought I heard him unlocking and opening a drawer. Presently he came out, in a great hurry: he ran past, saying, 'I can't stop now, mother.' I went into his room, and the first thing I noticed was the drawer of the writing-table left open. I knew it was the one where he keeps his revolver, and when I looked into it, I saw that the case was empty. Just then I suddenly got very faint, and they say I was unconscious for a long time. One of the maids says that she saw Jack running down towards the beach, about an hour ago. I believe numbers of people are there, searching. I said nothing to anyone about the revolver – perhaps I ought to have done so. What can he have wanted with it? I've been thinking that he may have intended to fire it off for a signal, if the night was very dark. Don't you think that is quite possible?'

'I don't know … I can't say,' I answered. At this moment a whole sequence of recollections stood out abruptly in my mind, as if my thoughts had been put under a stereoscope.

'Can you tell me whether there is an old, disused boat-house, perhaps a mile along the shore, built in a hollow between two banks?' I went on, impatiently adding what particulars I could, in hopes of prompting her memory, which seemed to be at fault.

'Yes, yes, there is one like that,' she said at last; 'in the direction of Mainforthing; I remember we walked as far as it not very long ago.'

'Someone ought to go there immediately,' I said, moving towards the door.

'Why?' exclaimed Mrs Lynn, following me. 'Is there any chance that the boys—?'

But I did not wait to explain my reasons, which, in truth, were scarcely intelligible to myself.

Hurrying down the lawn, and emerging on the beach, I fell in with a small group of men and lads, of whom I asked the way to Mainforthing. To the right, they told me by word and gesture, but the search party had set off in the opposite direction. I explained that my object was to find the old boat-house, whereupon they assured me that I would do so easy enough if I kept straight along by the strand for a mile and a bit, and two or three of them accompanied me as I started.

The stretches of crumbling, moon-bleached sand seemed to lengthen out interminably, but at last, round a corner I came breathlessly upon my goal. The door of the boat-house was wide open, and the moonlight streamed brightly through it, full in the face of a youth who, at the moment when I reached the threshold, was standing with his back to the wall, steadying himself by a hold on the window-ledge beside him, and looking as if he had just with difficulty scrambled to his feet. He was staring straight before him with a startled and bewildered expression, and saying 'Jack – I say, Jack, what the deuce are you up to?'

And not without adequate cause. For opposite to him stood John Lynn – altered, but still recognisable as my former acquaintance – who held in his hand a revolver, which he was raising slowly, slowly, to a level as it seemed with the other's head. The next instant I had sprung towards him, but he was too quick for me, and, shaking off my grasp on his arm, turned and faced me, still holding his weapon. 'Dr Harlowe! You here?' he said, and had scarcely spoken the words when he put the barrel to his temple, and before the echoes of the shot had died on the jarred silence, and while the smoke-wreaths were still eddying up to the boat-house roof, he lay dead at our feet with a bullet in his brain.

The coroner's jury, of course, returned their customary verdict, perhaps with better grounds than usual. Upon my own private verdict, I have deliberated often and long, but without arriving at any conclusive result. That crime that John Lynn had been about to commit – was it a premeditated one, or had he taken the revolver with some different intention, and then yielded to a sudden mad impulse? This question I can never hope to answer definitely, though my opinion inclines towards the latter. Upon the whole it seems clear to me that by his last act my unhappy friend took the easiest way out of a maze of mortal misery. Furthermore, I cannot avoid the conviction that but if he hadn't told me of his dream, or trance experiences, a fratricide's guilt would have been added to the burdens of his mind, and his passion mocked by Fate.

The Luck of Pitsey Hall

L.T. MEADE AND ROBERT EUSTACE (1899)

The benefits of scientific progress are manifold, but writers have found the nefarious potential of science to be just as fruitful. The following story is taken from a sequence entitled *The Brotherhood of Seven Kings*, in which the narrator does battle with an ancient organisation (currently headed by his ex-girlfriend) that uses scientific knowledge to criminal ends – including assassination by disease, sports fixing by means of a tsetse fly, and audacious, 'impossible' robberies.

AS THE DAYS AND WEEKS went on, Mme Koluchy became more than ever the talk of London. The medical world agitated itself about her to an extraordinary degree. It was useless to gainsay the fact that she performed marvellous cures. Under her influence and treatment weak people became strong again. Those who stood at the door of the Shadow of Death returned to their intercourse with the busy world. Beneath her spell, pain vanished. What she did and how she did it remained more than ever a secret. She dispensed her own prescriptions, but although some of her medicines were analysed by experts, nothing in the least extraordinary could be discovered in their composition. The cure did not therefore lie in drugs. In what did it consist?

Doctors asked this question one of another, and could find no satisfactory answer. The rage to consult Madame became stronger and stronger. Her patients adored her. The magnetic influence which she exercised was felt by each person with whom she came in contact.

Meanwhile Dufrayer and I watched and waited. The detective officers in Scotland Yard knew of some of our views with regard to this woman. Led by Dufrayer they were ceaselessly on the alert; but, try as the most able of their staff did, they could learn nothing of Mme Koluchy which was not to her credit. She was spoken of as a universal benefactress, taking, it is true, large fees from those who could afford to pay; but, on the other hand, giving her services freely to the people to whom money was scarce. This woman could scarcely walk down the street without heads being turned to look after her, and this not only on account of her remarkable beauty, but still more because of her genius and her goodness. As she passed by, blessings were showered upon her, and if the person who called down these benedictions was rewarded by even one glance from those lovely and brilliant eyes, he counted himself happy.

About the middle of January, the attention of London was diverted from Mme Koluchy to a murder of a particularly mysterious character. A member of the Cabinet by the name of Delacour was found dead in St James's Park. His body was discovered in the early morning, in the neighbourhood of Marlborough House, with a wound straight through the heart. Death must have been instantaneous. He was stabbed from behind, which showed the cowardly nature of the attack. I knew Delacour, and for many reasons was appalled when the tidings reached me. As far as anyone could tell, he had no enemies. He was a man in the prime of life, of singular power of mind and strength of character, and the only possible motive for the murder seemed to be to wrest some important State secrets from his possession. He had been attending a Cabinet meeting in Downing Street, and was on his way home when the dastardly deed was committed. Certain memoranda respecting a loan to a foreign Government were abstracted from his person, but his watch, a valuable ring, and some money were left intact. The police immediately put measures in active train to secure the murderer, but no clue could be obtained. Delacour's wife and only daughter were broken-hearted. His position as a Cabinet Minister was so well known, that not only his family but the whole country rang with horror at the dastardly crime, and it was fervently hoped that before long the murderer would be arrested, and receive the punishment which he so justly merited.

On a certain evening, about a fortnight after this event, as I was walking slowly down Welbeck Street, and was just about to pass the door of Mme Koluchy's splendid mansion, I saw a young girl come down the steps.

She was dressed in deep mourning, and glanced around from right to left, evidently searching for a passing hansom. Her face arrested me; her eyes met mine, and, with a slight cry, she took a step forward.

'You are Mr Head?' she exclaimed.

'And you are Vivien Delacour,' I replied. 'I am glad to meet you again. Don't you remember the Hotel Bellevue at Brussels?'

When I spoke her name, she coloured perceptibly and began to tremble. Suddenly putting out one of her hands, she laid it on my arm.

'I am glad to see you again,' she said, in a whisper. 'You know of our – our most terrible tragedy?'

'I do,' I replied.

'Mother is completely prostrated from the shock. The murder was so sudden and mysterious. If it were not for Mme—'

'Mme Koluchy?' I queried.

'Yes, Mr Head; Mme Koluchy, the best and dearest friend we have in the world. She was attending mother professionally at the time of the murder, and since then has been with her daily. On that first terrible day she scarcely left us. I don't know what we should have done were it not for her great tact and kindness. She is full of suggestions, too, for the capture of the wretch who took my dear father's life.'

'You look shaken yourself,' I said; 'ought you to be out alone at this hour?'

'I have just seen Madame with a message from mother, and am waiting here for a hansom. If you would be so kind as to call one, I should be much indebted to you.'

'Can I do anything to help you, Vivien?' I said; 'you know you have only to command me.'

A hansom drew up at the pavement as I spoke. Vivien's sad grey eyes were fixed on my face.

'Find the man who killed my father,' she said; 'we shall never rest until we know who took his life.'

'May I call at your house tomorrow morning?' I asked suddenly.

'If you will be satisfied with seeing me. Mother will admit no one to her presence but Mme Koluchy.'

'I will come to see you then; expect me at eleven.'

I helped Miss Delacour into her hansom, gave directions to the driver, and she was quickly bowled out of sight.

On my way home, many thoughts coursed through my brain. A year ago, the Delacours, a family of the name of Pitsey, and I had made friends when travelling through Belgium. The Pitseys, of old Italian origin, owned a magnificent place not far from Tunbridge Wells; the Pitseys and the Delacours were distant cousins. Vivien at that time was only sixteen, and she and I became special chums. She used to tell me all about her ambitions and hopes, and in particular descanted on the museum of rare curios which her cousins, the Pitseys, possessed at their splendid place, Pitsey Hall. I had a standing invitation to visit the Hall at any time when I happened to have leisure, but up to the present had not availed myself of it. Memories of that gay time thronged upon me as I hurried to my own house, but mixed with the old reminiscences was an inconceivable sensation of horror.

Why was Mme Koluchy a friend of the Delacours? My mind had got into such a disordered state that I, more or less, associated her with any crime which was committed. Hating myself for what I considered pure morbidness, I arrived at my own house. There I was told that Dufrayer was waiting to see me. I hurried into my study to greet him; he came eagerly forward.

'Have you any news?' I cried.

'If you allude to Delacour's murder, I have,' he answered.

'Then, pray speak quickly,' I said.

'Well,' he continued, 'a curious development, and one which may have the most profoundly important bearing on the murder, has just taken place; it is in connection with it that I have come to see you.' Dufrayer stood up as he spoke. He never liked to be interrupted, and I listened attentively without uttering a syllable.

'Yesterday,' he continued, 'a man was arrested on suspicion. He was examined this morning before the magistrate at Dow Street. His name is Walter Hunt; he is the keeper of a small marine store at Houndsditch.

'For several nights he has been found hovering in a suspicious manner round the Delacours' house. On being questioned he could give no straightforward account of himself, and the police thought it best to arrest him.

'On his person was discovered an envelope, addressed to himself, bearing the City post-mark and the date of the day the murder was committed. Inside the envelope was an absolutely blank sheet of paper. Thinking this might be a communication of importance it was submitted to George Lambert, the Government expert at Scotland Yard, for examination; he subjected it to every known test in order to see if it contained any writing on sympathetic ink, or some other secret cipher principles. The result is absolutely negative, and Lambert firmly declares that it is a blank sheet of paper and of no value. I heard all these particulars from Ford, the superintendent in charge of the case; and knowing of your knowledge of chemistry, and the quantity of odds and ends of curious information you possess on these matters, I obtained leave that you should come with me to Scotland Yard and submit the paper to any further tests you know of. I felt sure you would be willing to do this.'

'Certainly,' I replied; 'shall I come with you now?'

'I wish you would. If the paper contains any hidden cipher, the sooner it is known the better.'

'One moment first,' I said. 'I have just met Vivien Delacour. She was coming out of Mme Koluchy's house. It is strange how that woman gets to know all one's friends and acquaintances.'

'I forgot that you knew the Delacours,' said Dufrayer.

'A year ago,' I replied, 'I seemed to know them well. When we were in Brussels we were great friends.

'Vivien looked ill and in great trouble. I would give the world to help her; but I earnestly wish she did not know Madame. It may be morbidness on my part, but lately I never hear of any crime being committed in London without instantly associating Mme Koluchy with it. She has got that girl more or less under her spell, and Vivien herself informed me that she visits her mother daily. Be assured of this, Dufrayer, the woman is after no good.'

As I spoke I saw the lawyer's face darken, and the cold, hard expression I knew so well came into it, but he did not speak a word.

'I am at your service now,' I said. 'Just let me go to my laboratory first. I have some valuable notes on these ciphers which I will take with me.'

A moment later Dufrayer and I found ourselves in a hansom on our way to Scotland Yard. There we were met by Superintendent

Ford, and also by George Lambert, a particularly intelligent-looking man who favoured me with a keen glance from under shaggy brows.

'I have heard of you, Mr Head,' he said courteously, 'and shall be only too pleased if you can discover what I have failed to do. The sheet of paper in question is the sort on which ciphers are often written, but all my re-agents have failed to produce the slightest effect. My fear is that they may possibly have destroyed the cipher should such a thing exist.'

'That is certainly possible,' I said; 'but if you will take me to your laboratory I will submit the paper to some rather delicate tests of my own.'

The expert at once led the way, and Dufrayer, Superintendent Ford, and I followed him. When we reached the laboratory, Lambert put all possible tests at my disposal. A glance at the stain on the paper before me showed that cobalt, copper, etc., had been already applied. These tests had, in all probability, nullified any further chemical tests I might try, and had destroyed the result, even if there were some secret writing on the paper.

I spent some time trying the more delicate and less-known tests, with no success. Presently I rose to my feet.

'It is useless,' I said; 'I can do nothing with this paper. It is rather a presumption on my part to attempt it after you, Mr Lambert, have given your ultimatum. I am inclined to agree with you that the paper is valueless.'

Lambert bowed, and a look of satisfaction crept over his face. Dufrayer and I soon afterwards took our leave.

As we did so, I heard my friend utter a quick sigh.

'We are only beating the air as yet,' he said. 'We must trust that justice and right will win the day at last.'

He parted from me at the corner of the street, and I returned to my own house.

On the following day, at the appointed hour, I went to see Vivien Delacour. She received me in her mother's boudoir. Here the blinds were partly down, and the whole room had a desolate aspect. The young girl herself looked pale and sad, years older than she had done in the happy days at Brussels.

'Mother was pleased when I told her that I met you yesterday,' she exclaimed. 'Sit down, won't you, Mr Head? You and my father were great friends during that happy time at the Bellevue. Yes, I feel certain of your sympathy.'

'You may be assured of it,' I said, 'and I earnestly wish I could give you more than sympathy. Would it be too painful to give me some particulars in connection with the murder?'

She shuddered quite perceptibly.

'You must have read all there is to know in the newspapers,' she said; 'I can tell you nothing more. My father left us on that dreadful day to attend a Cabinet meeting at Downing Street. He never returned home. The police look in vain for the murderer. There seems no motive for the horrible crime … father had no enemies.'

Here the poor girl sobbed without restraint. I allowed her grief to have its way for a few moments, then I spoke.

'Listen, Vivien,' I said; 'I promise you that I will not leave a stone unturned to discover the man or woman who killed your father, but you must help me by being calm and self-collected. Grief like this is quite natural, but it does no good to anyone. Try, my dear girl, to compose yourself. You say there was no motive for the crime, but surely some important memoranda were stolen from your father?'

'His pocket-book in which he often made notes was removed, but nothing more, neither his watch nor his money. Surely no one would murder him for the sake of securing that pocket-book, Mr Head?'

'It is possible,' I answered gloomily. 'The memoranda contained in the book may have held clues to government secrets, remember.'

Vivien looked as if she scarcely understood. Once more my thoughts travelled to Mme Koluchy. She was a strange woman; she dealt in colossal crimes. Her influence permeated society through and through. With her a life more or less was not of the slightest consequence. And this terrible woman, whom, up to the present, the laws of England could not touch, was the intimate friend of the young girl by my side!

Vivien moved uneasily, and presently rose.

'I am glad you are going to help us,' she said, looking at me earnestly. 'Madame does all she can, but we cannot have too many friends on our side, and we are all aware of your wisdom, Mr Head. Why do you not consult Madame?'

I shook my head.

'But you are friends, are you not? I told her only this morning how I had met you.'

'We are acquaintances, but not friends,' I replied.

'Indeed, you astonish me. You cannot imagine how useful she is, and how many suggestions she throws out. By the way, mother and I leave London today.'

'Where are you going?' I asked.

'Away from here. It is quite too painful to remain any longer in this house. The shock has completely shattered mother's nerves, and she is now under Mme Koluchy's care. Madame has just taken a house in the country called Frome Manor – it is not far from our cousins, the Pitseys – you remember them? You met them in Brussels.'

I nodded.

'We are going there today,' continued Vivien. 'Of course, we shall see no one, but mother will be under the same roof with Madame, and thus will have the benefit of her treatment day and night.' Soon afterwards I took my leave. All was suspicion and uncertainty, and no definite clue had been obtained.

About this time, I began to be haunted by an air which had sprung like a mushroom into popularity. It was called the 'Queen Waltz', and it was scarcely possible to pick up a dance programme without seeing it. There was something fascinating about its swinging measure, its almost dreamy refrain, and its graceful alternations of harmony and unison. No one knew who had really composed it, and still less did any one for a moment dream that its pleasant chords contained a dark or subtle meaning. As I listened to it on more than one occasion, at more than one concert – for I am a passionate lover of music, and seldom spend an afternoon without listening to it – I little guessed all that the 'Queen Waltz' would bring forth. I was waiting for a clue.

How could I tell that all too late and by such unlikely means it would be put into my hands?

A month and even six weeks went by, and although the police were unceasing in their endeavours to gain a trace of the murderer, they were absolutely unsuccessful. Once or twice during this interval I had letters from Vivien Delacour. She wrote with the passion and impetuosity of a very young girl. She was anxious about her mother, who was growing steadily weaker, and was losing her self-restraint more and more as the long weeks glided by. Mme Koluchy was anxious about her. Madame's medicines, her treatment, her soothing powers, were on this occasion destitute of results.

'Nothing will rest her,' said Vivien, in conclusion, 'until the murderer is discovered. She dreams of him night after night. During the daytime she is absolutely silent, or she paces the room in violent agitation, crying out to God to help her to discover him. Oh, Mr Head, what is to be done?'

The child's letters appealed to me strongly. I was obliged to answer her with extreme care, as I knew that Madame would see what I wrote; but none the less were all my faculties at work on her behalf. From time to time I thought of the mysterious blank sheet of paper. Was it possible that it contained a cipher? Was one of those old, incomparable, magnificent undiscovered ciphers which belonged to the ancient Brotherhood really concealed beneath its blank surface? That blank sheet of paper mingled with my dreams and worried me during my wakeful hours. I became nearly as restless as Vivien herself, and when a letter of a more despairing nature than usual arrived on a certain morning towards the end of February, I felt that I could no longer remain inactive. I would answer Vivien's letter in person. To do so I had but to accept my standing invitation to Pitsey Hall. I wrote, therefore, to my friend, Leonardo Pitsey, suggesting that if it were convenient to him and his wife I should like to go to Pitsey Hall on the following Saturday.

The next afternoon Pitsey himself called to see me.

'I received your letter this morning, and having to come to town today, thought I would look you up,' he cried. 'I have to catch a train at 5.30, so cannot stay a minute. We shall be delighted to welcome you at the Hall. My wife and I have never forgotten you, Head. You will be, I assure you, a most welcome guest. By the way, have you heard of our burglary?'

'No,' I answered.

'You do not read your paper, then. It is an extraordinary affair – crime seems to be in the very air just now. The Hall was attacked by burglars last week – a most daring and cunningly planned affair. Some plate was stolen, but the plate-chest, built on the newest principles, was untampered with. There was a desperate attempt made, however, to get into the large drawing-room, where all our valuable curios are kept. Druco, the mastiff, who is loose about the house at night, was found poisoned outside the drawing-room door. Luckily the butler awoke in time, gave the alarm, and the rascals bolted. The country police have been after them, and in despair I have come up to Scotland Yard and engaged a couple of their best detectives. They come down with me tonight, and I trust we shall soon get the necessary clue to the capture of the burglars. My fear is that if they are not arrested they will try again, for, I assure you, the old place is worth robbing. But, there, I ought not to worry you about my domestic concerns. We shall have a gay party on Saturday, for my eldest boy Ottavio comes of age next week, and the event is to be celebrated by a great ball in his honour.'

'How are the Delacours?' I interrupted.

'Vivien keeps fairly well, but her mother is a source of great anxiety. Mme Koluchy and Vivien are constant guests at the Hall. The Delacours return to town before the ball, but Madame will attend it. It will be an honour and a great attraction to have such a lioness for the occasion. Do you know her, Head? She is quite charming.'

'I have met her,' I replied.

'Ah! that is capital; you and she are just the sort to hit it off. It's all right, then, and we shall expect you. A good train leaves Charing Cross at 4.30. I will send the trap to meet you.'

'Thank you,' I answered. 'I shall be glad to come to Pitsey Hall, but I do not know that I can stay as long as the night of the ball.'

'Once we get you into our clutches, Head, we won't let you go; my young people are all anxious to renew their acquaintance with you. Don't you remember little Antonia – my pretty songstress, as I call her? Vivien, too, talks of you as one of her greatest friends. Poor child! I pity her from my heart. She is a sweet, gentle girl; but such a shock as she has sustained may leave its mark for life. Poor Delacour … the very best of men. The fact is this: I should like to postpone the ball on account of the Delacours, although they are very distant cousins; but Ottavio only comes of age once in his life, and, under the circumstances, we feel that we must go through with it. 'Pon my word, Head, when I think of that poor child and her mother, I have little heart for festivities. However, that is neither here nor there – we shall expect you on Saturday.'

As Pitsey spoke, he took up his hat.

'I must be off now,' he said, 'for I have to meet the two detectives at Charing Cross by appointment.'

On the following Saturday, the 27th, I arrived at Pitsey Hall, where a warm welcome awaited me. The ball was to be on the following Tuesday, the 2nd of March. There was a large house party, and the late burglary was still the topic of conversation.

After dinner, when the ladies had left the dining-room, Pitsey and I drew our chairs together, and presently the conversation drifted to Mrs Delacour, the mysterious murder, and Mme Koluchy.

'The police are completely nonplussed,' said Pitsey. 'I doubt if the man who committed that rascally crime will ever be brought to justice. I was speaking to Madame on the subject today, and although she was very hopeful when she first arrived at Frome Manor, she is now almost inclined to agree with me. By the way, Mrs Delacour's state is most alarming – she loses strength hour by hour.'

'I can quite understand that,' I replied. 'If the murderer were discovered it would be an immense relief to her.'

'So Madame says. I know she is terribly anxious about her patient. By the way, knowing that she was an acquaintance of yours, I asked her here tonight, but unfortunately, she had another engagement which she could not postpone. What a wonderfully well-informed woman she is! She spent hours at the Hall this morning examining my curios; she gave me information about some of them which was news to me, but she has been many times now round my collection. It is a positive treat to talk with anyone so intelligent, and if she were not so keen about my Venetian goblet—'

'What!' I interrupted, 'the goblet you spoke to me about in Brussels, the one which has been in your family since 1500?'

'The same,' he answered, nodding his head, and lowering his voice a trifle. 'It has been in the family, as you say, since 1500. Madame has shown bad taste in the matter, and I am surprised at her.'

'Pray explain yourself,' I said.

'She first saw it last November, when she came here with the Delacours. I shall never forget her stare of astonishment. She stood perfectly still for at least two minutes, gazing at it without speaking. When she turned around at last she was as white as a ghost, and asked me where I got it from. I told her, and she offered me ten thousand pounds for it on the spot.'

'A large figure,' I remarked.

'I was much annoyed,' continued Pitsey, 'and told her I would not sell it at any price.'

'Did she give any reason for wishing to obtain it?'

'Yes, she said she had a goblet very like it in her own collection, and wished to purchase this one in order to complete one of the most unique collections of old Venetian glass in England. The woman must be fabulously rich, or even her passion for curios would not induce her to offer so preposterous a sum. Since her residence at Frome Manor she has been constantly here, and still takes, I can see, the deepest interest in the goblet, often remarking about it. She says it has got a remarkably pure musical note, very clear and distinct. But come, Head, you would like to see it. We will go into the drawing-room, and I will show it to you.'

As Pitsey spoke he rose and led me through the great central hall into the inner drawing-room, a colossal apartment supported by Corinthian pillars and magnificently decorated.

'As you know, the goblet has been in our family for many centuries,' he went on, 'and we call it, from Uhland's ballad of the old Cumberland tradition, "The Luck of Pitsey Hall". You know Longfellow's translation, of course? Here it is, Head. Is it not a wonderful piece of work? Have a close look at it, it is worth examining.'

The goblet in question stood about six feet from the ground on a pedestal of solid malachite, which was placed in a niche in the wall. One glance was sufficient to show me that it was a gem of art. The cup, which was eight inches in diameter, was made of thin glass of a pale ruby colour. Some mystical letters were etched on the outside of the glass, small portions of which could be seen; but screening them from any closer interpretation was some twisted fancy work, often to be observed on old Venetian goblets. If by any chance this fancy work were chipped off the letters would be plainly visible. The cup itself was supported on an open-work stem richly gilt and enamelled with coloured filigree work, the whole supported again on a base set with opal, agate, lapis lazuli, turquoise, and pearl. From the centre of the cup, and in reality supporting it, was a central column of pale green glass which bore what was apparently some heraldic design. Stepping up close I tapped the cup gently with my finger. It gave out, as Pitsey had described, a note of music singularly sweet and clear. I then proceeded to examine the stem, and saw at once that the design formed a row of separate crowns. Scarcely knowing why, I counted them. There were seven! A queer suspicion crept over me. The sequence of late events passed rapidly through my mind, and a strange relationship between circumstances apparently having no connection began to appear. I turned to Pitsey.

'Can you tell me how this goblet came into your possession?' I asked.

'Certainly,' he replied; 'the legend which is attached to the goblet is this. We are, as you know, descended from an old Italian family, the Pizzis, our present name being merely an Anglicised corruption of the Italian. My children and I still bear Italian Christian names, as you know, and our love for the old country amounts almost to a passion. The Pizzis were great people in Venice in the sixteenth century; at that time the city had an immense fame for its beautiful glass, the manufacturers forming a guild, and the secret being jealously kept. It was during this time that Catherine de Medici by her arbitrary and tyrannical administration roused the opposition of a Catholic party, at whose head was the Duke of Alenon, her own fourth son. Among the Duke's followers was my ancestor, Giovanni Pizzi. It was discovered that an order had been sent by Catherine de Medici to one of the manufacturers at Venice to construct that very goblet which you see there. After its construction it was for some secret purpose sent to the laboratory of an alchemist in Venice, where it was seized by Giovanni Pizzi, and has been handed down in our family ever since.'

'But what is the meaning of the seven crowns on the stem?' I asked.

'That I cannot tell. They have probably no special significance.'

I thought otherwise, but kept my ideas to myself.

We turned away. A beautiful young voice was filling the old drawing-room with sweetness. I went up to the piano to listen to Antonia Pitsey, while she sang an Italian song as only one who had Italian blood in her veins could.

Antonia was a beautiful girl, dark, with luminous eyes and an air of distinction about her.

'I wish you would tell me something about your friend Vivien,' I said, as she rose from the piano.

'Oh, Mr Head, I am so unhappy about her,' was the low reply. 'I see her very often – she is altogether changed; and as to Mrs Delacour, the shock has been so sudden, so terrible, that I doubt if she will ever recover. Mr Head, I am so glad you have come. Vivien constantly speaks of you. She wants to see you tomorrow.'

'Is she coming here?'

'No, but you can meet her in the park. She has sent you a message. Tomorrow is Sunday. Vivien is not going to church. May I take you to the rendezvous?'

I promised, and soon afterwards the evening came to an end.

That night I was haunted by three main thoughts: the old Italian legend of the goblet; the seven crowns, symbolic of the Brotherhood of the Seven Kings; and, finally, Madame's emotion when she first saw it, and her strong desire to obtain it. I wondered had the burglary been committed by her instigation? Sleep I could not, my brain was too active and busy. I was certain there was mischief ahead, but try as I would I could only lose myself in strange conjectures.

The following day I met Miss Delacour, as arranged, in the park. Antonia brought me to her, and then left us together. The young girl's worn face, the pathetic expression in her large grey eyes, her evident nervousness and want of self-control all appealed to me to a terrible degree. She asked me eagerly if any fresh clue had been obtained with regard to the murderer. I shook my head.

'If something is not done soon, mother will lose her senses,' she remarked. 'Even Mme Koluchy is in despair about her. All her ordinary modes of treatment fail in mother's case, and the strangest thing is that mother has begun to take a most queer and unaccountable dislike to Madame herself. She says that Madame's presence in the room gives her an uncontrollable feeling of nervousness. This has become so bad that mother and I return to town tomorrow; my cousin's house is too gay for us at present, and mother refuses to stay any longer under Mme Koluchy's roof.'

'But why?' I asked.

'That I cannot explain to you. For my part, I think Madame one of the best women on earth. She has been kindness itself to us, and I do not know what we should have done without her.'

I did not speak, and Vivien continued, after a pause:

'Mother's conduct makes Madame strangely unhappy. She told me so, and I pity her from my heart. We had a long talk on the subject yesterday. That was just before she began to speak of the goblet, and before Mr Lewisham arrived.'

'Mr Lewisham – who is he?' I asked.

'A great friend of Madame's. He comes to see her almost daily. He is very handsome, and I like him, but I did not know she was expecting him yesterday. She and I were in the drawing-room. She spoke of mother, and then alluded to the goblet, the one at the Hall. You have seen it, of course, Mr Head?'

I nodded; I was too much interested to interrupt the girl by words.

'My cousins call it "The Luck of Pitsey Hall". Well, Madame has set her heart on obtaining it, and she has gone to the length of offering Cousin Leonardo ten thousand pounds for it.'

'Mr Pitsey told me last night that Madame had offered an enormous sum for the vase,' I said, 'but it is useless, as he has no intention of selling.'

'I told Madame so,' replied Vivien. 'I know well what value my cousins place upon the old glass. I believe they think that their luck would really go if anything happened to it.'

'Heaven forbid!' I replied involuntarily. 'It is a perfect gem of its kind.'

'I know! I know! I never saw Madame so excited and unreasonable about anything. She begged of me to use my influence to try and get my cousin to let her have it. When I assured her that it was useless, she looked more annoyed than I had ever seen her. She took up a book, and pretended to read. I went and sat behind one of the curtains, near a window. The next moment Mr Lewisham was announced. He came eagerly up to Madame – I don't think he saw me. "Well!" he cried, "Any success? Have you secured it yet? If you have, we are absolutely safe. Has that child helped you?" I guessed that they were talking about me, and started up and disclosed myself. Madame did not take the slightest notice, but she motioned to Mr Lewisham to come into another room. What can it all mean, Mr Head?'

'That I cannot tell you, Vivien; but may I ask you one thing?'

'Certainly you may.'

'Will you promise me to keep what you have just told me a secret from anybody else? I allude to Madame's anxiety to obtain the old goblet. There may be nothing in what I ask, or there may be much. Will you do this?'

'Of course I will. How queer you look!'

I made no remark, and soon afterwards took my leave of her.

Late that same evening, Antonia Pitsey received a note from Vivien, in which she said that Mme Koluchy, her mother, and herself were returning to town by an early train the following morning. The Delacours did not intend to come back to Frome Manor, but Madame would do so on Tuesday in order to be in time for the great ball. She was going to town now in order to be present at an early performance of 'For the Crown' at the Lyceum, having secured a box on the grand tier for the occasion.

This note was commented on without any special interest being attached to it, but restless already, I now quickly made up my mind. I also would go up to town on the following day; I also would return to Pitsey Hall in time for the ball.

Accordingly, at an early hour on the following day, I found myself in Dufrayer's office.

'I tell you what it is,' I said, 'there is some plot deeper than we think brewing. Madame took Frome Manor after the murder of Delacour. She would not do so without a purpose. She is willing to spend ten thousand pounds in order to secure a goblet of old Venetian glass, which is one of the curios at Pitsey Hall.

A man called Lewisham, who doubtless bears another alias, is in her confidence. Madame returns to town tonight with a definite motive, I have not the slightest doubt.'

'This is all very well, Norman,' replied Dufrayer, 'but what we want are facts. You will lose your senses if you go on building up fantastic ideas. Madame comes up to town and is going to the Lyceum; at least, so you tell me?'

'Yes.'

'And you mean to follow her to see if she has any designs on Forbes Robertson or Mrs Patrick Campbell?'

'I mean to follow her,' I replied gravely. 'I mean to see what sort of man Lewisham is. It is possible that I may have seen him before.'

Dufrayer shrugged his shoulders and turned away somewhat impatiently. As he did so a wild thought suddenly struck me. 'What would you say,' I cried, 'if I suggested an idea to force Madame to divulge some clue to us?'

'My dear Norman, I should say that your fancies are getting the better of your reason, that is all.'

'Now listen to me,' I said. I sat down beside Dufrayer. 'I have an idea which may serve us well. It is, of course, a bare chance, and if you like you may call it the conception of a madman. Madame goes to the Lyceum tonight. She occupies a box on the grand tier. In all probability Lewisham will accompany her. Dufrayer, you and I will also be at the theatre, and, if possible, we will take a box on the second tier exactly opposite to hers. I will bring Robertson, the principal and the trainer of the new deaf and dumb college, with me. I happen to know him well.' Dufrayer stared at me with some alarm in his face.

'Don't you see?' I went on excitedly. 'Robertson is a master of the art of lip language. We will keep him in the back of the box. About the middle of the play, and in one of the intervals when the electric light is full on, we will send a note to Madame's box saying that the cipher on the blank sheet of paper has been read. The note will pretend to be an anonymous warning to her. We shall watch her, and by means of Robertson hear – yes, hear – what she says. Robertson will watch her through opera-glasses, and he will be able to understand every word she speaks, just as you or I could if we were in her box beside her. The whole thing is a bare chance, I know, but we may learn something by taking her unsuspecting and unawares.' Dufrayer thought for a minute, then he sprang to his feet.

'Magnificent!' he cried. 'Head, you are an extraordinary man! It is a unique idea. I will go off to the box-office at once and take a box if possible opposite Madame, or, failing that, the best seats we can get. I only hope you can secure Robertson. Go to his house at once and offer him any fee he wants. This is detection carried to a fine art with a vengeance. If successful, I shall class you as the smartest criminal agent of the day. We both meet at the Lyceum at a quarter to eight. Now, there is not a moment to lose.'

I drove down to Robertson's house in Brompton, found him at home, and told him my wish. I strongly impressed upon him that if he would help he would be aiding in the cause of justice. He became keenly interested, entered fully into the situation, and refused to accept any fee. At the appointed hour we met Dufrayer at the theatre door, and learned that he had secured a box on the second tier directly opposite Mme Koluchy's box on the grand tier. I had arranged to have my letter sent by a messenger at ten o'clock.

We took our seats, and a few moments later Mme Koluchy, in rose-coloured velvet and blazing with diamonds, accompanied by a tall, dark, clean-shaven man, entered her box. I drew back into the shadow of my own box and watched her. She bowed to one or two acquaintances in the stalls, then sat down, leaning her arm on the plush-covered edge of her box.

Robertson never took his eyes off her, and I felt reassured as he repeated to us the chance bits of conversation that he could catch between her and her companion.

The play began, and a few minutes past ten, in one of the intervals, I saw Madame turn and receive my note, with a slight gesture of surprise. She tore it open and her face paled perceptibly. Robertson, as I had instructed him, stood in front of me; his opera-glasses were fixed on the faces of Madame and her companion. I watched Madame as she read the note; she then handed it to Lewisham, who read it also.

They looked at each other, and I saw Madame's lips moving. Simultaneously, Robertson began to make the following report verbatim:

'Impossible ... some trick ... quite safe goblet ... key to cipher ... tomorrow night.'

Then followed a pause.

'Life and death to us ... Signed ... My name.'

There was another long pause, and I saw Madame twist the paper nervously in her fingers. I looked at Dufrayer, our eyes met. My heart was beating. His face had become drawn and grey. The ghastly truth and the explanation were slowly sealing their impress on our brains. The darkness of doubt had lifted, the stunning truth was clear. The paper which had defied us was a cipher written by Madame in her own name, and doubtless implicated her with Delacour's murder. Her anxiety to secure the goblet was very obvious. In some subtle way, handed down, doubtless, through generations, the goblet once in the possession of the ancient Brotherhood had held the key of the secret cipher.

But tomorrow night! Tomorrow night was the night of the ball, and Madame was to be there. The reasoning was so obvious that the chain of evidence struck Dufrayer and me simultaneously.

We immediately left the theatre. There was one thing to be

done, and that without delay. I must catch the first train in the morning to Pitsey Hall, examine the goblet afresh, and tell Pitsey everything, and thus secure and protect the goblet from harm. If possible, I would myself discover the key to the cipher, which, if our reasoning was true, would place Madame in a felon's dock and see the end of the Brotherhood.

At ten o'clock the following morning I reached Pitsey Hall. When I arrived I found, as I expected, the house in more or less confusion. Pitsey was busily engaged superintending arrangements and directing the servants in their work. It was some little time before I could see him alone.

'What is the matter, my dear fellow?' he said. 'I am very busy now.'

'Come into the library and I will tell you,' I replied.

As soon as ever we were alone I unfolded my story. Hardened by years of contact with the world, it was difficult to startle or shake the composure of Leonardo Pitsey, and before I had finished my strange tale I could see from his expression the difficulty I should have in convincing him of the truth.

'I have had my suspicions for a long time,' I said, in conclusion. 'These are not the first dealings I have had with Mme Koluchy. Hitherto she has eluded all my efforts to get her within the arm of the law, but I believe her time is near. Pitsey, your goblet is in danger. You will remove it to some place of safety?'

'Remove the Luck of Pitsey Hall on the night when my boy comes of age!' replied Pitsey, frowning as he spoke. 'It is good of you to be interested, Head; but really … well, I never knew you were such an imaginative man! As to any accident taking place tonight, that is quite outside the realms of probability.

'The band will be placed in front of the goblet, and it is impossible for anything to happen to it, as none of the dancers can come near it. Now, have you anything more to say?'

'I beg of you to be guided by me and to put the goblet into a place of safety,' I repeated. 'You don't suppose I would try to scare you with a cock-and-bull story. There is reason in what I say. I know that woman, my uneasiness is far more than due to mere imagination.'

'To please you, Head, I will place two of my footmen beside the goblet during the ball, in order to prevent the slightest chance of any one approaching it. There, will that satisfy you?'

I was obliged to bow my acquiescence, and Pitsey soon left me in order to attend to his multifarious duties.

I spent nearly an hour that morning examining the goblet afresh. The mystical writing on the cup, concealed by the open-work design, engrossed my most careful attention, but so well were the principal letters concealed by the outside ornaments, that I could make nothing of them. Was I, after all, entirely mistaken, or did this beautiful work of art contain hidden within itself the power for which I longed, the strange key to the mysterious paper which would convict Mme Koluchy of a capital charge?

The evening came at last, and about nine the guests began to arrive. The first dance had hardly come to an end before Mme Koluchy appeared on the scene. She wore a dress of cloth of silver, and her appearance caused an almost imperceptible lull in the dancing and conversation. As she walked slowly up the great ballroom on the arm of a county magnate all eyes turned to look at her. She passed me with a hardening about the corners of her mouth as she acknowledged my bow, and I fancy I saw her eyes wander in the direction of the goblet at the other end of the room. Soon afterwards Antonia Pitsey came to my side.

'How beautiful everything is,' she said. 'Did you ever see any one look quite so lovely as Madame? Her dress tonight gives her a regal appearance. Have you seen our dance programme? The "Queen Waltz" will be played just after supper.'

'So, you have fallen a victim to the popular taste?' I answered. 'I hear that waltz everywhere.'

'But you don't know who has composed it?' said the girl, with an arch look. 'Now, I don't mind confiding in you – it is Mme Koluchy.'

I could not help starting.

'I was unaware that she was a musician,' I remarked.

'She is, and a most accomplished one. We have included the waltz in our programme by her special request. I am so glad; it is the most lively and inspiriting air I ever danced to.'

Antonia was called away, and I leant against the wall, too ill at ease to dance or take any active part in the revels of the hour. The moments flew by, and at last the festive and brilliant notes of the 'Queen Waltz' sounded on my ears. Couples came thronging into the ballroom as soon as this most fascinating melody was heard. To listen to its seductive measures was enough to make your feet tingle and your heart beat.

Once again I watched Mme Koluchy as she moved through the throng. Ottavio Pitsey, the hero of the evening, was now her partner. There was a slight colour in her usually pale checks, and I had never seen her look more beautiful.

I was standing not far from the band, and could not help noticing how the dominant note, repeated in two bars when all the instruments played together in harmony, rang out with a peculiar and almost passionate insistence. Suddenly, without a moment's warning, and with a clap that struck the dancers motionless, a loud crash rang through the room. The music instantly ceased, and the priceless heirloom of the Pitseys lay in a thousand silvered splinters on the polished floor. There was a moment's pause of absolute silence, followed by a sharp cry from our host, and then a hum of voices as the dancers hurried towards the scene of the disaster.

The consternation and dismay were indescribable. Pitsey, with a face like death, was gazing horror-struck at the base and stem of the vase which still kept their place on the malachite stand, the cup alone being shivered to fragments. The two footmen, who had been standing under the pedestal, looked as if they had been struck by an unseen hand. Pushing my way almost roughly through the crowded throng I reached the spot. Nothing remained but the stem and jewelled base of the goblet.

Silent and gazing at the throng as one in a dream stood Mme Koluchy. Antonia had crept up close to her father; her face was as white as her dress.

'"The Luck of Pitsey Hall",' she murmured, 'and on this night of all nights!'

As for me, I felt my brain almost reeling with excitement. For the moment the thoughts which surged through it numbed my capacity for speech. I saw a servant gathering up the fragments. The evening was ended, and the party gradually broke up. To go on dancing would have been impossible.

It was not till some hours afterwards that the whole Satanic scheme burst upon me. The catastrophe admitted of but one explanation. The dominant note, repeated in two bars when all the instruments played together in harmony, must have been the note accordant with that of the cup of the goblet, and by the well-known laws of acoustics, when so played it shattered the goblet.

Next day there was an effort made to piece together the shattered fragments, but some were missing – how removed, by whom taken, no one could ever tell. Beyond doubt the characters cunningly concealed by the openwork pattern contained the key to the cipher. But once again Madame had escaped. The ingenuity, the genius, of the woman placed her beyond the ordinary consequences of crime.

Delacour's murder still remains unavenged. Will the truth ever come to light?

Lady Clanbevan's Baby

CLOTILDE GRAVES (1915)

Devious misapplications of science abound once again, as this time the Mad Scientist falls prey to a woman who turns out to be much more ruthless than he realises. In this story, Clotilde Graves undermines the self-serving narrative of the brilliant inventor winning a woman's heart with demonstrations of his genius, and it is up to the reader to decide whether Lady Clanbevan is a villain, or simply a woman playing the hand she's been dealt in order to live independently. Either way, this piece showcases Graves's wicked sense of humour.

THERE WAS A GREY, woolly October fog over Hyde Park. The railings wept grimy tears, and the damp yellow leaves dropped soddenly from the soaked trees. Pedestrians looked chilled and sulky; camphor chests and cedar-presses had yielded up their treasures of sables and sealskin, chinchilla and silver fox. A double stream of fashionable traffic rolled west and east, and the rich clarets and vivid crimsons of the automobiles burned through the fog like genial, warming fires.

A Baby-Bunting six horse-power petrol-car, in colour a chrysanthemum yellow, came jiggeting by. The driver stopped. He was a technical chemist and biologist of note and standing, and I had last heard him speak from the platform of the Royal Institution.

'I haven't seen you,' said the Professor, 'for years.'

'That must be because you haven't looked,' said I, 'for I have both seen and heard you quite recently. Only you were upon the platform and I was on the ground floor.'

'You are too much upon the ground floor now,' said the Professor, with a shudder of a Southern European at the dampness around and under foot, 'and I advise you to accept a seat in my car.'

And the Baby-Bunting, trembling with excitement at being in the company of so many highly varnished electric victorias and forty horse-power auto-cars, joined the steadily flowing stream going west.

'I wonder that you stoop to petrol, Professor,' I said, as the thin, skilful hand in the baggy chamois glove manipulated the driving-wheel, and the little car snaked in and out like a torpedo-boat picking her way between the giant warships of a Channel Squadron.

The Professor's black brows unbent under the cap peak, and his thin, tightly-gripped lips relaxed into a mirthless smile.

'Ah, yes; you think that I should drive my car by radio-activity, is it not? And so I could and would, if the pure radium chloride were not three thousand times the price of gold. From eight tons of uranium ore residues about one gramme – that is fifteen grains – can be extracted by fusing the residue with carbonates of soda, dissolving in hydrochloric acid, precipitating the lead and other metals in solution by the aid of hydrogen sulphide, and separating from the chlorides that remain – polonium, actinium, barium, and so forth – the chloride of radium. With a single pound of this I could not only drive an auto-car, my friend' – his olive cheek warmed, and his melancholy dark eyes grew oddly lustrous – 'I could stop the world!'

'And supposing it was necessary to make it go on again?' I suggested.

'When I speak of the world,' exclaimed the Professor, 'I do not refer to the planet upon which we revolve; I speak of the human race which inhabits it.'

'Would the human race be obliged to you, Professor?' I queried.

The Professor turned upon me with so sudden a verbal riposte that the Baby-Bunting swerved violently.

'You are not as young as you were when I met you first. To be plain, you are getting middle-aged. Do you like it?'

'I hate it!' I answered, with beautiful sincerity.

'Would you thank the man who should arrest, not the beneficent passage of Time, which means progress, but the wear and tear of nerve and muscle, tissue, and bone, the slow deterioration of the blood by the microbes of old age, for Metchnikoff has shown that there is no difference between the atrophy of senility and the atrophy caused by microbe poison? Would you thank him – the man who should do that for you? Tell me, my friend.'

I replied, briefly and succinctly: 'Wouldn't I?'

'Ha!' exclaimed the Professor, 'I thought so!'

'But I should have liked him to have begun earlier,' I said. 'Twenty-nine is a nice age, now … It is the age we all try to stop at, and can't, however much we try. Look there!'

A landau limousine, dark blue, beautifully varnished, nickel-plated, and upholstered in cream-white leather, came gliding gracefully through the press of vehicles. From the crest upon the panel to the sober workmanlike livery of the chauffeur, the turn-out was perfection. The pearl it contained was worthy of the setting.

'Look there?' I repeated, as the rose-cheeked, sapphire-eyed, smiling vision passed, wrapped in a voluminous coat of chinchilla and silver fox, with a toque of Parma violets under the shimmer of the silken veil that could only temper the burning glory of her wonderful Renaissance hair.

'There's the exception to the rule … There's a woman who doesn't need the aid of science or of Art to keep her at nine-and-twenty. There's a woman in whom "the wear and tear of nerve and muscle, tissue and bone" goes on – if it does go on – imperceptibly.

Her blood doesn't seem to be much deteriorated by the microbe of old age, Professor, does it? And she's forty-three! The alchemistical forty-three, that turns the gold of life back into lead! The gold remains gold in her case, for that hair, that complexion, that figure, are,' I solemnly declared, 'her own.'

At that moment Lady Clanbevan gave a smiling, gracious nod to the Professor, and he responded with a cold, grave bow. The glow of her gorgeous hair, the liquid sapphire of her eyes, were wasted on this stony man of science. She passed, going home to Stanhope Gate, I suppose, in which neighbourhood she has a house; I had barely a moment to notice the white-bonneted, blue-cloaked nurse on the front of the landau, holding a bundle of laces and cashmeres, and to reflect that I have never yet seen Lady Clanbevan taking the air without the company of a baby, when the Professor spoke:

'So Lady Clanbevan is the one woman who has no need of the aid of art or science to preserve her beauty and maintain her appearance of youth? Supposing I could prove to you otherwise, my friend, what then?'

'I should say,' I returned, 'that you had proved what everybody else denies. Even the enemies of that modern Ninon de l'Enclos, who has just passed—'

'With the nurse and the baby?' interpolated the Professor.

'With the nurse and the baby,' said I. 'Even her enemies – and they are legion – admit the genuineness of the charms they detest. Mentioning the baby, do you know that for twenty years I have never seen Lady Clanbevan out without a baby? She must have quite a regiment of children – children of all ages, sizes, and sexes.'

'Upon the contrary,' said the Professor, 'she has only one!'

'The others have all died young, then?' I asked sympathetically, and was rendered breathless by the rejoinder:

'Lady Clanbevan is a widow.'

'One never asks questions about the husband of a professional beauty,' I said. 'His individuality is merged in hers from the day upon which her latest photograph assumes a marketable value. Are you sure there isn't a Lord Clanbevan alive somewhere?'

'There is a Lord Clanbevan alive,' said the Professor coldly. 'You have just seen him, in his nurse's arms. He is the only child of his mother, and she has been a widow for nearly twenty years! You do not credit what I assert, my friend?'

'How can I, Professor?' I asked, turning to meet his full face, and noticed that his dark, somewhat opaque brown irises had lights and gleams of carbuncle-crimson in them. 'I have had Lady Clanbevan and her progeny under my occasional observation for years. The world grows older, if she doesn't, and she has invariably a baby – *toujours* a new baby – to add to the charming illusion of young motherhood which she sustains so well. And now you tell me that she is a twenty-years' widow with one child, who must be nearly of age – or it isn't proper. You puzzle me painfully!'

'Would you care,' asked the Professor after a moment's pause, 'to drive back to Harley Street with me? I am, as you know, a vegetarian, so I will not tax your politeness by inviting you to lunch. But I have something in my laboratory I should wish to show you.'

'Of all things, I should like to come,' I said. 'How many times haven't I fished fruitlessly for an invitation to visit the famous laboratory where nearly twenty years ago—'

'I traced,' said the Professor, 'the source of phenomena which heralded the evolution of the Rontgen Ray and the ultimate discovery of the radioactive salt they have christened radium. I called it "protium" twenty years ago, because of its various and protean qualities. Why did I not push on to perfect the discovery and anticipate Sir William C— and the X—'s? There was a reason. You will understand it before you leave my laboratory.'

The Baby-Bunting stopped at the unfashionable end of Harley Street, in front of the dingy yellow house with the black front door, flanked by dusty boxes of mildewed dwarf evergreens, and the Professor, relieved of his fur-lined coat and cap, led the way upstairs as lightly as a boy. Two garret-rooms had been knocked together for a laboratory. There was a tiled furnace at the darker end of the long skylighted room thus made, and solid wooden tables much stained with spilt chemicals, were covered with scales, glasses, jars, and retorts – all the tools of chemistry. From one of the many shelves running round the walls, the Professor took down a circular glass flask and placed it in my hands. The flask contained a handful of decayed and mouldy-looking wheat, and a number of peculiarly offensive-looking little beetles with tapir-like proboscides.

'The perfectly developed beetle of the *Calandria granaria*,' said the Professor, as I cheerfully resigned the flask, 'a common British weevil, whose larvae feed upon stored grain. Now look at this.' He reached down and handed me a precisely similar flask, containing another handful of grain, cleaner and sounder in appearance, and a number of grubs, sharp-ended chrysalis-like things buried in the grain, inert and inactive.

'The larvae of *Calandria granaria*,' said the Professor, in his drawling monotone. 'How long does it take to hatch the beetle from the grub? you ask. Less than a month. The perfect weevils that I have just shown you I placed in their flask a little more than three weeks back. The grubs you see in the flask you are holding, and which, as you will observe by their anxiety to bury themselves in the grain so as to avoid contact with the light, are still immature, I placed in the glass receptacle twenty years ago. Don't drop the flask – I value it.'

'Professor!' I gasped.

'Twenty years ago,' repeated the Professor, delicately handling the venerable grubs, 'I enclosed these grubs in this flask, with sufficient grain to fully nourish them and bring them to the perfect state. In another flask I placed a similar number of grubs in exactly the same quantity of wheat. Then for twenty-four hours I exposed flask number one to the rays emanating from what is now called radium. And as the electrons discharged from radium are obstructed by collision with air-atoms, I exhausted the air contained in the flask.' He paused.

'Then, when the grubs in flask number two hatched out,' I anticipated, 'and the larvae in flask number one remained stationary, you realised—'

'I realised that the rays from the salt arrested growth, and at the same time prolonged to an almost incalculable extent,' said the Professor, 'for you will understand that the grubs in flask number one had lived as grubs half a dozen times as long as grubs usually do ... And I said to myself that the discovery presented an immense, a tremendous field for future development. Suppose a young woman of, say, twenty-nine were enclosed in a glass receptacle of sufficient bulk to contain her, and exposed for a few hours to my protium rays, she would retain for many years to come – until she was a great-grandmother of ninety! – the same charming, youthful appearance—'

'As Lady Clanbevan!' I cried, as the truth rushed upon me and I grasped the meaning this astonishing man had intended to convey.

'As Lady Clanbevan presents today,' said the Professor, 'thanks to the discovery of a—'

'Of a great man,' said I, looking admiringly at the lean worn figure in the closely-buttoned black frock-coat.

'I loved her ... It was a delight to her to drag a disciple of science at her chariot-wheels. People talked of me as a coming man. Perhaps I was ... But I did not thirst for distinction, honours, fame ... I thirsted for that woman's love ... I told her of my discovery – as I told her everything. Bah!' His lean nostrils worked. 'You know the game that is played when one is in earnest and the other at play. She promised nothing, she walked delicately among the passions she sowed and fostered in the souls of men, as a beautiful tigress walks among the poison-plants of the jungle. She saw that rightly used, or wrongly used, my great discovery might save her beauty, her angelic, dazzling beauty that had as yet but felt the first touch of Time. She planned the whole thing, and when she said, "You do not love me if you will not do this," I did it. I was mad when I acceded to her wish, perhaps; but she is a woman to drive men frenzied. You have seen how coldly, how slightingly she looked at me when we encountered her in the Row? I tell you – you have guessed already – I went there to see her. I always go where she is to be encountered, when she is in town. And she bows, always; but her eyes are those of a stranger. Yet I have had her on her knees to me. She cried and begged and kissed my hands.'

He knotted his thin hands, their fingers brown-tipped with the stains of acids, and wrung and twisted them ferociously.

'And so I granted what she asked, carried out the experiment, and paid what you English call the piper. The giant glass bulb with the rubber-valve door was blown and finished in France. It involved an expense of three hundred pounds. The salt I used of – protium (christened radium now) – cost me all my savings – over two thousand pounds, for I had been a struggling man—'

'But the experiment?' I broke in. 'Good Heavens, Professor! How could a living being remain for any time in an exhausted receiver? Agony unspeakable, convulsions, syncope, death! One knows what the result would be. The merest common sense—'

'The merest common sense is not what one employs to make discoveries or carry out great experiments,' said the Professor. 'I will not disclose my method; I will only admit to you that the subjects were insensible; that I induced anaesthesia by the ordinary ether-pump apparatus, and that the strength of the ray obtained was concentrated to such a degree that the exposure was complete in three hours.' He looked about him haggardly. 'The experiment took place here nineteen years ago – nineteen years ago, and it seems to me as though it were yesterday.'

'And it must seem like yesterday to Lady Clanbevan whenever she looks in the glass,' I said. 'But you have pricked my curiosity, Professor, by the use of the plural. Who was the other subject?'

'Is it possible you don't guess?'The sad, hollow eyes questioned my face in surprise. Then they turned haggardly away. 'My friend, the other subject associated with Lady Clanbevan in my great experiment was – Her Baby!'

I could not speak. The dowdy little grubs in the flask became for me creatures imbued with dreadful potentialities ... The tragedy and the sublime absurdity of the thing I realised caught at my throat, and my brain grew dizzy with its horror.

'Oh! Professor!' I gurgled, 'how – how grimly, awfully, tragically ridiculous! To carry about with one wherever one goes a baby that never grows older – a baby—'

'A baby nearly twenty years old? Yes, it is as you say, ridiculous and horrible,' the Professor agreed.

'What could have induced the woman!' burst from me.

The Professor smiled bitterly.

'She is greedy of money. It is the only thing she loves except her beauty and her power over men; and during the boy's infancy – that word is used in the Will – she has full enjoyment of the estate. After he "attains to manhood" – I quote the Will again – hers is but a life-interest. Now you understand?'

I did understand, and the daring of the woman dazzled me. She had made the Professor doubly her tool.

'And so,' I gurgled between tears and laughter, 'Lord Clanbevan, who ought to be leaving Eton this year to commence his first Oxford term, is being carried about in the arms of a nurse, arrayed in the flowing garments of a six-months' baby! What an astonishing conspiracy!'

'His mother,' continued the Professor calmly, 'allows no one to approach him but the nurse. The family are only too glad to ignore what they consider a deplorable case of atavistic growth-arrest, and the boy himself—' He broke off. 'I have detained you,' he said, after a pause. 'I will not do so longer. Nor will I offer you my hand. I am as conscious as you are that it has committed a crime.' And he bowed me out with his hands sternly held behind him.

There were few more words between us, only I remember turning on the threshold of the laboratory, where I left him, to ask whether protium – radium, as it is now christened – checks the growth of every organic substance? The answer I received was curious:

'Certainly, with the exception of the nails and the hair!'

A week later the Professor was found dead in his laboratory … There were reports of suicide – hushed up. People said he had been more eccentric than ever of late, and theorised about brain-mischief; only I located the trouble in the heart. A year went by, and I had almost forgotten Lady Clanbevan – for she went abroad after the Professor's death – when at a little watering-place on the Dorset coast, I saw that lovely thing, as lovely as ever – she who was fifty if a day! With her were the blue-cloaked elderly nurse and Lord Clanbevan, borne, as usual, in the arms of his attendant, or wheeled in a luxurious perambulator. Day after day I encountered them – the lovely mother, the middle-aged nurse, and the mysterious child – until the sight began to get on my nerves. Had the Professor selected me as the recipient of a secret unrivalled in the records of biological discovery, or had he been the victim of some maniacal delusion that cold October day when we met in Rotten Row? One peep under the thick white lace veil with which the baby's face was invariably covered would clear everything up! Oh! for a chance to allay the pangs of curiosity!

The chance came. It was a hot, waspy August forenoon. Everybody was indoors with all the doors and windows open, lunching upon the innutritive viands alone procurable at health resorts – everybody but myself, Lord Clanbevan, and his nurse. She had fallen asleep upon a green-painted esplanade seat, gratuitously shielded by a striped awning. Lord Clanbevan's C-springed, white-hooded, cane-built perambulator stood close beside her. He was, as usual, a mass of embroidered cambric and cashmere, and, as always, thickly veiled, his regular breathing heaved his infant breast; the thick white lace drapery attached to his beribboned bonnet obscured the features upon which I so ardently longed to gaze! It was the chance, as I have said; and as the head of the blue-cloaked nurse dropped reassuringly upon her breast, as she emitted the snore that gave assurance of the soundness of her slumbers, I stepped silently on the gravel towards the baby's perambulator. Three seconds, and I stood over its apparently sleeping inmate; another, and I had lifted the veil from the face of the mystery – and dropped it with a stifled cry of horror!

The child had a moustache!

The Great Beast of Kafue

CLOTILDE GRAVES (1917)

The discovery of an extant dinosaur in the present day would be an astonishing scientific discovery; thus, it is hardly surprising that a number of cryptozoologists continue to pin their hopes on myths such as the Loch Ness Monster, or the *Mokèlé-mbèmbé* of the Congo River Basin. In the second Clotilde Graves story of this collection, we are presented with a character study of a damaged dinosaur-hunter, whose motives are much less noble than the furtherment of human knowledge.

IT HAPPENED at our homestead on the border of South-eastern Rhodesia, seventy miles from Tuli Concession, some three years after the War.

A September storm raged; the green, broad-leaved tobacco plants tossed like the waves of the ocean I had crossed and re-crossed, journeying to and coming back from my dead mother's wet, sad country of Ireland to this land of my father and his father's father.

The acacias and kameel thorns and the huge cactus-like euphorbia that fringed the water-courses and the irrigation channels had wrung their hands all day without ceasing; like Makalaka women at a native funeral. Night closed in: the wooden shutters were barred, the small-paned windows fastened, yet they shook and rattled as though human beings without were trying to force a way in. White-wash fell in scales from the big tie-beams and cross-rafters of the farm kitchen, and lay in little powdery drifts of whiteness on the solid table of brown locust-tree wood, and my father's Dutch Bible that lay open there. Upon my father's great black head that was bent over the Book were many streaks and patches of white that might not be shaken or brushed away.

It had fallen at the beginning of the War, that snow of sorrow streaking the heavy curling locks of coarse black hair. My pretty young mother – an Irishwoman of the North – had been killed in the Women's Laager at Gueldersdorp during the Siege. My father served as Staats gunner during the Investment – and now you know the dreadful doubt that heaped upon those mighty shoulders a bending load, and sprinkled the black hair with white.

You are to see me in my blue drill roundabout and little homespun breeches sitting on a cricket in the shadow of the table-edge, over against the grim *sterk* figure in the big, thong-seated armchair.

There would be no going to bed that night. The dam was over-full already, and the next spate from the hill sluits might crack the great wall of mud-cemented saw-squared boulders, or overflow it, and lick away the work of years. The farm-house roof had been rebuilt since the shell from the English naval gun had wrecked it, but the work of men today is not like that of the men of old. My father shook his head, contemplating the new masonry, and the whitewash fell as though in confirmation of his expressed doubts.

I had begged to stay up rather than lie alone in the big bed in my father's room. Nodding with sleepiness I should have denied, I carved with my two-bladed American knife at a little canoe I meant to swim in the shallower river-pools. And as I shaped the prow I dreamed of something I had heard on the previous night.

A traveller of the better middle-class, overseer of a coal-mine working 'up Buluwayo way', who had stayed with us the previous night and gone on to Tuli that morning, had told the story. What he had failed to tell I had haltingly spelled out of the three-weeks-old English newspaper he had left behind.

So I wrought, and remembered, and my little canoe swelled and grew in my hands. I was carrying it on my back through a forest of tall reeds and high grasses, forcing a painful way between the tough wrist-thick stems with the salt sweat running down into my eyes ... Then I was in the canoe, wielding the single paddle, working my frail crank craft through sluggish pools of black water, overgrown with broad spiny leaves of water-plants cradling flowers of marvellous hue. In the canoe bows leaned my grandfather's elephant-gun, the inlaid, browned-steel-barrelled weapon with the diamond-patterned stock and breech, that had always seemed to my childish eyes the most utterly desirable, absolutely magnificent possession a grown-up man might call his own.

A *paauw* made a great commotion getting up amongst the reeds; but does a hunter go after *paauw* with his grandfather's elephant-gun? Duck were feeding in the open spaces of sluggish black water. I heard what seemed to be the plop! of a jumping fish, on the other side of a twenty-foot high barrier of reeds and grasses. I looked up then, and saw, glaring down upon me from inconceivable heights of sheer horror, the Thing of which I had heard and read.

At this juncture I dropped the little canoe and clutched my father round the leg.

'What is it, *mijn jongen?*'

He, too, seemed to rouse out of a waking dream. You are to see the wide, burnt-out-looking grey eyes that were staring sorrowfully out of their shadowy caves under the shaggy eyebrows, lighten out of their deep abstraction and drop to the level of my childish face.

'You were thinking of the great beast of Kafue Valley, and you want to ask me if I will lend you my father's elephant-rifle when you are big enough to carry it that you may go and hunt for the beast and kill it; is that so?'

My father grasped his great black beard in one huge knotted brown hand, and made a rope of it, as was his way. He looked from my chubby face to the old-fashioned black-powder 8-bore that hung upon the wall against a leopard kaross, and back again, and something like a smile curved the grim mouth under the shaggy black and white moustache.

'The gun you shall have, boy, when you are of age to use it, or a 450-Mannlicher or a 600-Mauser, the best that may be bought north of the Transvaal, to shoot explosive or conical bullets from cordite cartridges. But not unless you give me your promise never to kill that beast, shall money of mine go to the buying of such a gun for you. Come now, let me have your word!'

Even to my childish vanity the notion of my solemnly entering into a compact binding my hand against the slaying of the semi-fabulous beast-marvel of the Upper Rhodesian swamps smacked of the fantastic if not of the absurd. But my father's eyes had no twinkle in them, and I faltered out the promise they commanded.

'*Nooit* – *nooit* will I kill that beast! It should kill me, rather!'

'Your mother's son will not be *valsch* to a vow. For so would you, son of my body, make of me, your father, a traitor to an oath that I have sworn!'

The great voice boomed in the rafters of the farm kitchen, vying with the baffled roaring of the wind that was trying to get in, as I had told myself, and lie down, folding wide quivering wings and panting still, upon the sheepskin that was spread before the hearth.

'But – but why did you swear?'

I faltered out the question, staring at the great bearded figure in homespun jacket and tan-cord breeches and *veldschoens*, and thought again that it had the hairy skin of Esau and the haunted face of Saul.

Said my father, grimly –

'Had I questioned my father so at twice your age, he would have skinned my back and I should have deserved it. But I cannot beat your mother's son, though the Lord punish me for my weakness … And you have the spirit of the *jager* in you, even as I. What I saw you may one day see. What I might have killed, that shall you spare, because of me and my oath. Why did I take it upon me, do you ask? Even though I told you, how should a child understand? What is it you are saying? Did I really see the beast? Ay, by the Lord!' said my father thoughtfully, 'I saw him. And never can a man who has seen, forget that sight. What are you saying?'

The words tumbled over one another as I stammered in my hurry –

'But – but the English traveller said only one white man besides the Mashona hunter has seen the beast, and the newspaper says so too.'

'*Natuurlijk*. And the white man is me,' thundered the deep voice.

I hesitated.

'But since the planting of the tobacco you have not left the *plaats*. And the newspaper is of only three weeks back.'

'*Dat spreekt*, but the story is older than that, *mijn jongen*. It is the third time it has been dished up in the *Buluwayo Courant*, sauced up with lies to change the taste as belly-lovers have their meat. But I am the man who saw the beast of Kafue, and the story that is told is my story, nevertheless!'

I felt my cheeks beginning to burn. Wonderful as were the things I knew to be true of the man, my father, this promised to be the most wonderful of all.

'It was when I was hunting in the Zambezi Country,' said my father, 'three months after the *Commandaants* of the Forces of the United Republics met at Klerkadorp to arrange conditions of peace—'

'With the English Generals,' I put in.

'With the English, as I have said. You had been sent to your – to her people in Ireland. I had not then thought of rebuilding the farm. For more than a house of stones had been thrown down for me, and more than so many thousand acres of land laid waste …

'Where did I go? *Ik wiet niet*. I wandered *op en neer* like the evil spirit in the Scriptures.' The great corded hand shut the Book and reached over and snuffed the tallow-dip that hung over at the top, smoking and smelling, and pitched the black wick-end angrily on the red hearth-embers. 'I sought rest and found none, either for the sole of my foot or the soul in my body. There is bitterness in my mouth as though I have eaten the spotted lily-root of the swamps. I cannot taste the food I swallow, and when I lie down at night something lies down with me, and when I rise up, it rises too and goes by my side all day.'

I clung to the leg of the table, not daring to clutch my father's. For his eyes did not seem to see me anymore, and a blob of foam quivered on his beard that hung over his great breast in a shadowy cascade dappled with patches of white. He went on, I scarcely daring to breathe –

'For, after all, do I know it is not I who killed her? That accursed day, was I not on duty as ever since the beginning of the Investment, and was it not a splinter from a Maxim Nordenfeld fired from an eastern gun-position, that—' Great drops stood on my father's forehead.

His huge frame shook. The clenched hand resting on the solid table of locust-beam shook that also, shaking me, clinging to the table-leg with my heart thumping violently, and a cold, crawling sensation among the roots of my curls.

'At first, I seem to remember there was a man hunting with me. He had many servants, four Mashona hunters, wagons drawn by salted tailless spans, fine guns and costly tents, plenty of stores and medicine in little sugar-pills, in bottles with silver tops. But he sickened in spite of all his quinine, and the salted oxen died, just like beasts with tails; and besides, he was afraid of the Makwakwa and the Mashengwa with their slender poisoned spears of reeds. He turned back at last. I pushed on.'

There was a pause. The strange, iron-grey, burnt-out eyes looked through me and beyond me, then the deep, trembling voice repeated, once more changing the past into the present tense –

'I push on west. My life is of value to none. The boy – is he not with her people? Shall I live to have him back under my roof and see in his face one day the knowledge that I have killed his mother? Nay, nay, I will push on!'

There was so long a silence after this that I ventured to move. Then my father looked at me, and spoke to me, not as though I were a child, but as if I had been another man.

'I pushed on, crossing the rivers on a blown-up goatskin and some calabashes, keeping my father's elephant-gun and my cartridges dry by holding them above my head. For food there were thorny orange cucumbers with green pulp, and the native women at the kraals gave me cakes of maize and milk. I hunted and killed rhino and elephant and hippo and lion, until the head-men of the Mashengwa said that the beast was a god of theirs, and the slaying of it would bring a pestilence upon their tribe; so, I killed no more. And one day I shot a cow hippo with her calf, and she stood to suckle the ugly little thing while her life was bleeding out of her, and after that I ceased to kill. I needed little, and there were yet the green-fleshed cucumbers, and ground-nuts, and things like those.'

He made a rope of his great beard, twisting it with a rasping sound.

'Thus, I reached the Upper Kafue Valley where the great grass swamps are. No railway then, running like an iron snake up from Buluwayo to bring the ore down from the silver-mines that are there.

'Six days' trek from the mines – I went on foot always, you will understand – six days' journey from the mines, above where L'uengwe River is wedded to Kafue, as the Badanga say, is a big water.

'It is a lake – or rather, two lakes – not round, but shaped like the bowls of two wooden spoons. A shore of black, stone-like baked mud round them, and a bridge of the same stone is between them, so that they make the figure that is for 8.'

The big, hairy forefinger of my father's right hand traced the numeral in the powdered whitewash that lay in drifts upon the table.

'That is the shape of the lakes, and the Badanga say that they have no bottom, and that fish taken from their waters remain raw and alive, even on the red-hot embers of their cooking stove. And they gave me tortoise to eat and told me, partly in words of my own *moder Taal* they had picked up somehow, partly in sign language, about the Great Beast that lives in the double lake that is haunted by the spirits of their dead.'

I waited, my heart pumping at the bottom of my throat, my blood running horribly, delightfully chill, to hear the rest.

'The hunting spirit revives in a man, even at death's door, to hear of an animal the like of which no living hunter has ever brought down. The Badanga tell me of this one, tales, tales, tales! They draw it for me with a pointed stick on a broad green leaf, or in the ashes of their cooking-fires. And I have seen many a great beast, but, *voor den donder!* never a beast such as that!'

I held on to my stool with both hands.

'I ask the Badanga to guide me to the lair of the beast for all the money I have upon me. They care not for gold, but for the old silver hunting-watch I carry they will risk offending the spirits of their dead. The old man who has drawn the creature for me, he will take me. And it is January, the time of year in which he has been before known to rise and bellow – *Maar!* – bellow like twenty buffalo bulls in spring-time, for his mate to rise from those bottomless deeps below and drink the air and sun.'

So there are two great beasts! Neither the traveller nor the newspaper nor my father, until this moment, had hinted at that!

'The she-beast is much the smaller and has no horns. This my old man makes clear to me, drawing her with the point of his fish-spear on smooth mud. She is very sick the last time my old man has seen her. Her great moon-eyes are dim, and the stinking spume dribbles from her jaws. She can only float in the trough of the wave that her mate makes with his wallowings, her long scaly neck lying like a dead python on the oily black water. My old man thinks she was then near death. I ask him how long ago that is? Twenty times have the blue lake-lilies blossomed since, the lilies with the sweet seeds that the Badanga make bread of. And the great bull has twice been heard bellowing, but never has he been seen of man since then.'

My father folded his great arms upon the black-and-white cascade of beard that swept down over his shirt of homespun and went on –

'Twenty years. Perhaps, think I, my old man has lied to me! But we are at the end of the last day's journey. The sun has set and night has come. My old man makes me signs we are near the lakes and I climb a high mahogo, holding by the limbs of the wild fig that is hugging the tree to death.'

My father spat into the heart of the glowing wood ashes, and said –

'I see the twin lakes lying in the midst of the high grass-swamps, barely a mile away. The black, shining waters cradle the new moon of January in their bosom, and the blue star that hangs beneath her horn, and there is no ripple on the surface, or sign of a beast, big or little. I am coming down the tree, when through the night comes a long, hollow, booming, bellowing roar that is not the cry of any beast I know. Thrice it comes, and my old man of the Badanga, squatting among the roots of the mahogo, nods his wrinkled bald head, and says, squinting up at me, "Now you have heard, will you go back or go on?"

'I answer, *"Al recht uit!"* For something of the hunting spirit has wakened in me. And I see to the cleaning of the elephant-gun and load it carefully before I sleep that night.'

I would have liked to ask a question but the words stuck in my throat.

'By dawn of day we have reached the lakes,' went on my father. 'The high grass and the tall reeds march out into the black water as far as they may, then the black stone beach shelves off into depths unknown.

'He who has written up the story for the Buluwayo newspaper says that the lake was once a volcano and that the crumbly black stone is lava. It may be so. But volcanoes are holes in the tops of mountains, while the lakes lie in a valley-bottom, and he who wrote cannot have been there, or he would know there are two, and not one.

'All the next night, camping on the belt of stony shore that divides lake from lake, we heard nothing. We ate the parched grain and baked grubs that my old man carried in a little bag. We lighted no fire because of the spirits of the dead Badanga that would come crowding about it to warm themselves, and poison us with their breath. My old man said so, and I humoured him. My dead needed no fire to bring her to me. She was there always …

'All the day and the night through we heard and saw nothing. But at the dawn of the next day I saw a great curving ripple cross the upper lake, which may have been a mile and a half wide; and the reeds upon the nearer shore were wetted to the knees as by the wave that is left in the wake of a steamer, and oily patches of scum, each as big as a barn floor, befouled the calm water, and there was a cold, strange smell upon the breeze, but nothing more.

'Until at sunset of the next day, when I stood upon the mid-most belt of shore between lake and lake. With my back to the blood-red wonder of the west and my eyes sheltered by my hand as I looked out to where I had seen the waters divided as a man furrows earth with the ploughshare, I felt a shadow fall over me from behind, and turned … and saw… *Alamachtig!*'

I could not breathe. At last, at last, it was coming!

'I am no coward,' said my father, in his deep resounding bass, 'but that was a sight of terror. My old man of the Badanga had bolted like a rock-rabbit. I could hear the dry reeds crashing as he broke through. And the horned head of the beast, that was as big as a wagon-trunk, shaking about on the top of a python-neck that topped the tallest of the teak-trees, seemed as if it were looking for the little human creature that was trying to run away.

'*Voor den donder!* how the water rises up in columns of smoke-spray as the great beast lashes it with his crocodile-tail! His head is crocodile also, with horns of rhino, his body has the bulk of six hippo bulls together. He is covered with armour of scales, yellow-white as the scales of leprosy, and he has paddles like a tortoise. God of my fathers, what a beast to see! I forget the gun I hold against my hip – I can only stand and look, while the cold, thick puffs of stinking musk are brought to my nostrils and my ear-drums are well-nigh split with the bellowing of the beast. Ay! and the wave of his wallowings that wets one to the neck is foul with clammy ooze and oily scum.

'Why did the thing not see me? I did not try to hide from those scaly-lidded great eyes, yellow with half-moon-shaped pupils; I stood like an idol of stone. Perhaps that saved me, or I was too little a thing to vent a wrath so great upon. He Who in the beginning made herds of beasts like that to move upon the face of the waters, and let this one live to show the world of today what creatures were of old – He knows. I do not. I was dazed with the noise of its roaring and the thundering blows of its huge tail upon the water; I was drenched with the spume of its snortings and sickened with the stench it gave forth. But I never took my eyes from it, as it spent its fury, and little by little I came to understand.

'*Het is jammer* to see anything suffer as that beast was suffering. Another man in my place would have thought as much, and when it lay still at last on the frothing black water, a bullet from the elephant-rifle would have lodged in the little stupid brain behind the great moon-eye, and there would have been an end …

'But I did not shoot!'

It seemed an age before my father spoke again, though the cuck-oo-clock had only ticked eight times.

'No! I would not shoot and spare the beast, dinosaurus or brontosaurus, or whatever the wiseacres who have not seen him may name him, the anguish that none had spared me. *"Let him go on!"* said I. *"Let him go on seeking her in the abysses that no lead-line may ever fathom, without consolation, without hope! Let him rise to the sun and the breeze of spring through miles of the cold black water, and find her not, year after year until the ending of the world. Let him call her through the mateless nights until Day and Night rush together at the sound of the Trumpet of the Judgment, and Time shall be no more!"*'

Crash!

The great hand came down upon the solid locust-wood table, breaking the spell that had bound my tongue.

'I – do not understand,' I heard my own child-voice saying. 'Why was the Great Beast so sorry? What was he looking for?'

'His mate who died. Ay, at the lower end of the second lake, where the water shallows, her bones were sticking up like the bleached timbers of a wrecked ship. And He and She being the last of their kind upon the earth, he knows desolation … and shall know it till death brings forgetfulness and rest. Boy, the wind is fallen, the rain has spent itself, it is time that you go to bed.'

The Sorcerer

CHARLOTTE McMANUS (1922)

In the early twentieth century, old traditions became a topic of heated discussion for Irish republicans. To some, the issue boiled down to a question of how much of its old culture Ireland would be willing to cast aside to join the modern world. This question is central to much of the work of Charlotte McManus, who is best known as the author of *The Professor in Erin* (1912), set in a parallel universe where Hugh O'Neill defeated the English at the Battle of Kinsale (1601). The following story explores the same theme on a more intimate scale, with a sly nod to Yeats's Cathleen Ni Houlihan to signal McManus's intent.

THERE WAS A MAN living in one of the Congested Districts Board's new houses – those ugly houses with thin cold slate roofs and big windows – who had a charm. No one cared to cross him because of it. He lived there alone with his brother, and Anthony wanted to get a wife. But no girl would marry Anthony because of William's charm. There were farmers who looked at his land, thirty acres of tillage and pasture, who would have given him their daughters. More than once there had been embassies, and negotiations, and dowry-fixing in the match-room of the town; but everything had fallen through when the girls were told.

These failures troubled Anthony, yet heightened his respect for his brother. Once he had wondered what measure of sorrow he would feel if he were to see William's coffin carried down the boreen, and a wife come tripping up. Sorrow sank the scale at one moment as he gazed into the airy fields of possibility; then he saw the comely figure of a woman, and he thought of the comforts her presence would bring.

The thought stood waiting for him on the threshold as he entered the house after a girl's refusal. He took it, and sighed. The silent kitchen had invited the light in through the staring panes of the windows. Its width and length were shamelessly exposed. All that should have been softened or hidden, the light had touched; the disorder, the dust, the unwashed delph on the dresser, the rent in the coarse red quilt that covered the sleeper's figure. The fire had faded before it. It had thrust itself into the throat of the chimney. It had wiped up the shadows in the sooty corners. The silence, in which sound seemed encamped, the hard unsparing light, gave the man a cheerless feeling, an irritation beyond the comfort of an oath. He filled his pipe, drove the bowl into a coal, gave some angry puffs, and looked towards the bed.

The sleeper's lips were pressed together. He breathed through a long straight nose without sound, like a child. The face and head of the man belonged to the dolichocephalous type, and a lock of black hair streaked with grey hung over the forehead. His brother's head was the other type, broad and round.

When Anthony had made up the fire, put on the kettle, and laid the soda-cake on the table, the man on the bed opened his eyes. They were blue, set in deeply wrinkled flesh. He got off the bed, and as he limped across the room, asked if the match were made. It was not, Anthony said; there had been a dispute over the stock. The man took off his hat, blessed himself, and ate in silence. When they had finished the meal, a woman came to the door.

Her face was half hidden in a brown shawl, and she spoke in a nasal drawl.

'Good evening, sirs,' she said. 'Is it here that the gentleman, Mr William Carney, lives?'

Anthony looked at his brother. Many visitors came to William, seeking help through his charm. Some came openly; some went out silent and mysterious from their homes and asked for the cure. The shrouding shawl over the woman's face suggested mystery, and her voice said she was what Connacht calls 'a Yank'.

'Is it me you're wanting?' William asked. He sat without moving, looking at the wall in front of him. There was a remoteness in his manner and air.

The woman came in. She pushed the shawl a little from her face. It was thin and colourless. A movement of the hands showed a blue silk blouse and a white neck. She sat down on the chair Anthony placed for her.

'I'm told you have a charm,' she said.

'I have.'

'I guess it's good for most things.'

'Do you want it done over you?'

'You are real smart, Mr Carney, I do, but I don't like to speak before the other gentleman.'

Anthony went towards the door. William rose and followed him. 'This is the wife for you,' he said when they stood outside.

'She's too old,' Anthony objected.

'She's a returned Yank, and has a fortune.'

'Well, I might.'

'Say if you will, or you will not, before I do the charm.'

'Well I might, but I must see the money first – if we can settle the match.'

William called the woman. 'If you come out, I'll do the charm,' he said, and went over to the wall, and sat upon it.

She came from the kitchen with an unhesitating step, her face uncovered. The only beauty left her in her fight with the seasons and hard work was her red-brown hair. But she had the confident air of success; of one whose life has been widened by the knowledge of New York kitchens; by the freedom of her evening; by the money that enabled her to buy finery. The man asked what was wrong with her.

She told him in a clear business-like way. She had returned home from the States three months before, and if her friends there knew she was asking him for a charm they would joke her 'til she died. They didn't believe in charms; neither did she, but it would be real clever of him if he could make a girl look like herself again.

'Do you want to be made young?'

'I guess I am young enough, but I want to look as I did when I went to the States,' she said.

The man picked three blades of grass, measured them, and got off the wall. 'In the name of the Holy Trinity, and in the name of the saint of the muscles of the body. Amen,' he said. 'Now do you walk three times after me round the little bush over there.'

She obeyed, and they went thrice round the hawthorn, going by the left to the right. Then he got a bowl with clean water, and put the pieces of grass into it, and told her to look into the bowl. The grass floated slowly on the surface. He took a little stick from his pocket and stirred the water, and said the prayer of the saint of the muscles in Irish. 'Take out the blade that comes nearest to you.' he said.

She drew out the short blade.

'As long as you keep that bitteen of grass, you will look young to any man wanting a wife. It will be eighteen you'll look – a slip of a girl.' He emptied the bowl, walked back to the house, and slammed the door.

Anthony heard steps drawing near as he sat on a bank. He had discreetly turned his back on the rite, bending his gaze on the ground. The closing door told him that the charm had been done. He sat modestly motionless.

The woman stopped before him, and the scope of his gaze took in a thin white hand with a pound note. 'Give that to your brother,' she said.

She was two yards away as he still stared at it, and a mellow, ruminating look settled on his face. When he raised his eyes she was some distance off, and he thought she walked like a young girl.

The woman went on her way. She took a shortcut over the fields to the Big House, the semi-derelict grey limestone building, where with two servants, a young man and a little girl, she had kept house for the Experimenter for a month. He had hired the house half a year before; he was a bald-headed, lively little man who had theories.

He called her from the door of his laboratory as she crossed the hall; she went into the room. Instruments, coils, and jars stood on a table. There was a flow of commingled odours. One coil, attached to a mouthpiece, was fastened to a battery, and a mirror beside it reflected a sunbeam. Not far from the table stood John Naughton and Bridgie, and she was told to join them.

The Experimenter spoke some words to himself. The three had a value as human units with vocal chords and throats and differences of sound, and this was their pre-eminent interest to him. He was engaged on experiments of light, and sound, and electric waves, and psycho-activities, and was just then experimenting on sound in its relation to the rest. He asked Mary Nally to speak into the receiver.

She did so readily, and taking observations, he scarcely noticed the child's snigger. For the woman had said, 'I am eighteen and beautiful.'

She spoke the same words three times, and his eyes puckered. It seemed as if something unexpected had happened.

He told the young man and the child to speak into the receiver in turn. Both said that Mary Nally was eighteen and beautiful. The Experimenter waved them back, and seized the tube. But the words he meant to say melted into 'She's eighteen and beautiful.'

He examined his instruments; he read the sunbeam on the mirrors; a look of interest showed on his face. He began speaking, to himself more than to the three. Something remarkable had happened. A magnetic field had been created round the receiver, so that they spoke words directed by animal magnetism, or odic force. Miss Nally, he conjectured, had either a powerful magnet about her which prevented the results he had expected from his experiments, or had become a magnet herself, as if she had been subjected to N-rays. These rays exercised a great influence on the nerve centres increasing the activities of muscles and nerves, and were produced by muscular contractions and nervous activity. He would put her to further tests.

But the woman had backed to the door. The cakes were in the oven; it was time to get the tea. There was a dark poppy-tint in each cheek as she went out of the room. It lasted till she reached the great stone-flagged kitchen. Then she went grey-white; she had dropped the charm. She sat down and thought about where it might be. John Naughton's and Bridgie's step came on the stair, and she got up and stood by the fire till they had passed through the kitchen. Then she fled upstairs. Standing by his coil, the Experimenter saw the door open, and his abstracted gaze rested on the woman as she came in and bent over the floor. A blade of grass fluttered from the paper she took up. Her hand swept the air like a wing; she bent again and she seized it. The door opened wider, and closed, and she was gone.

Mary's big brass-bound American trunk stood at the foot of the bed in her room off the kitchen. She put the charm in the trinket case with her eight-carat gold bracelets. She dressed herself in her purple suit and re-did her red-brown hair, her mind prepared for any attack. She had words ready, like splinters of an iceberg. She was composed, cold. There was no one in the kitchen when she went back.

The man seeking a wife coughed outside. He looked though the doorway and came in. The pound note was in his hand. 'I hope I'm not after giving you a start, Miss Nally,' he said. 'I've brought the pound back.'

She looked at him and it. 'Well, I guess, Mr Carney, that's good money.'

'The best,' he said deferentially. 'But it's what my brother does take but nine coppers, or nine pieces of silver, or nine pieces of gold.'

'Is that so? I suppose it's coppers he mostly gets.'

'I won't be denying it. There's not been anyone but one Yank who could show him nine pieces of gold. And as many come back from the States with the name of a fortune they haven't got, it's small wonder.'

'Then I guess, Mr Carney, I'm to give you nine coppers, and you give me back the pound. I'm real pleased at the charm being so cheap.'

She took the note his fingers seemed reluctant to release, and his eyes lingered on her. 'Have ye the grass safe?' he asked.

The answer had jerked from her lips, 'I threw it away,' when the Experimenter came down the stairs. His voice went before him; he was calling on his household. Everyone was to come up to the laboratory again. He pattered into the kitchen, threw one glance at the stranger, and swept him into the party.

The little girl was not of it; she had wandered off into the mushroom field, and, eyes earthward, was moving among the red cows.

Mary Nally was the first to speak. Her lower lip drooped, the white edge of a tooth showed as she bent over the mouth-piece. She dealt with the weather. The two men followed; and as each spoke, the Experimenter examined the plates, coils, and instruments, setting something in motion that interrupted by timed intervals the light of the sunbeam on the mirror. He appeared pleased, straightened himself, tapped the table with a finger, and addressed the three as he would have done a row of students. The sounds, he told them, had acted as he had anticipated. The magnetic field, mysteriously created, was no longer present. They had spoken their thoughts under natural conditions. There was no compulsion to follow a set formula of words.

The molecules of the body loosened, as it were, by that unknown magnetic current had produced a hypnotic effect. They had been magnetised in the first experiment by induction – that was magnetised by another body which had been strongly magnetised. A magnetic field was created that held up and deflected the energies and activities of his instruments; and why it had done so (for it had not acted in such a way as the current might be expected to act), and where it had come from, was still a matter of conjecture to him.

The human beings addressed bore varying expressions on their faces. The wife-seeker's was full of the gravity that a fellow scientist might give. Words stood on his lips. His voice shot into the pause when the Experimenter ceased.

'There's not a man in Ireland, north, south, east, or west, that can do a better charm than my brother William,' he said, and swelled with pride.

The Experimenter's eyes wandered out of the imaginary classroom, and he had an exact vision of the three. His mind reached for the words that had stopped at his ears. 'Ah, indeed. What charms?' he said.

'I seen him take a bitteen of grass,' said the wife-seeker, 'and put it in a bowl of water and say the prayer of the saint of the muscles over it. That would be one charm. Many do be corning to him for it.'

Mary Nally had reached the door. It opened and closed behind her with the speed of a gust of wind. Some minutes later Anthony appeared in the kitchen. He had not put any harm on what he had said, he told her; he had not let on that she had been to William.

She thrust the one pound into his hand as if she were a wild thing about to claw him, and said some words, and he went away. In the field he met the little girl, and he stayed and talked to her. 'She can't do you a ha'penny worth of harm,' he concluded, and walked on.

The child came back to the house with the mushrooms in her blue apron. As her hands rattled the tea-cups in the basin of water, she watched Mary from the corner of her eyes. She watched her, as, dressed for visiting, she crossed the yard. When she was out of sight the child ran swiftly to the bedroom door and as swiftly ran back. Three times she pattered across the flags, and three times returned. And on each excursion to the door she carried a face of resolve, and each time she ran back, the resolution was broken and there was alarm in its place. On the fourth adventure the door fell open before her, and darting into the bedroom, she swooped upon the trunk.

The Experimenter went out the next morning. About eleven, he reached the boreen that led to the slated house. He followed the boreen and saw a man going before him driving a donkey with creels of turf. The man limped. He and the donkey stopped before a half-built rick. The sods were thudding to the ground as the Experimenter reached them. 'Good morning,' he said. 'Are you William Carney?'

The stooping figure straightened up and looked round at the voice. 'Good morning. That's my name.'

'You have a charm, I hear; a magnet. You charge a piece of grass. How do you do it?'

The sods thudded again. The man's coat spread out like the brown wings of a hen as he stooped over them.

'I am a scientist, and interested in your magnet. I wish to learn your method.'

The answer was the sound of falling sods.

The Experimenter raised his voice. 'I ask you to show me how to magnetise a blade of grass so that it will create a wide magnetic field. I will pay you for your secret.'

The hen-like wings swung up. William turned and studied the Experimenter's face. 'Do you want it done over yourself?' he asked.

'Yes, if that is the only way you can demonstrate.'

'Are your muscles knotted?'

'I am not rheumatic.'

'What's wrong with ye then?'

'Nothing. I wish to investigate. I wish to learn if your charm is a real activity, or whether you are a humbug. I see you are lame. Why do you not cure yourself?'

The sods fell again. That was a rhythm in the sway of the man's arms; in the answering thud. Some minutes passed.

Then he stood up, and his closed lips parted. He drew a deep breath, looked towards the fairy tree, and wiped the brown dust of his hands on has coat. 'Come back to the house and I'll make a cure,' he said.

He led the way, limping. The Experimenter followed with a sprightly step. He watched the rites closely. He took the bowl with the three blades of grass, and went after the man three times round the hawthorn tree. But the circle was made not sun-wise, from left to right, but left-hand wise. The water in the bowl was stirred, and the Experimenter told to take the grass that floated nearest to him.

'Now carry it in your left hand and the bowl in your right, and walk back to the house.'

The Experimenter did as directed. Suddenly he found that something had happened to his right foot; he was limping.

It was early that morning that Mary Nally began to think of Anthony. She had thought of him before, but that was in a dream at the time that Bridgie met Anthony as he went by with a bullock to the fair. She remembered she had said some insulting things to him. She wondered how she could have thought of marrying a young fellow like John Naughton, instead of a sober, settled prudent man of years. About eleven she went to shake out the folds of her various suits, and take a glance at her bank-receipt. Before she reached the lower layers of her garments she knew that the charm had gone. Dramatically, slowly, she removed everything; then slowly, automatically, refilled the trunk. She sat for a space with tightened lips and eyes of steel. Who was the thief?

The Experimenter! He had seen the grass!

Then she went up the stair, putting her feet down heavily as a woman might who called on all to see her wrong. The laboratory door was locked. She shook it; beat on it, and turned angrily away. Prudence came and sat by her side as she waited in the hall, and laid calming hands upon her. Another thought stole in. She put on her silk suit, her rose-garlanded hat, her eight-carat bracelets, and left the house.

It was noon, and the sun was breaking through the long-drawn white-grey clouds as she reached the boreen. A man was coming along the road. It was Anthony with the price of the bullock in his pocket. He was sober – that is, he had only had enough to show that he had been to a fair, a degree of sobriety that is not classed with 'a drop taken' – and the elegant figure by the boreen caught his eye. It was the rich 'Yank', the woman with whom he must match.

And to her – Anthony in his good black suit, the green felt hat on his head, with his broad, red, matured face, his eyes just pleasantly brilliant – the man she had pictured in her matrimonial attains. His loud hearty greeting rang before him; they drew together. He swung her hand up and down for a minute. 'Here's the pound I borrowed off you!' he said, 'and another with it for interest!'

William heard their voices and steps as they came down the boreen some minutes later. He stopped building the rick, and studied them for a few minutes. 'Is the match made between ye?' he called.

The wife-seeker shouted it was, the pride of success on his face. The Experimenter sitting on the bank looked at Mary Nally. Her flinty eyes were upon him.

He got off the bank, and standing by it, offered his congratulations. He spoke of happy married lives, of true love, of his pleasure in the happiness of a woman who had every quality to make the man she had chosen blessed. The wedding gift that he wished to give her should be one that she herself should name. It should be beautiful, it should be useful. And the woman with her man won, the new slated house before her, was pacified.

He had a question to ask her, he said; was he lame? He asked it as a scientist. He had another thing to ask – a favour. Would she stand before him, and look straight into his eyes, and say, five times in a loud commanding voice, that he was not lame; that he was to walk without a limp down the lane. He was not joking. It was an experiment.

She laughed gaily; stood before him, and did what he asked. Five times she spoke. He put one step forward, hesitated, moved again, gave one limp, and then walked with a firm and equal step down the boreen.

William's eyes followed him, wide gaping. He threw the sod in his hand on the ground, and went after the Experimenter. Anthony pulled the woman's arm. 'Lookit, lookit!' he exclaimed, 'the limp's gone from William!'

The Experimenter heard the steps and looked back. He walked on with strong strides till the man's voice called twice. Then he stopped. Bare-headed, his black locks ruffled over his high forehead, William came towards him.

There was deep respect in his tone. 'Will you wait a minute, sir, I would ask you a question.'

The Experimenter waited.

'You made her spake five times. It's nine or seven I've seen used. What would be the reason of the five?'

'What is the secret in the blades of grass? And why have you never cured yourself till now?'

'I swear by the Gospels that I know no more than that the charm is by the power of the saint of the muscles of the body. And I didn't cure myself because I'd have to give my lameness to someone.'

'You didn't mind giving it to me!'

'I heard you had gifts yourself, and ye vexed me with the questions ye were putting. I'll be greatly thankful to you, sir, if you will say why you used the five.'

'Five had no merit in it. Any other number would have done as well. But I was nervous. I used the power of suggestion. Good day!'

A Story Without an End
(For N.C.)

DOROTHY MACARDLE
(Mountjoy Gaol, December 1922)

The War of Independence (or Anglo-Irish War) brought bloodshed and atrocity to nearly every corner of the island of Ireland between 1919 and 1921. The Anglo-Irish Treaty that ended it partitioned the island into Northern Ireland and the Irish Free State, leading to a Civil War between Pro-Treaty and Anti-Treaty forces a few months later (1922–1923). Against that traumatic backdrop, this subtly weird story by Dorothy Macardle, written while she was imprisoned for her Anti-Treaty activities, might make us wonder what a 'vision' really is – a precognitive dream, or a warning sent backwards through time?

IT WAS SOON AFTER the truce began that Nesta McAllister came to Philadelphia. A little shyly she came among us and a little critically she was received; many of us had worked with Roger McAllister and delighted in him as the wittiest, believed in him as the most creative and inspiring of Ireland's men, and we wondered, when we heard of his marriage, whether he had been lucky and wise.

We liked Nesta; very young, very dark, she was, very serious at times, without the defiant gaiety that is the only armour for such a war as she had to wage.

She contributed little to the talk and storytelling of those evenings, but loved to listen, and one felt in her a sensitive response to one's precise meaning, one's more discriminate thought, which made the talk grow subtler when she was there. Una, who knew her best, said of her: 'She has lost herself in Roger's life and mind.' Frank said: 'She is a little woman who'll get hurt.'

It was on one evening when we had been recalling old prophecies and forebodings and telling of omens and dreams that she told us her troubling story; she told it, I think, chiefly to hear us assure her that the dream could never come true.

It had happened in January when she and Roger were living in hiding in the mountains of County Cork, he waging with his pen a campaign so dangerous to the enemy and so infuriating that we dreaded capture for him more than death. No man in Ireland was more remorselessly hunted then.

'It was in the middle of the worst time of all,' she said, 'when martial law had been proclaimed and men were being tried by drum-head Court-Martial and shot on any pretext at all. You could be shot for "harbouring rebels", you know. We didn't harbour rebels, of course, because Roger's work had all to be done "underground"; we lived without even a servant in a little four-roomed cottage in the hills. When it was necessary for Roger to meet the staff, he used to go off alone on his bicycle at night and come back just when there came a chance. Those, of course, were my worst times.

'It was on a night when he was away that I had the dream. You know,' she said, hesitating a little, 'that I have had dreams sometimes that came true. I dreamed of my father's stroke, though he was quite well, just before it came – I saw his face change – and my sister's baby – before it was born. I saw it under the sea – and afterwards, in the *Leinster*, they were both drowned. It is terrible to dream like that.[2]

'As a rule, when Roger was away I couldn't sleep, but that night I was very tired and fell asleep before twelve o'clock. In the dream we were sitting, he and I, in a room lighted only by candles – the living-room of the cottage it was – I saw the makeshift couch by the fire and the door that opened straight on to

2. Editor's note: the *HMS Leinster*, a mailboat sunk by a German submarine on its way from Dublin to Holyhead in October 1918, killing 500 people.

the road. It was night; the door and shutters were bolted and there was no sound. I think I was looking into the fire – I was looking at something, anyhow, that shaped itself into a face – a thin, long face with hollow eyes. I hated it, I tried to drive it away. Then we were in the room, just as before, Roger writing by the candlelight, with no sound – I was waiting for a sound. Then it came – footsteps on the gravel outside, and a long, low, hissing call, then a knock, someone knocking with his knuckles on the door. Roger stood up and crossed the room quickly and opened the door and four men carrying a stretcher came in; they came walking slowly like figures in a play; there was a man lying on the stretcher – a dead man, with that long, thin face and those deep eyes; there was a blood-stained bandage round his head – I hated him – I was afraid – such terror gripped me that I woke. I woke cold and shuddering, but I didn't wake properly. I fell asleep again and then – then came the other dream.'

Her face had gone white and her eyes wide and dark. 'Better not be telling it,' Frank said. But she crushed her hands together and said, 'No, no – I'll get rid of it – 'tis better for me to tell.'

'In this dream I was not present myself – I knew in a way that I was asleep – there was a mad feeling that if only I could wake – if only I could cry out – but I had no power.

'There were high stone walls and a dark yard; everything was cold; it was dawn. The yard was full of stones; it was narrow and long; there was a dark hole dug in the earth. There was a man standing near it, against the wall; his hands were behind his back and his eyes were bandaged; there was a bright red mark over his heart. It was Roger; he was going to be killed. Soldiers formed up with rifles and stood covering him. There were nine; I counted them; it was all quite clear. Then a tall man stood behind them, an officer, with a revolver, covering them. I looked at him and tried to scream – I tried to stop him, but I couldn't, I had no power.

He was the dead man – he had a great scar on his brow and hollow eyes, and that long, cadaverous face. I heard him shout "Fire!" and heard the volley, and saw Roger fall, and saw that man go over to him with his revolver and shoot – Oh, it was horrible. I can't.'

She broke off. For a while none of us could think of anything to say, then Liam Daly said laughingly, 'One of the uncounted terrors of martial law! I suppose our misfortunate wives and mothers were dreaming our executions every night! God pity them,' he added soberly, 'the time they had.'

Nesta looked up gratefully. 'Yes, it was very natural,' she said, 'and there was one thing that showed how it was – just a crazy combination of hopes and fears. The uniforms of the soldiers were *green*! That comforted me, of course, but – the first part of the dream came true.'

'The wounded man?' I exclaimed.

'That evening', she said, 'Roger came home. He was in splendid spirits; everything was going well; one man who'd been sentenced was reprieved, and another who was to have been executed in the morning had escaped. We had a leisurely supper and afterwards sat resting by the firelight, as usual, before beginning the night's work. You know Roger,' she said, smiling: 'One resolves to conceal things from him, but it's no good. In a few minutes I was telling him my dream. He knew, of course, that I had dreamed things that came true, and when I came to the execution he looked startled until I told him "the soldiers were in green".

'"In green!" he exclaimed. "In the uniform of the IRA?" and I said "Yes." Then he laughed and began inventing nonsense, delightedly – "Victory for the Republic," he said, "our army all swank in uniform and me charged with high treason and shot at dawn!" It was so absurd that the whole dread that had been over me fell away and I laughed too, and we lit the lamps and pulled out the files and papers and began work.

'We both loved, for writing, the unbroken quiet of the midnight hours, and we worked in dead silence until after one o'clock; then the lamp began to flicker out, and Roger muttered, "Sorry, I forgot the oil," so I had to light candles.

'It was that, I suppose, the candles – that brought it back – the face out of my dream – suddenly I saw it before me in the shadows, ghastly clear, and my heart crumpled up with dread. I sat down at the table again, trying not to tell Roger, waiting – but I couldn't work, couldn't think.

'At last it came, a sound of slow footsteps on the gravel and a long, low, hissing call. Roger sprang up instinctively and opened the drawer in which he kept his automatic, but then the knock came – someone knocking with his knuckles – and he put it back and crossed to open the door.

'I cried out and stood against the door. I cried out to him, "Don't open, don't open!" He put his arm around me and drew me away, smiling. "It isn't raiders," he said.

'He flung the door open and they came in, four men in dark coats, walking slowly, and laid the stretcher down. I saw the white face of the man who lay on it, the long, lean, hollow face – the bandaged head – the blood – Oh, I was not brave; I could do nothing; I sank down on a chair in the shadow and did nothing at all. I heard the men whispering with Roger and heard them go away. They had laid the man on the couch, and he was moaning – that was the dreadful thing – he was not dead.

'Roger came over to me, smiling. "Nesta, we've got to harbour a rebel," he said. He said that to call up my courage, of course, and it did make me ashamed. I stood up and went to the couch; then I looked at Roger and told him, "It's the face in my dream." "This boy was to be executed tomorrow," he said gravely. "It was a great rescue: he was fired after and hit; it's a bad wound, but I think he needn't die." I – I couldn't help it – I said again, stupidly, "It's the face in my dream." Roger looked at me almost – he was almost stern – and said, "Nesta, we can't let dreams—" I took off the bandage then and examined the wound; it wasn't dangerous, only he'd lost so much blood; he'd need long, careful nursing I could see; but he needn't die. He was five weeks in the house.'

'Tell me, did you like him?' Una asked.

'No,' Nesta said, frankly. 'Roger did. Roger said he was a splendid fellow with a fine record since nineteen-sixteen – one of Mick Collins's right-hand men. But I – I was ashamed – I could see nothing to hate, yet I – I hated him. But I did my best, he went away strong and well.'

'And that's the end of the story,' Liam said.

'Yes, that's the end,' said Nesta, looking up. 'You see – the war will break out again of course, we all know that – but the green uniforms … it couldn't come true.'

A Vision

ART Ó RIAIN (1927)

Science, religion and tradition are seemingly reconciled in this story, in which the narrator is afforded a glimpse of the future not in a dream, but by technological means. The 'Professor' is a gifted autodidact in true sci-fi tradition, but he's not a fully fledged Mad Scientist, probably due to his religious beliefs; the narrator and the reader, on the other hand, must decide for themselves if the Professor's response to the unsettling nature of time is satisfactory. This story was originally published in Irish as 'Aisling'; this translation is by the editor.

ON THE TOP OF THE HILL lives my friend the Professor. We all call him 'The Professor', but it wasn't in any university in the world that he got his learning; I say he drank it straight from the Well of Knowledge itself. It's a lonely, bleak spot that he lives in, but he is thus able to keep himself far away from gossips and chatterboxes, and the general sordidness of life. If you go up that hill, you better have a good reason for doing so. I myself climb Carrauntoohil to talk with the Professor – or, more accurately, to listen to him.

'You've come at just the right moment,' he said to me when I called in to see him that afternoon. 'I have something new to show you.' He led me into the room where he did all his work.

'I've seen that device that's been around for a while – the one that allows you to see and hear a person at a huge distance? When you compare that device to the far-viewer, you'll see that the old appliance has an advantage over the new thing – that is, that with the old thing you can watch anything you want. For a long while now, I've been trying to fix that deficiency, so that it will be possible to aim the new device at any point on Earth; it was hard work, but I've finally done it. You will be the first person, after myself, to try it out.'

I

There was a remote village on the edge of the sea. The music of the waves could be heard clearly in the little house, and sometimes sand would blow in through the door. The children were listening, their eyes wide, to the talk that was going on at the fireside between their mother, their father, and the man from the big town.

'It's true for you,' the father said, 'staying here is a huge effort for us, and nothing to show for it but loneliness and hardship, when we could be living in the city. We'll go to Dublin as soon as I've gathered the money for it. We're bound to find contentment there.'

II

An upper room in a big house in the city. An exhausted woman with eight family members in the room with her, all aggrieved by the heat and the lack of space; the noise and clamour of the street coming in through the window.

The man came in, took off his jacket, and sat as far away from the fire as he could. 'I have great news, Kate,' he said. 'I'm going to be Head of the Workforce from next Monday.'

'Thanks be to God!' she said. 'We'll be able to get out of this accursed street, and move to someplace outside the city with peace and quiet and fresh air! Nobody could expect to be healthy, living in a place like this.'

III

I recognised from the design of the houses, and from the number of vehicles that were coming and going, that I was in one of the suburbs of the city now. The couple were sitting in the garden and conversing; the woman was elegantly dressed, and the man had the air of one who has risen through life through his own efforts, relying on none but himself.

'I've been considering the situation for a while now,' he said, 'and I'm certain that I'm right. This country is too small for me. If I was over in England, there would be no limits to the business I could do. We'll leave for London as soon as possible.'

IV

He was a young man, but I understood from the behaviour of those around him that he was the owner of this large house. It would be more accurate to call it a 'castle', albeit a false one. The electric lights were all on, and there was truly a need for them, as the entire house was surrounded by a thick, sallow fog. That same fog was always outside the house, turning day into an ugly, man-made night. The young man grabbed a telephone; he seemed irritable.

'Is this the bank? Get the manager for me, please … Are you there? Listen to me, I am not going to stay in this country for one more day. I should wait until the inheritance comes to me in a year's time, but I'm sick of business and streets and rain and fog. I'm flying to Italy tonight, and after that, any country that takes my fancy. No, I have no desire to return to England. I'm leaving the company to you.'

V

I had never seen such a beautiful place. There were thousands of flowers, of every kind; vineyards and orange trees weighed down with their fruit; powerful sunshine beaming down over everything. It was difficult to say which was bluer, the sky above or the sea below. It must have been some part of the Tyrrhenian Sea.

I heard a car approaching. The staff of the Chateau emerged to welcome the person who had arrived: a worn, weather-beaten man, in whose features some sort of dissatisfaction could be clearly read. I understood from the conversation that surrounded him that he had been travelling for quite some time, and that this was his habit.

The rich man ascended to the library – a beautiful bright room with a view of the sea. He sat at the desk and turned to the letters that were there for him to read, but he did so without any enthusiasm. When he had read half a dozen, he jumped to his feet suddenly and threw the lot of them away from him in anger and disdain.

'I'm sick of it all!' he said aloud. 'No matter where I go, word of my money precedes me. I have no appetite for anything – I might as well be Midas. It's clear I'll never know peace or satisfaction as long as I have this wealth.

'But I'd be rid of them, the toadying liars! I could throw away every penny I have, and turn my face towards the place where my ancestors lived before me. It's in a remote village on the edge of the sea that I'll find rest and tranquillity.'

I stopped there out of sheer astonishment. 'Good God, it's a circle! Where's the peace in that?' My voice was rising.

'In the centre of the circle,' the Professor answered.

'But what *is* the centre of the circle?'

He took me by the elbow and led me to the window. It was a bright, moonlit night, and all the stars were glittering brightly above our heads.

'Each one of those stars has its own path,' he said, 'and each one of those paths is a circle, of a kind. What is the centre of all those circles? It's the centre of your circle, too.'

I didn't give him any answer, because I knew that he would provide it himself.

'The will of God is what it is,' he said.

The Chronotron

TARLACH Ó hUID (1946)

The history-altering potential of time-travel stories has significant pros and cons. On the one hand, if it is possible to re-write history, then free will *does* exist after all, and traumatic events such as the Anglo-Irish War and the Irish Civil War are not inevitable. On the other hand, if you succeed in changing anything, the universe will more than likely ruin your life and tie your brain in knots. The final Mad Scientist of this collection learns this the hard way, in Tarlach Ó hUid's wry treatment of nationalist wish-fulfilment fantasies. This story was originally published in Irish as 'An Cianadóir'; this translation is by the editor.

I AM GOING OUT OF MY MIND, and that is a fortunate thing, for the madness I have endured of late is far, far worse. That thing called the 'Chronotron' is the source of this mental anguish. I cannot help but think back to that difficult question; it will drive me into a red rage, and I am powerless to stop it. Only one thing will banish these thoughts, and that is the advance of insanity; I've tried all else and failed. If I had a needle or a keen blade or a piece of glass in my possession, I would open my veins and let the life pour out of me onto the floor; in this place, there is no stake, post, spike or spar that would allow me to hang myself. I tried to strangle myself with my own two hands, but it was no use. It goes without saying that as I was fervently constricting my throat, to the point where my tongue and eyes were bulging out, I fainted and could not accomplish the deed! And if I spent an entire day trying to bash my brains out against a wall, that would do nothing but knock me into a stupor, because this entire cell

– the walls, floor, ceiling and all – is lined with rubber, just as the Chronotron was on the inside.

I knew, of course, that Professor Ó Néill had been trying for ten years to create a contraption that could travel through Time as an aeroplane travels through the Air or a trawler travels through Water. Well, I didn't believe he would do it. What's over and done with can't be revisited, and we have no choice but to wait for what has yet to come – that was my attitude to the whole thing. And although I knew that there was nobody in Ireland more renowned for their grasp of science and philosophy than Professor Ó Néill, I couldn't see anything in it other than silly daydreaming. Though I had little interest in the Professor's work, we spent many a meal in each other's company, as next-door neighbours often do. Thus, it wasn't any great surprise when he asked me to come around for dinner one November evening in 1985. I took him up on that invitation, and my God, woe is me forever more that I went!

The Professor didn't say much until the coffee was on the table. I could tell, from the way that he was glancing at his watch between every second sentence, that his mind was very much preoccupied. The time came, however, and he lit a cigarette and looked into my eyes.

'Seosamh,' he said, 'I am about to tell you a secret, and bind you to it. Seosamh, my friend, I have completed the Chronotron!'

I laughed apprehensively, worried that he might realise my lack of faith in his invention.

'Well, I hope you knock some enjoyment out of it!' I said, sort of tamely.

He peered at me from under his bushy eyebrows.

'You have a quiet life at the moment, don't you?' he asked, as though that question was somehow relevant to this business of the Chronotron.

'Och, terribly! There's no describing how unchanging it is.'

'And you have a desire for adventure and wonder?'

'You can say that again! But as you know, since I got that limp while hunting lions in Africa—'

'I know, I know,' he said, impatiently, 'I remember you telling that story before. But here, I will lay the whole lot out, ready to hand. Would you be willing to risk death on a wondrous adventure?'

'I'd step through the gates of Hell itself for some novelty!' I said, eagerly.

The Professor leaped forward out of the chair, his expression keen.

'Come with me into the Chronotron!' he said.

I was in two minds about what answer I should give to this kind of peculiar invitation, but I had to hold in my laughter, for fear I would hurt his feelings.

'What are the dangers of travelling in – in a Chronotron?'

'There are plenty of dangers. For example, if it loses its steering, it could take us back millions of years, to the beginning of the world, and we'd be roasted alive! Joking aside, the slightest mishap could leave us stranded in the Middle Ages, and wouldn't that be enough of a disaster?'

I stared at him doubtfully, but it was clear that he was deadly serious.

'And – and you've travelled through Time?'

He grinned.

'Well, I've travelled to the future, but then, who isn't able to do that? But to go *back!* You don't believe it? Think about it. Time is like a kind of music; it's only a mathematical mode imagined by humanity. Do you understand me?'

'I understand that understanding is hard,' said I. 'But time *has to* exist. Night follows day, winter follows autumn; people get older, they lose their vigour, and they die.'

'That's all true, but that's only change, and there's no use in talking about that or wrestling with it. Come back a couple of years with me tonight, and you'll get some proof that will shut you up!'

I don't know what sense there was in doing so, but I said I would go. It's true that I was hungry for adventure, and that I had a craving for weird and wonderful things, but the fact was that I did not believe for one minute that there was anything in the 'Chronotron' …

The Professor led me through his laboratory and into a sort of garage, where a young man was tinkering with a thing that looked sort of like a new-fangled car, but of a strange make.

'Behold the Chronotron!' the Professor said, proudly.

He introduced me to the youngfella. 'This is Colonel Michael Mac Reachtain,' he said. 'The Colonel is my engineer, and a hell of an engineer he is, too – there's none better than him in the whole Air Force. The government loaned him to me.'

A moment or two later, I had an opportunity to approach the Colonel alone.

'I want to ask you something,' I said. 'Do you think that Professor Ó Néill … that he's right in the head?'

He let out a hearty laugh.

'That's a very broad question! They say that genius and madness are close to one another. But you can be sure there's genius in him anyway, whatever about the madness.'

'You don't mean to tell me that this Chronotron *works*!'

'Did he not tell you that we've already tried it out? Well, we did, and let me tell you, friend, it was astonishing! Back to 1641 we went, to watch Phelim O'Neill's army advancing on Drogheda – and a tattered, bedraggled army it was, too!'

I was left speechless, and the Colonel went back to messing about with the Chronotron, a tyre pump in his hand. The Professor returned to us moments later.

'Is it in some sort of working order, Colonel?'

'Ready for departure,' the other man said.

'Well then, unless you're feeling anxious, Seosamh, we'll take it out.'

It was a quiet night, and the light of the Moon shone down on Loch Neagh. We embarked.

'I'm afraid you'll have to sit on the floor,' the Professor said. 'We're going to be packed in like herring in a barrel. Colonel, 1920!'

The Colonel started fiddling with levers, buttons and the throttle. I heard a low humming that only lasted for the blink of an eye, a shock went through me, and I felt the Chronotron pulsing beneath me, as if it were alive. I looked out the porthole. There was no starlight to be seen anymore; there was nothing to see but pitch darkness. The pulsing stopped, and my eyes were suddenly blinded by sunlight streaming in through the porthole.

'We're in 1921, Professor,' said the Colonel. 'I couldn't get any closer to it.'

The Professor spoke with an impatient tone. 'It's close enough,' he said.

I let out a croak of astonishment. 'We're in the same place that we were before, but now it's day! I can see Loch Neagh over yonder!'

'Yes,' said the Professor. 'Loch Neagh, on a summer's day in 1921. London, Colonel!'

The Colonel pushed another button, and the Chronotron rose from the ground with the speed of a bullet. It took me by surprise and laid me flat on my back.

'The Chronotron isn't exactly how I'd like it to be,' the Professor said, levelly, 'but it will improve once it is able to move through Space and Time in the same go. As it stands, it will take us ten minutes to reach London. I should explain to you why I'm going there. Here's a question for you, Seosamh – in your opinion, which event from Irish history is most to blame for the hideous state of the country today?'

I thought about it for a second.

'The Coming of the Normans,' I said, 'or the Famine, maybe, or the legacy of the Civil War.'

'Exactly! Now, I'm not confident enough in the Chronotron to go all the way back to the time of the Normans, and I don't yet know how I would go about erasing the Famine, but I think I can save Ireland from the Civil War.'

'You're blathering, man! There's no—'

He grabbed me by the shoulders, and there was a strange glow in his eyes.

'It isn't blathering at all. Imagine it, Seosamh – if it were possible to wipe London off the face of the Earth in 1920, along with the British government, the monarchy, the docks and the armouries. The IRA would win the day. We have the means to do it – with an atomic bomb! Isn't it a striking image? Hiroshima in '45, and the capital city of England twenty years before that!'

I knew then that I was dealing with the worst kind of maniac, and that he would do exactly as he said. Overcome with horror, I tried to calm him down.

'Don't do it, Professor! It's not right to oppose God's will! What's done is done. And think of the millions of innocent English—'

The Professor gave a wry smile. 'Innocent English!' he said, mockingly. 'There's no such thing!'

My mouth was dry, and my heart was turning over with fear and revulsion.

'Does – does the Colonel know what we're involving him in?'

'I don't think he'd care that much. He's an engineer, and his expertise is limited to engines. He doesn't have an imagination. He's really only an engine himself.'

The Colonel stuck his head back. 'London,' he said, all relaxed.

The Professor scrambled up beside him and examined the measuring and telemetry instruments.

'Another few degrees north, Colonel,' he said, 'to avoid the Thames.'

The Professor took a tiny little bomb out of the back, and a small trap-door opened in the floor of the Chronotron.

'Now, Colonel, rise a couple of hundred feet, and as soon as this explodes – back to Ireland as fast as the wind!'

'Ready?' asked the Colonel a moment later.

'Ready!' said the Professor, and the little bomb dropped out of sight. The Professor pulled the trapdoor shut. I shut my eyes and covered my ears with my palms …

It seemed to me that I was waiting for ages before the piercing blast of the conflagration came. The Chronotron was tossed back and forth like a feather caught by the wind, but the Colonel managed to steady it somehow, and I felt it recover.

We must have been halfway home to Ireland before I found the courage to raise my head and open my eyes. The Colonel was bent forward and cursing anxiously under his breath. And the Professor? I was dumbfounded. There was no Professor at all there! Wherever he was, there wasn't hide nor hair of him to be found on the Chronotron.

I grabbed hold of the Colonel's arm.

'Where did the Professor go?'

He pulled his head back, and he was saucer-eyed with astonishment.

'He must have fallen out the trapdoor,' I said, shaking with fear.

'He didn't fall, or anything like it, because he was on his knees beside me at the exact moment of the explosion. After that I was too busy trying to regain control of the ship to take much notice of him. But never mind that. Whatever that blast did to the thruster, we're losing speed ...'

I moved back and huddled against the wall. My head was spinning with the horrors and wonders of this adventure, and worries about the Professor. What terrible, mysterious thing had taken him? God, what *could* have taken him? And the whole time, there was a memory way back in the back of my mind, annoying me and tormenting me, a memory connected with that date in 1921, a memory that could possibly explain Professor Ó Néill's absence. I pressed my fingers to my temples, trying to find it ...

The Chronotron was rocking back and forth alarmingly as the Colonel struggled to keep control of it. Then, in the depths of my memory, I saw a couple of lines I had read in some newspaper once:

'This renowned scientist was born in London, England, in 1921...'

And then, I thought, I understood the whole thing. What had happened was – it would stop your heart to think of it – that the Professor's mother had been killed in 1921 by the atomic bomb that the Professor himself had dropped on London! Thus – oh, how horrible to imagine it! – *the Professor was never born!*

The whole thing was like a nightmare, a dream that only a lunatic would have, a dream to make the sanest man go mad.

Suddenly, while my head was reeling from the tempest of horrific thoughts inside it, the Colonel let out an urgent shout:

'Save yourself, man! It's out of control! We're falling into Loch Neagh!'

When I came to, I was lying on my belly, soaked through. A small crowd had gathered all around me.

'Where's the Colonel?' I asked, half-gasping.

'You'll meet him soon,' said one of them, sort of evasively.

'And the Chronotron?'

They glanced knowingly at each other.

'Stay calm, friend. I'm sure the doctor will be able to provide you with a Chronotron, or whatever you call it.'

And then they took me here and locked me in this cell, a place where there is nothing that I could hang myself with. Yes, they left me in here, teasing apart that question until my senses were deranged and I lost my reason. I have never been able to forget that question; no such deliverance has come to me. It is an unbelievable tangle, to be sure, for if it was true that the Professor's mother was killed in the atomic explosion, he couldn't have been born. Thus, he never built any Chronotron, and he never dropped any bomb.

But if that's true, his mother was *not* killed in an atomic explosion in 1921, and thus, as the newspaper account had it, he *was* born, was brought home to Ireland, grew up, found respect and renown as a scientist, invented the Chronotron, invited me to dinner, took me back through the years, dropped the bomb on London, and killed his own mother! But if so …

… but …

The Exile

CATHAL Ó SÁNDAIR (1960)

The final story of this collection comes to us from the glittering future of Cathal Ó Sándair's *Captaen Spéirling* series. In between averting World War III, fending off a Martian invasion and preventing a war between Earth and Venus, the eponymous Space-Pilot helps to establish trade relations with the moon (Luna) and the other civilisations of the solar system. The more things change, however, the more they stay the same, and even in this wonderful space-opera world, Irish youngsters still emigrate in search of a decent living. This story was originally published in Irish as 'An Deoraí', which appeared as an appendix to *Captaen Spéirling agus an Phláinéad do Phléasc* (1960). This translation is by the editor.

SEÁN MURPHY had decided to return from Luna to this world, and to spend the end of his life in his native land – Erin's emerald isle.

'Yes,' he said to himself, 'to be back in a place without any need for an artificial atmosphere or space suits; that's what would cheer my heart.'

A long time before this, when Seán was a strong young man in County Kerry, he saw an advertisement in one of the newspapers:

EMPLOYMENT ON LUNA
The Government of Luna welcomes young men and women between 18 and 25 years of age. The Government will cover the cost of the journey from Earth, and migrants will be employed as soon as they arrive. Additional information and a free booklet, *Your New Life on Luna*, can be obtained on request from the Lunar Information Office, O'Connell Street, Dublin.

For a good while before he spotted this ad, Seán Murphy had been entranced by all aspects of space travel. In addition, there were few households in the community that did not already have a family member that had gone to the Moon to seek their fortune. There were good wages to be had in the glass-canopied Lunar cities, and there was no rain up there either. Seán already knew all of that, but his mother never dreamed that he would ever actually consider going. She never imagined it – until she saw the envelope of the letter that came for him from the Selenites' office in Dublin.

She left the letter in a place where Seán would see it; having done so, she gave a broken-hearted sigh. Her husband was long dead, and except for Seán, her children were all married, and none were living nearby. She had been hoping that Seán might marry one of the local girls, and that they might keep her company in her old age.

That afternoon, Seán spent a long time reading the booklet that the Lunar Information Office had sent; of course, the images contained therein were delightful. One of them was a picture of a spaceship that had just landed at a Lunar airport (the famed Airport of the Moon, obviously), full of passengers from Earth. There were three stages to that journey. For the first stage, passengers would ascend to the Space Platform that orbited the Earth like a satellite; this stage was carried out in a 'ferry' ship, whose purpose was identical to that of ferry-boats in the old days when bigger ships still crossed the ocean. For the second stage, passengers would board a bigger, sturdier spaceship to cross the firmament to Luna's Space Platform. There, they would board another 'ferry' ship for the third stage, the journey from the Platform to the surface.

The other pictures in the booklet were just as enticing: pictures of Luna's capital city; pictures of the wonderful factories situated there; pictures of its theatres, and its elegant hotels – and yes, pictures of the statues, monuments and works of art that had been created in honour of Captain Spéirling, the Irish space-pilot who first established contact with the Selenites in 2007.

Seán Murphy's mother did not ask him any questions about the letter. Over the following week, however, her heart was almost torn asunder with worry – and, in fairness to the poor creature, this worry was not baseless. A week after the letter arrived, Seán spoke to her about it.

'Mam,' he said, 'I'm about to … I'm going to be leaving you. At the end of the month, I'll he setting off for Luna.'

His poor mother did not know what to do or to say. She wanted to hug him and beg him not to leave her there, old and lonely, but she did not give in to this urge. She remembered those young men whose mothers kept them at home; and she remembered how some of those men turned sour, as if they had suddenly aged.

'Well, Seán my love, I won't stand in your way,' she said. 'Go, if you think that you'll do well out of it – and I hope that you will!'

Seán was deeply moved to hear this, and the tears were not far from his eyes in that moment, because he knew how impossibly difficult it was for his mother to let him go.

'I'll be back in five years, Mam,' he said. 'I will, without a doubt. I'll be back with a power of money then, you'll see. I'll buy a fancy car, and I'll bring you to see every nook and cranny of Ireland.'

'Indeed, I'd love to take a trip like that, Seán,' his mother said. 'May we both be safe and sound to see it!'

Even so, that night she cried herself to sleep. She had little hope that Seán would return as early as he said he would. Of those she had seen go to Luna, few of them came home before twenty years had passed, and she was sure that she would be dead and gone before that time was up.

The end of the month came, and Seán went. He got the atomic train up to Dublin, and after that, he boarded the space-ferry. He got a good job in one of the huge Lunar mines, and three years later, he had been promoted to a kind of manager. A week after this promotion, however, he received a message from home – his mother was dead, and she had already been buried alongside his father.

For a good while after that, it seemed to Seán that his life was not worth living. Very often, while he was in the middle of his work, he could not help but think that he had failed his mother. He had been too hopeful that she would live longer than she did, that she would not be heartsick after him. However, he eventually shed that sorrow – especially after he and Nora Ryan got to know each other.

Nora was a steward on one of the space-ferries. She and Seán met each other in the Irish Club in Luna City. They got along with each other immediately, and a year later they were married.

'My goodness, it's a long way from here to there!' Seán said to himself, on one of the days when he was thinking about returning to Ireland. He and Nora ended up together for forty years, and they saw their seven children disperse in all directions: Brian was an engineer on Mars; Pádraig was there too, working as a nuclear physicist, and Séamas was working all over Africa. Máire, meanwhile, was married to a man who had a job near the North Pole; Brigid had gone to Venus, where she was working as a nurse. Poor Peadar died when the spaceship he was travelling on was destroyed, and Mícheál, the youngest, was a space-pilot, and he spent more time flying around the void than he did on solid ground anywhere.

All of them gone! Them, and their mother Nora, who had passed away three years before. And so it was that at the age of seventy, Seán Murphy was left all alone in the house where his seven children had grown up.

Hans Marsden was the name of his next-door neighbour; Hans had a good pension, and he and his beloved wife Irma had a fine, comfortable way of life. Seán told Hans that he had decided to return to Earth, 'to die there'.

'Hans,' he said, 'before I go, I want one more view of the nicest place under the sun. I'll take a coach trip around Killarney, and after that, I won't do any more travelling. I'll find lodgings in some friendly house, and on my death-bed, I'll bequeath them whatever I have.'

Hans shook his head sadly. 'That's what you think right now, Seán,' he said, 'but I fear that you'll be greatly disappointed. The Irish climate will not suit you, with you having lived on Luna for as long as you have. And another thing, Seán – very few are left of the people you knew when you were young.'

Hans did his best to convince Seán to stay where he was, but his efforts were futile. However, Seán did accept one piece of advice from him: Hans told him not to sell his house on Luna yet, and Seán agreed.

'Perhaps you're right, Hans,' Seán said, laughing. 'Maybe I shouldn't sell the old nest until I have a new one sorted. I'll leave the keys with you. I'll let you know as soon as I've found a place, and then you can sell the house for me.'

After that, he went to the Luna City Bank. He had a good amount of money stored there – a little over £10,000 in Irish money, he reckoned. He took a fifth of it in cash, and instructed the bank to credit the rest to a particular bank in Killarney. At the start of the summer, he bade farewell to Hans and Irma; they were as old as he was, and they were sure that they would not see him again. They said goodbye to him sorrowfully, and it was not without sadness that Seán wished them well.

When he reached Ireland, he stayed in Dublin for a few days. At the start, he enjoyed being out in the open air, instead of being under Luna City's glass canopy; before long, however, he was reminded that the air here can get very cold indeed. The following day, he was shivering, and he started to suffer from frequent bouts of coughing.

After spending a week in Dublin, he took the atomic train to Kerry. He arrived in Killarney as night was setting in, and as he was walking down the main street, he saw the Moon high above.

'Luna!' he said to himself. 'I can hardly believe that I spent most of my life up there!'

He went into a shop to buy some tobacco, and the shopkeeper guessed from his accent that he was a returned Moon-migrant. 'Have you just come back to the old sod, sir? I'd say things have changed quite a bit since you left.'

Seán replied that it seemed to him that the place still looked like the Old Country, and that was how he preferred it. The shopkeeper laughed, and gave Seán a strange look.

'Sir,' he said, 'are you by any chance the son of Pádraig Murphy of the Boats?'

'Indeed I am, without a doubt,' Seán said, with sparks of joy in his eyes. 'Did you know my father?'

'I can't say that I did,' the shopkeeper said, 'but I've seen his picture – a picture of the greatest hurler that was ever in this area; no sooner did I see you than I remembered him.'

Seán went to a hotel and asked to book a room for the night; he was not there long, however, before a newspaper reporter approached him, looking for his comments for an article to be called 'There's No Place Like Home'.

'Most young Irish men and women are emigrating to Luna, or Mars or Venus,' the reporter said. 'It's an awful shame!'

'It probably is,' Seán said, 'but sense comes with age. Can't you see that sense came to me, and I returned?'

The following day was a wet one, but Seán went out to see the village anyway. Before long, though, he felt the cold starting to hurt him, and his cough was getting worse. He returned to the hotel and asked the maid to have an old-fashioned fire lit in his room.

'A fine turf fire,' he said, half-smiling. 'There's no turf on the Moon, you know.'

The maid found it odd that anyone would ask for a fire to be lit – especially in the middle of the summer. The age of fires in fireplaces was over; for a long time, central heating had been provided by atomic power. However, plenty of hotels kept their old fireplaces, on the off-chance that guests might enjoy them. In any case, she did as she was asked, and Seán kept his coat on until all the turf in the fireplace was ablaze.

He sat beside the fire, and he started to think of Hans and Irma. He had promised them that he would send a letter before long, and he felt now that he should fulfil his promise without any further delay. He would enjoy telling them how much he loved being back in his native land. He gathered a pen and paper, but no sooner had he done so than he lost all desire to write.

'*Yerra*, it's hard for me at the moment. I'm still tired from the voyage; it'd be better to wait until I'm feeling like myself again.'

The following day, he felt strange pains in his bones. This worried him, because he could not remember ever having pains like that before. He went to a doctor, and the diagnosis was not difficult to reach.

'Neuralgia, without a doubt,' the doctor said. 'It happens to everyone who returns to Ireland after a long time spent on Luna – and you're going to suffer with it as long as you're here.'

Seán was shocked. 'Hah? What are you saying, Doctor? Surely you can't be saying that there's no cure for it? I have plenty money, and I can pay for the finest treatment available.'

The doctor shook his head and smirked. He knew well that the likes of Seán believed that there was no cure that money could not buy; even though it was difficult for him, once again he said that Seán could not hope to be free of his neuralgia as long as he was living on this planet. He was right, and that much became painfully clear to Seán after he had stayed in the hotel for a couple of months. In all that time, he was not able to find a new home for himself; nor was he able to write anything to Hans.

The first week of August was very wet, and cold with it.

'It'll be a fine story in another few months!' Seán said to himself one day, as the cold was chilling him to the marrow. He went to bed early that night, and he arose early the following morning. While he was sitting at the breakfast table, the maid told him that she would light the fire in his room as soon as she was able.

'*Yerra*, don't bother with the fire, love,' he said. 'I'll be leaving ye today. Bring me my bill, please.'

The maid did as she was asked, and brought Seán his bill. He gave her a hundred Lunar dollars for herself, and she was extremely grateful for it.

'I'm … I'm getting married next month,' she said, 'and this will be a great help.'

'Good! Well, may God send good fortune to you and your beloved!'

Shortly after that, he went back to Dublin, and began the journey back to Luna.

When Seán Murphy reached Luna City, he quickly went back to his old neighbourhood. Hans saw him approach, and was clearly amazed at the sight of him.

'You're back, Seán,' he said, as casually as if he had last spoken to him an hour ago.

'I am, Hans,' said Seán. 'You were thinking that I'd return, and you were right. There's no place like home!'

About the Authors

JANE BARLOW (1856–1917) was born in Dublin. She wrote under a couple of different pseudonyms, most notably Felix Ryark and Antares Skorpios, the latter of which she shared with her father, the Reverend James William Barlow, Vice-Provost of Trinity College Dublin. As Felix Ryark, she published *A Strange Land* (1908), a 'lost world' story which is of some interest from a speculative fiction standpoint.

FRANCES POWER COBBE (1822–1904) was born in Dublin, the daughter of the prominent landowning Cobbe family. An outspoken social reformer, she campaigned for women's suffrage and published numerous treatises on the subjection of women, and she is also remembered for her fierce opposition to vivisection and her advocacy of animal rights; she was a founder of the National Anti-Vivisection Society and the British Union for the Abolition of Vivisection. Cobbe was a regular correspondent with Charles Darwin, and wrote extensively on the moral implications of his theory of evolution. She is buried beside her partner Mary Lloyd in the cemetery of St Illtyd's Church in Gwynedd, Wales.

CLOTILDE ('CLO') GRAVES (1863–1932) was born in Buttevant, Co. Cork, and published her first novel at the age of forty-six, under the pseudonym 'Richard Dehan'. Prior to this, she enjoyed considerable success as a playwright under her own name, having also briefly worked as a freelance journalist and a cartoonist. Despite her fervent Catholicism, she presented herself in an unconventional manner for her time, cutting her hair short, smoking in public and wearing masculine clothes. During her lifetime, she was perhaps best known for her controversial 1911 novel *The Dop Doctor*, which lionised the British side of the Second Boer War (1899–1902).

MARGARET WOLFE HUNGERFORD (1855–1897) was born in Rosscarbery, Co. Cork, and later married a Dublin solicitor. Her first novel was written to support herself and her three young children following the sudden death of her husband. After becoming a professional author, she wrote under the pseudonym of The Duchess, and sometimes as Mrs Hungerford. She is perhaps most famous as the originator of the phrase, 'Beauty is in the eye of the beholder,' which first appeared in her second novel, *Molly Bawn* (1878).

DOROTHY MACARDLE (1889–1958) was born in Dundalk, Co. Louth, into the famed Macardle brewing family. She studied at University College Dublin, and subsequently taught English at Alexandra College, the girls' school at which she herself had been educated. As a member of Cumann na mBan and the Gaelic League, her political activities and opinions resulted in her being arrested twice – first by the Royal Irish Constabulary in 1918, during the War of Independence, and then by the Free State government in 1922, during the Civil War. Although she was best known as the author of *The Irish Republic* (1937), her 1942 novel *Uneasy Freehold* – adapted to film as *The Uninvited* (1944) and subsequently published under that title – is now acknowledged as a modern classic ghost story.

WILLIAM MAGINN (1794–1842) was a native of Cork and a prolific writer of short fiction, contributing pieces to *Blackwood's Magazine*, *Fraser's Magazine*, and *Bentley's Miscellany*, the latter edited by Charles Dickens. A resident of London from 1824, he was a frequent contributor to various newspapers, and in 1836 he fought a duel with the Honourable Grantley Berkeley over the fallout from a negative review Maginn had written of the Whig MP's debut novel. Also of genre interest is his 1827 novel *Whitehall*, presented as a historical novel about the 1820s from the year 2227.

CHARLOTTE ELIZABETH ('L') MCMANUS (1853–1944), a native of Castlebar, Co. Mayo, is best remembered today for her novel *The Professor in Erin*, originally serialised in Arthur Griffith's *Sinn Féin Weekly* in 1912. A nationalist and a member of the Gaelic League, she is also known for her patriotic historical novels, and during the Civil War, she supported the Anti-Treaty side. She also helped to establish the second branch of the Gaelic League in Co. Mayo, and was an esteemed member of the Irish Literary Society.

L.T. MEADE, or ELIZABETH THOMASINA MEADE SMITH (1844–1914) was a prolific author, mostly of children's stories. She was born in Bandon, Co. Cork, and later resided in London. *The Brotherhood of Seven Kings* was one of several works Meade created in collaboration with the English author Dr Robert Eustace. She was also a member of the Pioneer Club, a progressive feminist group based in London.

AMELIA GARLAND MEARS (1842–1920) was born in Freshford, Co. Kilkenny, the daughter of the poet John Garland. She achieved some renown as a short story writer, with most of her material set in or around Hartlepool and the Yorkshire country-side, where she lived with her husband. The full novel version of *Mercia, the Astronomer Royal* indicates that she was passionately interested in the culture and history of the Indian subcontinent, and a supporter of Indian independence.

FITZ-JAMES O'BRIEN (1828–1862) was born in Cork, and grew up in Castleconnell, Co. Limerick. He wrote poetry calling for the establishment of relief programmes during the Great Famine, and emigrated to the US in the early 1850s. Evidently a hot-tempered man, he broke his nose in a fistfight in 1858, and he later fought for the Union in the American Civil War, serving under Brigadier General Lander at the Bloomery Gap Skirmish of 1862.

TARLACH Ó hUID (1917–1990) was born Augustus Walter Hood, after his father, in London. His parents were English Methodists, associated with the Orange Order; however, he identified with Ireland so strongly that he joined the Gaelic League, learned to speak and write in Irish, changed his name to its Gaelicised form and converted to Catholicism in 1937, in the belief that such a conversion was necessary to properly identify as an Irishman. He was a member of the Social Credit Party of Great Britain and Northern Ireland, and later a member of the IRA. For his IRA activities (mostly pamphleteering), he was jailed from 1940–1945, and he continued working for the Gaelic League after his release.

ART Ó RIAIN (1893–1968), a native of Thurles in Co. Tipperary, was a civil servant who wrote under the pseudonym 'Barra Ó Caochlaigh' (since civil servants were not permitted to publish under their own names at the time); under this name, he wrote the Oireachtas Literary Award-winning novella *An Tost* [*Silence*], a short family saga that becomes explicitly science-fictional in its latter half. He went on to produce a number of well-received novels for the state Irish-language publishing company An Gúm, and he was also well-known as a pianist and organist.

CATHAL Ó SÁNDAIR (1922–1996) was born in Weston-super-Mare to an English father and an Irish mother, and he published his first Irish-language short story at the age of sixteen. A prolific author of genre fiction in Irish, he is reputed to have written 160 books, most of which were intended for schoolchildren. Among his most famous creations are the intrepid detective Réics Carló, the cowboy Réamonn Óg, and the space-pilot Captaen Spéirling. As well as Irish, Ó Sándair was fluent in Scots Gaelic (*Gaidhlig*), Welsh, Cornish, Manx and Breton, and semi-fluent in German, French, Spanish, Dutch and Russian.

Æ (GEORGE WILLIAM RUSSELL) (1867–1935) was born in Lurgan, Co. Armagh. A committed Home Rule nationalist, he was instrumental in the Co-operative Movement, and a vocal critic of the 1913 Lock-Out, the 1916 Rising, and the partitioning of Ireland. As a poet, novelist, essayist and painter, he was well respected and fondly regarded by Dublin's bohemians, and he appears as a character in James Joyce's *Ulysses*. Much of his work was influenced by his Theosophical beliefs, as can be seen in his story in this collection, and his pseudonym 'Æ' was abbreviated from the ambiguous spiritualist term 'Æon'.

Acknowledgements

Many thanks to the estate of Dorothy Macardle for their permission to reprint 'A Story Without an End', and to Gráinne Ní Uid, Maelíosa Ó Riain and Joe Saunders for permission to translate and re-print 'An Cianadóir', 'Aisling' and 'An Deoraí', respectively. This collection is enhanced immeasurably by these stories' inclusion.

This book would not exist at all if not for the hard work of everyone involved in its production. Huge thanks are due to Lisa Coen, Sarah Davis-Goff, Fiachra McCarthy and Marsha Swan for their insight, humour, patience and aesthetic flair. Much gratitude also to Peter O'Connell for his help in bringing *A Brilliant Void* to the wider world.